BLOOD GAMBLE

T0051112

By Melissa F. Olson

Disrupted Magic series

Midnight Curse

Boundary Magic series

Boundary Crossed
Boundary Lines
Boundary Born

Scarlett Bernard novels

Dead Spots
Trail of Dead
Hunter's Trail

Short Fiction

Sell-By Date: An Old World Short Story
Bloodsick: An Old World Tale
Malediction: An Old World Story

Also by Melissa

The Big Keep: A Lena Dane Mystery
Nightshades

BLOOD GAMBLE

DISRUPTED MAGIC BOOK TWO

MELISSA F. OLSON

This is a work of fiction. Names, characters, organizations, places, events, and incidents are either products of the author's imagination or are used fictitiously. Any resemblance to actual persons, living or dead, or actual events is purely coincidental.

Text copyright © 2017 by Melissa F. Olson
All rights reserved.

No part of this book may be reproduced, or stored in a retrieval system, or transmitted in any form or by any means, electronic, mechanical, photocopying, recording, or otherwise, without express written permission of the publisher.

Published by 47North, Seattle

www.apub.com

Amazon, the Amazon logo, and 47North are trademarks of Amazon.com, Inc., or its affiliates.

ISBN-13: 9781542045834
ISBN-10: 1542045835

Cover design by Mike Heath, Magnus Creative
Cover photography by Gene Mollica

Printed in the United States of America

"Ah, well, poor girl, there is peace for her at last.
It is the end!"
He turned to me, and said with grave solemnity:—
"Not so; alas! not so. It is only the beginning!"

—Bram Stoker, *Dracula*

Prologue

Pasadena, CA
Four years ago

The girl in the cell paced and paced, trying to ignore the new signals from her body. Everything hurt, and the blasted emptiness in her belly cried out—for *food*, of all wretched things. She screamed with frustration, smacking her palms against the bars of the cage, but that hurt too. How did anyone do this? How did those fragile little humans survive in these soft shells of skin and blood? She *hated* it.

She sat down once more on the bed, huddling under the thin cotton sheet. The cold was another old-new experience she now had to endure. The basement cells weren't damp, she had to give him credit for that, but they were eternally cold—*as the grave*, she thought manically, and laughed at her own joke. They had given her a plain shift to wear, little more than a glorified sheet, but it was better than the torn and shredded cocktail dress she'd arrived in, which lay discarded in one corner, still covered in blood. Blood that now meant nothing to her. It no longer knew how to call her name.

It was all his fault. He had come to her several times, her John— she refused to call him by the name he now used. Each time, he would silently draw her blood into syringes, check her pulse and her pupils, and depart without a word, leaving behind a tray of *food*, like a final slap in the face. At first she refused to cooperate, kicking and scratching with her frail human body, but he'd calmly pressed her mind to make her obedient. Imagine that—being pressed by a vampire! Was there no greater humiliation? She had decided she would rather be still than be used as a puppet.

But whether or not she submitted, her time was running out. When he completed his tests, she knew that her long, turbulent life would end. All those years . . . the days and nights spent with distinguished men, the child she'd borne, the efforts she'd made, first to be with greatness, and then to be great herself. She had had so many adventures, so much passion! She had saved vampires from themselves; she *knew* she had. But no one would give her any credit, and now they never would.

After that, after her one heroic attempt to alter the current of history had ended in a sort of meaningless success, there had been years and years of sulking in her rotting mansion, trying to devise a way to regain relevance. Then an opportunity to stage a coup had fallen into her lap, and there'd seemed to be a sort of poetry to it. After all, John had brought her into all of this. He had been her maker. Wasn't it only fair that she unmake him in return?

She had come so *close*.

She lost track of time in her cell, of course—her body suddenly required *sleep*, like a common animal. But after perhaps three or four days, John came again, with no tools this time, no tray of food. She knew he would be able to smell the fear that this provoked in her, but she held her chin high. She would show him nothing.

"So you've had enough of playing mad scientist?" she said crisply. "Did you figure out what that . . . that *creature* did to me?"

He looked at her with eyes that hadn't aged, but which had become ancient all the same. "You know what she did, Claire," he said in his quiet way. "She's cured you."

She snorted. "Cured. *Cured*. I cannot believe you would say such a thing after all we have been through, as humans, and then as vampires. After all I have done for you."

His eyes narrowed. "Be very careful, Claire. The last thing you did for me was try to kill my wife in my presence."

She waved a hand. "I was upset. You were being unreasonable."

He just looked at her, his face etched with sadness. To her disgust, she felt her lower lip begin to tremble. Would this body never cease to betray her? "If you're waiting for an apology, it will not come," she snapped, meeting his eyes. She knew it was dangerous, but what did it matter now? "Feeding Stoker the book united us. It pushed us past the infighting and forced us to find order—choosing cities, taking care with our prey. Kill me for that if you must, but I regret nothing. I *saved* us."

He regarded her with an expression she could no longer read. She fought the human desire to squirm. She would not show him a prey response, not now. "Maybe you did," he said at last. "And maybe not. Either way, that is not why you will die today."

She tossed her hair out of her eyes.

"Why, then?"

He smiled then, the old wry smile she had known forever. "Because you lost."

In the end, he pressed her mind, so that as her spine twisted sideways and snapped, she felt nothing but a pleasant daze. She didn't particularly deserve such mercy, Dashiell knew, but he did it more out of respect for the past than respect for her. He had been Claire's maker, and in many distasteful ways, she had been his.

He never told anyone that he pressed Claire before her death, not even his wife. Instead, as he returned to her he gave the appearance of a man who had just taken the garbage to the curb. His wife probably suspected, of course, because of all those who still walked the planet, she alone knew that he kept the fading ember of a Romantic still alive within him. But she had kept that secret for a very long time, and would keep this one for longer still.

Chapter 1

On a Thursday evening in the middle of March, I was sitting on the floor of a werewolf's condo, delivering on what might be the world's most awkward favor.

I couldn't leave my spot on the carpet, but I'd at least come prepared, with big-ass headphones, magazines, and snacks. Shadow, the enormous bargest who had decided to adopt me, was draped across my feet, her head turned to watch the bedroom door. Her body language was sort of amused-but-puzzled. Even a regular dog could have figured out what was happening in the next bedroom, and Shadow was miles from a regular dog. Every now and then she would tilt her head backward to check my face, as if to say, "I know we do some weird shit, but . . . really?"

Each time, I just kind of had to shrug.

Two weeks earlier, my friend (and knife trainer) Marko had brought up a personal problem, for probably the first time since I'd met him. Marko was a werewolf, and werewolf magic causes its victims to become sterile. He and his (human) wife really wanted a baby. They couldn't afford options like international adoption or IVF with sperm donors, and they were both in their early forties now, running out of time.

Which is how I ended up being the only one who could help. As a null, I don't have any particular magic powers—just the opposite, really. I negate all the magic within a certain radius around me, creating a magic-free bubble that has me as its center. In theory, if Marko stayed within that area, I could keep him human for a short time, and he and his wife could make a baby the old-fashioned way. Assuming, of course, we could all get past the extreme awkwardness that would be involved.

It was weird, but it was far from the weirdest thing I'd done lately. The leaders of the Los Angeles vampires, werewolves, and witches all paid me a retainer to clean up supernatural problems that arose in the city. When things were quiet, as they'd been for the past couple of months, I was free to pick up freelance work.

Most of the time this involved shepherding vampires around during daylight activities, but two weeks earlier, I had been paid to attend a witch's beach volleyball tournament so I could make sure her opponent wasn't using magic to cheat. A few days before *that*, I'd accompanied a crowd-shy werewolf to a taping of his favorite sitcom, to help him stay calm in the midst of all that teeming humanity. I might have actually enjoyed that outing, except the sitcom was one of those "fat slovenly husband vs. shrill anorexic wife" crapfests. Freelance work could be kind of a gamble.

Compared to that, sitting around with loud music and magazines wasn't exactly hard on me. "Besides, it's not like I had anything better to do," I muttered to myself, causing Shadow to briefly raise her head and look at me inquiringly. Whoops. I'd probably said that a lot louder than I meant to. It was true, though: since I had split up with Eli, my werewolf ex-boyfriend, I'd had an awful lot of free time. I exercised (reluctantly), ran security drills with Dashiell's daytime (human) crew, let my friend Jesse drag me to the shooting range to practice with his stupid guns, and hung out with Molly, my vampire roommate. Occasionally someone would make a mess in the Old World, and I'd go clean it up. But I had what currently boiled down to a part-time job, exactly two friends, and zero romantic interests. And, insult to injury, most of my TV shows were going on hiatus.

I was bored.

My phone buzzed, cutting off Courtney Barnett's voice in my ears. The screen showed a smiling picture of my brother, Jack. Ignoring the sounds behind me, I picked up the phone and hit Answer.

"Hey, Scarbo," he said cheerfully. "How are you?"

"I'm fine, Jack," I said, really hoping the sounds of sex weren't audible through the headphone mic.

"I can hear the eye-roll in your voice, you know," Jack replied. And I could hear the smile in his. "Are you working tonight?"

Jack thought I was a professional house cleaner who specialized in preparing homes for big events—hence my need to work nights. "Uh, sort of." I was busy, but I wouldn't be taking any money from Marko for this. He was a friend, not to mention the only member of the Los Angeles wolf pack who wasn't currently treating me like something smelly they'd stepped in. That's what happens when you break up with a beloved pack member. "But look, you don't have to call me every other day to check on me," I said to my brother. "I'm fine."

"I know," he insisted. "But it's still hard to go from being in a committed relationship to being single, under any circumstances. I just want to make sure my baby sister is okay."

For just a second, an old hurt resurfaced. What about the year after our parents' deaths, when Jack had basically ignored eighteen-year-old me so he could grieve alone? I'd been so vulnerable, and being alone then had led to some bad things later.

But I reminded myself that I wasn't being fair. Jack was here *now*, and he was trying. "I know. But I really am fine. How are Juliet and the kids?"

After years of awkward singlehood, my shy, gangly big brother had recently gotten married, to a widowed guidance counselor from

Bakersfield. Juliet was lovely, and her two kids had taken a shine to me. The feeling was mutual.

"They're great," he chirped, and we spent a few minutes talking about how he was coaching Riley's soccer team. The image of quiet Jack running up and down a field screaming at preteen girls made me grin.

"And Logan?" I asked. "Are the billing people still being a bag of dicks?"

"Ugh. Don't remind me." Jack's new stepson, Logan, had spent almost a year in the hospital being treated for tumors on his spinal cord. That was how my brother had met them, while he was on rotation in the children's cancer ward.

Logan was in remission now, and his prognosis was excellent, but Juliet had had really shitty insurance when he was diagnosed. Now she and Jack were dealing with a ridiculous amount of debt for Logan's medical care. He wouldn't tell me how much it was, but I got the impression that it ran into six digits.

I had been quietly stashing away most of my freelance money to give to them, but it wouldn't make much of a dent yet. "I'll take that as an affirmative on the dick-bag scenario," I said mildly.

"Yeah," Jack grumped. "Anyway. I was gonna ask you—" The phone beeped again, and when I looked at the screen, I saw Dashiell's name above a cartoon Dracula image. Great. Molly had been messing with my phone again. If Dashiell ever saw that picture, I'd suffer the Glare of All Glares. "Hey, Jack, I gotta go. Work call."

"Okay, gotcha. Real quick: Can you come for dinner Sunday night?"

"I don't need your pity invite."

"I know, I know, it'll hurt your antisocial street cred, but Juliet's making those hot dog things you like," he wheedled.

"With the bread around them?" I said hopefully.

"Uh-huh."

"Then I'm in, as long as you promise never to use the phrase 'street cred' ever again."

Smiling, I clicked over to Dashiell without giving Jack a chance to respond.

"Good *eve*ning," I said in a fakey vampire voice.

There was a pause, and then the cardinal vampire of Los Angeles said formally, "No, that has not gotten any funnier since the last time you said it."

"It's funny to me," I replied, but I kept my tone light. Even if I could push Dashiell a little further these days, I was still not a moron.

"Indeed," he said, his voice dry as dust. "If you're quite finished, I'd like you to come to the mansion."

"Really?" I checked my watch. Eight thirty on a Thursday night. It wasn't an unusual time for me to get called to work, but usually Dashiell just texted me an address. Before I could check myself, I blurted, "Please tell me you didn't kill anyone at your own house. That's just tacky."

I expected him to snap at me, but he just said in the same brittle voice, "No. I want to offer you a freelance assignment."

He couldn't see it, but my eyebrows climbed up into my scalp. Dashiell barely approved of me taking "unofficial" jobs at all; I certainly hadn't expected him to offer me one. Despite myself, I was intrigued.

At the same time, I had made a promise to Marko. He knew I might have to leave for an Old World emergency, but I wouldn't ditch him if I didn't have to. "Can you give me an hour?" I said into the headphone mic. "I have a previous obligation."

There was another brief pause—*don't listen to the noises behind you, Scarlett!*—and then Dashiell agreed that it could wait an hour.

Which set off a red flag all on its own. In Los Angeles, the three branches of the supernatural share power more or less equally, and I'm considered a partner, which means that in theory I'm on the same level as them. But for the really important, life-threatening stuff, we all look to Dashiell. I can't help but think of him as my boss, and as a cardinal vampire, he's used to getting what he wants, the moment he wants it. Which meant that Dashiell being accommodating might be an actual sign of the apocalypse.

Or a sign that I was about to get myself in serious trouble.

As previously arranged, Marko just texted me a brief *Thanks, Scarlett!* when he and his wife . . . no longer needed my services. My feet had fallen asleep thanks to the hundred-eighty-pound bargest on top of them, so I shook them out, packed up my stuff, and took off for Pasadena.

When I finally arrived at the enormous Pasadena mansion that Dashiell shared with his wife, Beatrice, Shadow trotted off into . . . well, the shadows. It's not just a clever name. Dashiell's place was secure and spacious, not to mention completely fenced in, so it was one of the few places where the bargest could comfortably wander around, taking in smells and organizing a contained squirrel genocide. Which worked out well for everyone, since Beatrice didn't really like having Shadow around. This may or may not have had something to do with me encouraging her to poop on the fancy Spanish tiles in the driveway.

After Shadow left to go exploring, one of the ubiquitous vampire lackeys ushered me straight into Dashiell's office. Beatrice had decorated the rest of the house in a Spanish Revival style—or that was what they told me; I knew as much about interior design as I did about life in zero gravity—but this one room was a weird combination of Victorian-era furnishings and expensive technology. It was all very Dashiell.

He was sitting behind an enormous carved-oak desk, and when I came into the room he simultaneously stood up and winced. Like most vampires, Dashiell doesn't like being in my radius, which makes him human again. Humanity comes with weakness and vulnerability, not to mention petty human problems like hunger and bladder control. Sometimes it really throws vampires to have that thrust on them again, but Dashiell had spent enough time around me to adjust fairly quickly. Before I could say more than "hello," he was pointing me to the leather visitor's chair across the desk.

"How much do you know about the Las Vegas entertainment world?" he asked abruptly. I'll say this for Dashiell: the man doesn't dick around with small talk. "Specifically the big casino shows?"

I blinked hard for a moment, not even trying to keep the surprise off my face. I had not anticipated a Cirque du Soleil quiz. "Um, as little as possible?" I said honestly. "I saw a Cirque show like six years back, but I'm not a fan of Vegas." Understatement.

"Hmm." He spun in his chair, picked up a sheet of paper from the state-of-the-art printer behind the desk, and turned back to hand it to me. It was an article from the *Las Vegas Sun* about a new production opening at the Bellagio. I scanned the headline and first few paragraphs, and noticed that it was a vampire-themed show. The entertainment company producing it wasn't actually Cirque du Soleil, but the show itself sounded pretty similar to other stuff I'd heard about in Vegas: acrobats, mentalists, magic tricks . . . that kind of crap. It would bring vampires back into the spotlight again—literally—but I didn't see anything we could do about it that wouldn't make the problem worse.

I lifted my eyes back to Dashiell, who was watching me expectantly. "I mean . . . as I understand it, Vegas has shows based on topless zombies and giant bugs," I said with a shrug, setting the paper on the desk in front of me. "This is like when we were dealing with the *Twilight* movies. It'll blow over."

"Finish the article," he instructed, his face unreadable.

Okay, that made me nervous. I picked up the printout again and kept reading, more carefully this time. The vampire-themed show was called *Demeter*, and it was being put on by a new entertainment company run by a husband-and-wife team, the Holmwoods. That name sounded just the tiniest bit familiar, but nothing in the article seemed particularly worrying. Then I got to this paragraph:

Arthur and Lucy Holmwood came onto the Vegas scene rather abruptly, and have been given an unheard-of opportunity to leapfrog the entertainment stepladder to the very top: a headlining show at the Bellagio. Little is known about the couple other than their stage names, which are a reference to characters in Bram Stoker's infamous vampire novel, Dracula.

Okay, that explained the familiar name. I'd reread the book a few years earlier, after I'd first learned about Dashiell's own weird connection to *Dracula*. Back in the early 1800s, he had turned his nutty ex-girlfriend, Claire, into a vampire. Decades later, when the Old World was still in chaos after the fall of the vampire council that had previously led it, Claire had persuaded a stage manager/personal assistant named Abraham Stoker to write a book about vampires, which, of course, became as famous in human culture as anything could in a pre-Twitter world. Come to think of it, wasn't *Demeter* the name of the ship that Dracula had taken to England?

At any rate, *Dracula* was still the most famous vampire novel in history, and had been adapted hundreds of times. Why would this bother Dashiell? Unless—

I looked back up at Dashiell. "You don't actually think these two are real vampires, just because they took the names of characters from *Dracula*?"

Dashiell leaned forward and rubbed at his face. He was still close enough to me to be human, and he looked tired. "It's the other way around, I'm afraid. The characters in that infernal book were based on the real couple."

Chapter 2

It took me a moment to process that, because it was just so ridiculous. "No way," I said to arguably the most powerful man in Los Angeles. Besides Spielberg, of course.

But he was already nodding. "The last name was fictionalized, but Lucy and Arthur are very real. I haven't met them myself, but they're well known in the Old World."

"Well known?" I echoed. Like . . . vampire celebrities? There was a time when I would have laughed out loud at the idea, but instead I pushed out a slow breath, thinking it over. Unfortunately, the first question that popped into my head wasn't terribly mature. "Wait! Is Dracula real, too?"

"No," he said firmly. Then he inclined his head a little. "Well . . . Stoker's character is an amalgamation of a number of real vampires, particularly Claire. But there is no single person who was fictionalized into Count Dracula."

"Okay," I said, feeling surprisingly relieved. It was kind of silly, since I dealt with vampires on a daily basis, but Count Dracula had scared me back in middle school, and old fears are the hardest to shrug off. "Good."

He gestured to the article. "The Holmwoods, however . . . that part of the story really happened."

"But in the book, doesn't Arthur behead Lucy and die as a human?"

"Yes, because Victorian audiences wouldn't have accepted the truth," Dashiell replied. "At the moment when Arthur meant to behead her, he faltered. Instead, he lied to his friends, and went back to Lucy's grave that evening. He begged her to turn him so he could be with her forever." He gave me a thin smile. "In the vampire world it was considered very romantic."

"Uh, okay," I said, trying to take that in. This was like finding out that Batman was based on a real dude. "So you're saying the real vampires Lucy and Arthur adopted a last name to match the book, moved to Vegas, and are now putting on a stage show."

He jerked his head in one crisp nod. "I believe so, yes."

"That seems . . ." I tried to think of an even remotely appropriate term, and finally settled on "incongruous."

Now Dashiell gave me a tiny, approving smile, though I didn't know if it was because of the insight or my awesome word choice. Vampires—at least, every one I'd ever known or heard of—are invisible predators who prefer to pop out of shadows, take what they need, and vanish again. They occasionally take a vampire spouse, but mostly they hunt alone, and they *avoid* attention.

"Which is one of the reasons I want you to go to Las Vegas and view the show," Dashiell replied.

I jerked in my seat. "What? No." I hated Las Vegas—the crowds and the attitudes and the sweat-tinged smell of desperation in the air. But that wouldn't be a good enough reason for Dashiell. "I mean, uh . . ." I gestured at the printout. "This is really interesting, but I don't see what it has to do with us."

"Do you remember Carlos?"

I opened my mouth to say no, but then an image flashed in my head: a short, squat vampire in a bad suit. He had come to Dashiell's house three years ago, intent on helping another vampire stage a coup. Unfortunately for him, they made their move the same night a very bad man brought a teenage null to the house as a hostage. Jesse and I came to save her, and both Carlos and the kidnapper were killed in the melee that followed.

"You said he was a cardinal vampire," I remembered.

"Of Las Vegas," Dashiell supplied.

"Oh," I said in a small voice. We had killed the cardinal vampire of Vegas? Why hadn't anyone told me about that?

Um, because you were unconscious after accidentally curing Ariadne of vampirism? I reminded myself. I hadn't meant to do it. At the time, I hadn't even known that I *could* concentrate my null-ness to the point of permanently removing someone else's connection to magic. It was only after I woke up in the hospital that I understood what I had done— which was also when Dashiell explained that Ariadne was actually his own vampire descendent, Claire. He wasn't upset with me, though, since Claire had been trying to usurp him. And since turning her into a human had made her very easy for him to kill.

"Since then," Dashiell was saying, and I reminded myself that we were supposed to be talking about Carlos, "Las Vegas has been experiencing a power vacuum. It is a mecca for vampire activity, for obvious reasons, but in the last four years no vampire has been able to secure control and keep it. Several have died trying."

"And now you think this Lucy and Arthur are trying to take control?" I asked, tapping the printout.

"That, or they're simply taking advantage of an opening," he replied.

I did *not* say, "That's what she said." Not out loud, anyway. "But what are they planning to do with it?" Dashiell continued. "Why take an American city, and why now?"

I chewed on my lip for a second. It was interesting, and problematic, but . . . "Again, and with respect, how is this our problem?"

"It's not," he said, to my surprise. "But it may well be *my* problem. If, during the show, the Holmwoods announce that they are vampires, they may be risking exposure for all of us, and therefore all of the Old World. That is why I want to hire you to go see the show. And, of course, to make sure it's safe for humans," he added, trying not to sound like it was an afterthought. "I don't expect you to actually move against them by yourself, Scarlett. I just need you there as a scout."

I automatically shook my head. "I can't. I have Shadow." The bargest was not allowed to leave LA County, a deal we'd made with the people who'd created her.

"Corry's spring break begins this weekend," Dashiell reminded me. "She can take care of the bargest. I'll pay her for her time. And you, too, of course." He named a figure, and I couldn't help but widen my eyes. That would take a chunk out of Logan's hospital debt. And all I had to do was spend a couple of days on what amounted to a vacation.

But something about the situation felt wrong. For one thing, diving into an enormous, completely unknown vampire population all by myself was more reckless than I was willing to be. I was a little bored, sure, but I wasn't looking for actual physical danger. I'd found plenty of that right here in LA, and I was in no hurry to repeat the experience.

Besides, I *hated* Las Vegas. You know that expression "You couldn't pay me to go there"? Yeah.

Happily, Dashiell couldn't *make* me go. I didn't work for him individually; I worked *with* him, Kirsten, and Will as a team. So I shook my head.

"I'm sorry, Dashiell, but no. If I randomly show up at one of their performances, those two are going to know exactly what you're doing, and they'll see it as a declaration of war, or—at the very least—a challenge. If they *are* doing something sinister, they'll come after me. And you can't send people to protect me without making it look like even more of a threat." I stood up. "This is above my pay grade, and risky as hell. Send one of your vampires."

He tilted his head, considering this for a long, silent moment, while I tried not to fidget. "You may have a point," he allowed at last.

It took an effort, but I managed to keep my mouth from dropping open. Dashiell agreed with my assessment of danger? That was a first.

"I will give the matter more consideration," he added. To my further surprise, Dashiell rose from behind the desk. "Let me walk you out."

"Um, okay." Did he think I'd forgotten the way?

But his motive became clear almost immediately. "So, how is Jack adjusting to married life?" he asked, in a perfectly civil, conversational tone.

My fists clenched. My brother Jack was human, which meant he didn't know anything about the Old World or what I could do. As a way of keeping leverage on me, Dashiell had given him a job at one of his business endeavors, a company that made medical equipment. He'd even paid most of Jack's way through med school. I'd hoped Jack would finally be out from under Dashiell's thumb after he finished his residency, but that had been naive: Dashiell had offered him a part-time job, and now my brother worked thirty-five hours a week at the ER and twenty hours at Dashiell's company, testing the equipment in his lab.

I knew Jack was probably a great employee—Dashiell didn't suffer fools—but I was always aware that he was being used as leverage against me. Whenever Dashiell brought him up, I got half a panic attack—something the cardinal vampire had undoubtedly realized.

"He's fine," I said stiffly. "Juliet and the kids, too."

"Good, good."

I expected Dashiell to push his request again, now that he'd shown me the stick. At the very least, I figured he'd tell me we were going to revisit the topic soon. But the cardinal vampire of the city just bade me good night at the door, watching as Shadow rejoined me, her eyes bright and happy from chasing squirrels. There was probably a pile of them somewhere, a grisly present for Dashiell's groundskeeper. Together we walked down the front steps and around the path to the van.

It was, of course, impossible, but I could swear I felt his eyes on me all the way home.

Chapter 3

"OMG, *the* Lucy and Arthur?" Molly squealed, a half hour later.

My vampire roommate was lounging on the couch in our little Marina Del Rey cottage, trying to pull open a bag of tortilla chips. Vampires can't eat people food, so she'd been saving them until I arrived to turn her human again. Molly was used to vampire strength, and not at all used to the storage of modern food, so her attempts to open the bag were actually pretty funny. I could have helped her, but I hated to give up the comedy value.

"What do you mean, *the* Lucy and Arthur?" I asked, watching her try to pull at the top of the bag with her dull human teeth. "They're really that famous?"

"Hell yeah, they are. They're, like, vampire royalty."

I finally took pity on her, grabbing the bag from her hands and pulling the top open. "Yessss," Molly said greedily, practically snatching the bag back. Around a mouthful of chips, she added, "Do we have any of that green dippy stuff?"

I rolled my eyes. "Guacamole." Expanding my radius so she would stay within it, I went into the little kitchen and retrieved the container from the fridge for her. After scooping some onto her chip, Molly continued, "You gotta understand, other than the cardinal vampires who run big cities, we don't really have celebrities in the vampire community. Hell, we don't really have a *community*, just a power hierarchy." She popped the chip in her mouth, chewed appreciatively, and added, "Lucy and Arthur are the big anomaly. They're like the JFK and Jackie of the undead." She paused, considering that for a moment. "Or maybe the Obamas? Pre-divorce Brad and Angelina?"

"I get it. So why am I just hearing about them now?"

"Because they've always been in Europe and Asia," Molly replied. "Look, you know we don't travel around, not the way humans do— every ten or twenty years we just move to a new town, and when that happens there's all this negotiating between cardinal vampires, and it's a whole big thing. Lucy and Arthur are different. They've got, like, a free pass to wander around Europe meeting with cardinal vampires, telling stories, passing news. I heard they've got a tricked-out tour bus and a bunch of human roadies, whatever that means." She shook her head. "But I don't think they've ever toured the US."

"Have you met them?"

"Not me, no. But I've met vampires who have, and they say Lucy and Arthur are charming as hell. They're not like most of us. They *socialize*."

"Huh." I watched her eat another chip, thinking that Molly socialized too, but then, she was also kind of an anomaly. Decades ago, Molly had been an unwilling sex worker at a vampire brothel. All these years later, she still seemed most comfortable with other women around her. A few months ago, some human friends of Molly's had been forced to become vampires, and she now visited them regularly.

"This Vegas thing, though . . . that *is* pretty weird," Molly went on. "I've never heard of vampires putting on a show. I get why Dashiell's freaked out."

I scoffed at her word choice. "Dashiell doesn't get freaked out."

She raised an eyebrow. "He waited an hour for you, and he said please several times?"

"Well, yeah."

I thought about that for all of two seconds. "He's freaked out," we said at the same time.

Molly laughed, and a chunk of avocado slipped off the precarious pile on her chip and dripped onto her pricey black sweater, which made her curse cheerfully. Expensive things meant nothing to Molly, or most of the vampires I'd met. If you could walk up to any rich guy leaving a bank and press him to give you a wad of cash whenever you wanted, what did money matter?

"What do you think he'll do now that you said no?" she asked me. There was no judgment in her voice, but I still squirmed a little. *Not my circus, not my monkeys*, I reminded myself. For once, I really didn't have to get sucked into Dashiell's current supernatural crisis.

"I think he might send one of his vampire toadies," I replied. "They can scope it out from the cheap seats and report back. Then Dashiell will decide if he needs to take action."

She grunted, still inhaling chips. When she finished the bite, she added, "You know, if the show does get the okay from Dashiell, I'd really like to go, maybe in a few weeks or something. I've always wanted to see Lucy and Arthur." She gave me a speculative look.

"I'm *not* going to Vegas with you," I said immediately.

Molly wrinkled her nose. "You are zero fun."

After that, she changed the subject, and then we put in a movie, and while I won't say that I forgot about the vampires-take-Vegas problem, I did sort of let it fall off my mental list of things to worry about. Los Angeles was my territory. Southern California, at a stretch. I could understand how this Vegas thing was a vampire problem, but it still wasn't *my* problem.

Until, of course, it was.

• • •

On Sunday evening, just a few days later, Shadow and I were at Jack and Juliet's new condo in Sherman Oaks, listening to ten-year-old Riley tell a story about a boy at her school who had arrived wearing two different shoes. "And they didn't even *look* alike. He was obviously super embarrassed about it. So my friend Ella—she's on my soccer team—and I traded *our* left shoes during gym class," she said, her big brown eyes sparkling. "And then two of the boys did the same thing at recess, and by lunchtime Mrs. Turner just did *not* know what to do with us."

She was sort of earnestly mischievous about it, and we were all laughing. Under the table, I could even feel Shadow's clubbed tail thumping in solidarity.

Riley preened a little, savoring the attention the way only kids can. Jack shot Juliet a little smile, one that was full of pride and awe at the cool little person Juliet had created. I'd never expected to see an expression like that on my brother's face. It was kind of amazing, and made me a little sad, too.

Riley's brother, Logan, meanwhile, slipped yet another bite of hot dog under the table. We were eating one of Juliet's specialties: gourmet hot dogs with bread wrapped right around them, plus corn on the cob and a quinoa salad. Shadow had wedged herself under the small table with her head turned toward the kids, who, as far as I could tell, snuck Shadow more of their food than they ate. I said nothing about this. It wasn't every day you got to see a thoroughly delighted bargest.

Logan, who was the most serious seven-year-old I'd ever met in my life, turned to face me, pushing up his glasses. "Aunt Scarlett," he began, and my heart thrilled at the words. They both called my brother Jack, but they called me Aunt Scarlett, which made me smug as hell. "My friend Aidan, from support group, just got a service dog like Shadow."

"Aidan had eye cancer," Juliet supplied. My sister-in-law was about my height, with Tina Fey–style square glasses and a curvy figure. Her mother was Korean, which was where she got the glossy black hair. "He's been very excited about getting the dog."

"That's cool," I replied, a little cautious. Jack and his family had bought the cover story that I needed a seizure-alert dog because I'd suffered a minor brain injury in a car accident while Jack and I were estranged. It hadn't been easy to convince my doctor brother that I really had epileptic-type seizures, especially since I never seemed to have one in his presence, but I had showed him a letter from my neurologist, and by now they were all used to Shadow accompanying me everywhere.

"Aidan's dog is a black *Labrador*," Logan went on, pronouncing it carefully, "and he says everybody knows Labradors make the best service dogs. So I was wondering, what breed of dog is Shadow?"

Hearing her name, the bargest thumped her tail again. "Well," I said, trying for as much honesty as possible, "she's a mutt, or a dog that has more than one breed mixed together."

Eager nod from Logan, obviously wanting me to continue. "She's partly a breed called Peruvian Hairless, which is a very funny-looking dog with no hair, just like it sounds. And I think she's got some kind of tracking dog, like maybe a bloodhound, and maybe even a tiny bit of wolf. Or husky," I added, glancing at Juliet. If she was bothered by the idea that Shadow might be part wolf, it didn't show in the smile she shot me.

"Do you think I could take a picture of Shadow to group so I can show Aidan?" Logan asked hopefully. "Mom said I could."

"I said you could *ask* Scarlett," she corrected.

I smiled at him, but there was just no way I could put photos of Shadow out in the world. How to explain that to a seven-year-old who wasn't allowed to know about my life? "I'm sorry, buddy," I said, "Shadow is a really special dog, and I'm not sure I want other people looking at pictures of her."

He thought about that for a moment, while Jack and Riley made faces at each other over glasses of orange juice. "Are you afraid people will make fun of her," Logan asked, then lowered his voice to a whisper, "because she's ugly?"

I kind of wanted to duck my head under the table to see how Shadow responded to *that*, but instead I suppressed my smile and tilted my head to the side, pretending to think it over. "Maybe a little bit," I told Logan. "Tell you what: How about after supper I'll help you find a picture of a Peruvian Hairless online, and you can bring *that* to school?"

His lips twisted sideways as he considered this. "Trust me," I added. "They're *really* weird-looking." This was true, although from what I'd read those dogs topped out around sixty pounds, and Shadow weighed three times that. She really did look like something Dr. Frankenstein had cooked up in a lab, minus the whole "using dead parts" bit. But the idea cheered Logan up, and he nodded happily.

Later, as we were clearing the table, Juliet's cell phone rang. She dug it out of her back pants pocket and checked the screen, her brow furrowing. "Why would your boss be calling me on a Sunday night?" she said to both Jack and me. It was common knowledge that Jack and I shared an employer . . . but I couldn't think of a good reason for him to call Juliet. A wave of fear stirred in my extremely full stomach, but I managed to shrug at the same time Jack suggested, "Butt dial?"

Juliet held out her free hand, palm up, like "what are you gonna do," and answered the phone. "Oh, hello, Beatrice," she said, giving us a confused glance. "No, I can talk."

At that moment, Logan raced through the kitchen with Riley at his heels, shouting at him about her tablet. Juliet winced and said, "One second, please," into the phone. She gave Jack a look that said "all yours, dude" and retreated into their bedroom.

While Jack got the kids calmed down, I finished cleaning up the kitchen, my thoughts whirring. My humans-only world and the Old World didn't collide often, but I freaked out whenever they did. A vampire calling my sister-in-law at home, on a Sunday night? Definitely cause for alarm.

The only thing I could think of was that the call could be wedding-related. Jack and Juliet had only been married for a couple of months, and Dashiell was Jack's boss, too. Maybe Beatrice wanted to see if Juliet had received a late gift? Dashiell and Beatrice had made a brief stop at the small reception—the wedding itself had taken place during the day—but perhaps she'd forgotten the gift that night?

It didn't seem likely. Not when Beatrice had three separate assistants, two of whom were human.

I got more and more nervous as the minutes ticked past without a sign of Juliet. I helped Logan find a picture of a Peruvian Hairless online, which took all of two seconds on Wikipedia, and then he disappeared into his room to play with his Legos. Jack invited me to play Settlers of Catan, which he'd been teaching to Riley. I tried to focus on setting up the complicated game, but Juliet still hadn't returned by the time all the pieces were organized.

The bedroom door finally opened right after Riley managed to swipe the Longest Road card from Jack. Juliet practically bounded out of the bedroom. "You're not going to believe this!" she crowed, her cheeks flushed with excitement. "Beatrice is throwing me a bachelorette party! Well, belated bachelorette party," she added hastily. "In *Vegas*!"

Chapter 4

Oh, *no*.

It hadn't even occurred to me that the phone call could be related to the Vegas thing. All that delicious food in my stomach suddenly turned into a heavy block of ice.

Sensing a longer adult conversation, Riley got up and went to use the bathroom. "Seriously?" my brother asked Juliet, standing up and going around the table to stand next to her. "I mean . . . when? Why?"

Juliet, who hadn't seemed this excited since Jack first proposed, began to bounce on her feet. "Next weekend! I guess Beatrice and Dashiell had show tickets and a suite reserved, and everything is paid for, but now they can't go." The words were tumbling out of her so fast, it would have been funny if my world hadn't just caved in. "And Beatrice knew I never had a bachelorette party, so she hatched this whole plan to send us there at the last minute! All the bridesmaids are invited! Is it okay?" she asked Jack, suddenly anxious. "Can you be with the kids?"

"Of course." Jack was smiling at her.

Abruptly, my shock was replaced with serious rage. How fucking *dare* he? How could Dashiell set up this situation behind my back? How could he pull Juliet, a completely innocent human, into it?

Oh, right, because he needed to manipulate me into going on the trip. This was just like him, to use family against me.

Juliet turned to me. "Oh, and they especially invited you, because I guess Dashiell wants you to do a little work while you're there? Something about meeting with cleaning companies . . . Scarlett? Are you okay?"

I was still standing behind the kitchen table, frozen in place. My palm hurt from the little house figure that was clenched in one of my fists. "Scarbo?" Jack asked, concern in his voice. He took one step toward me. "You look pale . . ."

Shadow had gotten up from her place under the table and moved soundlessly over to me, putting her head under my hand. She had to duck to do it.

"I . . . I . . ." I swallowed hard, forcing myself to take a deep breath. Anger would not be an appropriate response in this company, I reminded myself. *You have to say something.*

Ordinarily I'd make an excuse about needing to work, but Juliet already knew Dashiell had given me the time off. And everyone knew I wasn't exactly in the dating game these days. Besides, I couldn't just duck out of the trip. I needed to make sure Juliet didn't go at all. "Are you sure that's a good idea?" I managed to say. "I thought you said you were too old for penis necklaces and screen-printed tank tops."

Juliet deflated, just a little bit, and I felt like an ass. My brother glared at me, rather rightfully. I was going to *murder* Dashiell. "I'm sorry," I said before she could reply. "I'm just . . . um . . . Vegas isn't my favorite."

Jack's face softened. He took a step back to his wife, putting an arm around her shoulders. "We went to Las Vegas for my twenty-first birthday, right before our parents died," he told her. "It was our last family trip."

"Oh," Juliet said, understanding flooding her face. "*Oh.* Scarlett!"

I winced. "That's not . . . that isn't the only reason," I said lamely. But Juliet had already darted forward and thrown her arms around me. I awkwardly patted her back. I am not a hugger.

It was true that the family trip to Vegas had been rough, though it took me years to figure out why. Vegas is a vampire town, and every time we left our hotel rooms, vampires were stumbling in and out of my radius. Only I didn't know what I was yet, so I didn't know how to process the endless weird sensations and the strange looks I kept getting from people I didn't know. Most of them were hateful, although a few looked at me the way I suspect pedophiles look at kids. Like I was something to be used up.

And they didn't *just* stare. Every time Jack and my dad went to the bathroom or the blackjack table, I was propositioned for what I thought at the time was sex. As a body-shy seventeen-year-old, it was a nightmare.

Juliet took a step back so she could touch my face with her cool, dry palms. "Listen," she said, sympathy in her voice. "Vegas has changed so much in the last eight years; you probably won't even recognize it. And we're not doing the penis necklace, matching tank tops, club thing," she added sternly. "I was very clear about that. We'll take in a show—Beatrice got more tickets so we can all go—do some shopping, maybe hit the spa." Her eyes were sparkling. "The three big S's of female bonding, right? It'll be so much fun. Beatrice and Bethany have got it all planned."

"Bethany?" I said faintly. Ugh, talk about making matters worse.

Bethany Sibowski was Juliet's older stepsister, a chiropractor in Reseda. I wouldn't say she was my nemesis—I didn't see her often enough, and really, there were a lot of other people who hated me more. There just wasn't room for human Bethany on my nemesis short list. But she was an uptight, severe woman who probably organized the contents of her change purse.

Even I had to admit that Bethany had made an excellent matron of honor for Juliet, given her obsession with details. But she thought I was a useless slacker who naturally sucked at all the important things in life: organization, bridal shower games, personal grooming, and returning phone calls in a timely manner. She wasn't exactly *wrong* about any of that, but still. If Bethany was planning the weekend, I would bet a year's salary that there was a printed itinerary in my near future. Probably in goddamned calligraphy.

But of course, Bethany was far from my biggest problem. I couldn't put Juliet and a bunch of innocent humans in the middle of a possible vampire skirmish. I had to nip this in the bud before my sister-in-law got any more excited. And I needed to have a conversation with Dashiell about using humans as cannon fodder. Especially *my* humans.

I mumbled something about needing to sleep on it, and made some excuses. I don't think I even said goodbye to Riley and Logan before I bolted for the van with Shadow trotting after me. It wasn't until I saw my shaking hands on the steering wheel that I realized I was *furious*.

I drove to Pasadena in a blind rage—though since this was LA, anger-driving probably put me in the majority. I parked on the fancy Spanish-tiled driveway and stormed up the sculpted path toward the front door. Shadow had sensed my obvious tension and made no effort to go explore Dashiell's yard. Instead, she was in full-on silent predator mode, stalking along beside me with the hunt in her eyes.

As soon as the vampire lackey opened the door, I marched past him toward Dashiell's office. The lackey let us go by without so much as a comment, which probably meant that Dashiell had warned him I was coming—which in turn meant he had known *exactly* how I would feel about this, and he'd done it anyway.

Just when I thought I couldn't get any angrier.

I slammed Dashiell's office door open, hard enough to make it hit the wall. Shadow surged in ahead of me to check the room for threats.

There was a pretty frickin' big threat sitting behind the desk. Dashiell gazed at me calmly. A thin, fashionably dressed brunette woman stood next to him, looking slightly flustered. Beatrice, Dashiell's vampire wife. She'd probably been sitting in his lap before I stormed in.

"Good evening, Scarlett," Dashiell said mildly. There was a slight edge to his voice as he added, "Please, do come in."

Not finding any strangers, or any immediate source of danger, Shadow returned to my side, clearly a little confused, but ready to back my play. "You win, *boss*," I spat. "I'll go to Vegas and be your little spy. Now call it off."

He raised an eyebrow. "Call what off?"

I ground my teeth. "The bachelorette weekend." I pointed to the cell phone sitting on the desk. "Call Juliet and cancel."

Beatrice made a little clucking noise, and Dashiell gave me a disapproving frown. "Scarlett. Do you know how hard Beatrice worked to plan a full bachelorette weekend so quickly?"

"I don't care!" My voice came out shrill.

Beatrice gave me a look that I'd seen on my mother's face: I sounded petulant. No one would take me seriously until I calmed down. I threw myself into the chair, glaring at them as I took a couple of deep breaths. "I'll go see your stupid fucking show," I said in the calmest tone I could manage. "Hell, I'll go tonight, right now, if you want. But leave my family out of this."

"I'm afraid it's not that simple," Dashiell said smoothly. "The situation has changed."

"How?"

Beatrice stepped back to perch on a table behind the desk, while Dashiell picked up his cell phone and pressed the screen. "I took your advice," he said, his eyes on the phone. "I sent one of my vampires to see the opening performance on Friday night."

"Who did you send?" I instantly regretted the digression, which sort of took the wind out of my angry sails.

"Margaret," he replied nonchalantly. I had met her: a plump, sexy vampire who radiated confidence and charm—when she wanted to. I could see how she'd be a good choice for a mission that involved interacting with humans. "She sent me several photos from the opening night reception, and was supposed to call me after the show."

"She didn't call," I guessed, temporarily distracted by the story.

"No. I presume she has been killed." His voice was still completely calm, and before I could really absorb that idea, he handed the phone across the desk to me. "These were taken right before the performance," he explained. "Scroll right."

I shot him a glare, but now I was too curious to resist. Accepting the phone, I saw that the photos had been taken in an elegant ballroom, with everyone in formalwear. There were a couple of surreptitious shots of a gorgeous couple, the same man and woman pictured in the newspaper article. I scrolled again. The last photo was of just the man, Arthur Holmwood, with a second man leaning down to say something in his ear. The second man was in profile, with only part of his face visible to the camera, but his body language was deferential. "I know him," I said absently. I swiped my fingers on the screen to zoom in, my brow furrowing. Then I looked at Dashiell in disbelief. "No fucking way. It's gotta be a mistake."

Dashiell shook his head. "No mistake. It's him."

The second man in the photo was Jameson Thomas, formerly of New York City. And he was a null.

Chapter 5

Years earlier, I had been betrayed by my psycho ex-mentor, Olivia, the woman who had first introduced me to the Old World. Olivia's crimes included, but were not limited to, killing my parents, attempting to slowly brainwash me into becoming her clone, stalking and threatening my loved ones, and trying to turn me into a vampire. I managed to get away from her, but afterward I felt like I couldn't trust anything she'd taught me. Which, at the time, was everything I knew about the Old World.

Shaken and lost, I had wanted to get out of town for a while, and to learn more about nulls who were *not* homicidal maniacs. To my surprise, Dashiell had agreed on both counts. He'd suggested I go to New York and stay with Jameson, who worked for a cardinal vampire named Malcolm. Partly, I think, he wanted to keep me out of Olivia's reach, but at the time, I had also thought he wanted me to see what an ideal relationship between a null and a cardinal vampire looked like. Stupid, naive Scarlett.

Dashiell arranged for a sort of null exchange visit, but when I arrived in New York I learned very quickly that Malcolm didn't just employ Jameson, he *controlled* him, with a combination of threats, passive-aggressive demands, and fervent praise. He acted as a sort of father/

minor deity to Jameson, who was aware of some of it, and manipulated by the rest. Malcolm didn't take the manipulation as far as Olivia had, but in many ways he was worse than her. He was just better at hiding his tracks. I probably wouldn't even have noticed how controlling he was if I hadn't just been through a similar experience.

Eventually, I realized that Malcolm's twisted treatment of Jameson *was* what Dashiell wanted me to see. The point was to show me that as confused and lost as I felt, it could all be a hell of a lot worse. It was a very Dashiell-like demonstration . . . and a lesson I hadn't forgotten.

Despite all that, though, I had liked Jameson. We'd even had a little chemistry, although I was struggling with complicated relationships back home, and we never acted on it. Since my visit, Jameson and I had texted sporadically, usually when we were thinking of one of the movies we'd watched together. And one time he'd wanted to know how to get blood out of wool. My life is weird. Anyway, the last time I'd heard from him, a few months earlier, he was definitely still in New York.

As I stared at the grainy photo of Jameson in Las Vegas, obviously deferring to Arthur Holmwood, my first reaction was to feel like an idiot. I should have figured out last week that the Holmwoods had a null. Arthur and Lucy were putting on an incredibly costly show at an incredibly costly casino property. Of *course* they would need to make appearances during the day, and for a vampire, that would only be possible with someone like me.

But at the same time, I couldn't believe that the null in question was Jameson.

Well, actually, I couldn't believe that Jameson had left New York. "This . . . it doesn't make any sense," I sputtered. "Jameson works for Malcolm the way I work for you. He always has."

Malcolm was the cardinal vampire of New York City, but unlike Dashiell, he didn't believe in sharing power. Actually, as far as I could tell, he didn't believe in sharing *anything*. I couldn't see him letting his null go to Las Vegas to work for the Holmwoods.

Unless he hadn't? Had Malcolm sent Jameson to spy, the way Dashiell wanted to send me? If so, why? I doubted that Malcolm gave a shit about the Holmwoods risking exposure or hurting humans.

Too much didn't add up here.

I handed the phone back to Dashiell. "Like I said," I began in a calmer voice, "I'll go to Vegas and look into the show for you. But call off the bachelorette party. I'm not risking Juliet."

"And we're not risking *you*," Beatrice replied, squeezing Dashiell's shoulder. "You were right when you told Dashiell that showing up as his representative would look . . ." she searched for a word, and settled on, "aggressive. This gives you a nice cover story to explain why you're in town. And all the reservations have been made in Juliet's name, which is different from yours." Juliet hadn't taken my brother's last name, at least not yet.

"But Jameson knows me," I argued. "He's not going to believe me being there is a coincidence."

"He doesn't have to," Dashiell countered. "It just has to be plausible."

I rolled my eyes. Ah yes, Old World politics. You can't attack someone with a perfectly acceptable story, even if you think they're lying. It's not like putting up a controversial Facebook post. Proof is the only thing that matters.

"But what if they come after me?" I demanded. "What if these Holmwoods decide I'm a threat anyway? Juliet and her friends will be caught in the crossfire."

"That's why we have arranged for one of Hayne's men to serve as the party's 'driver,'" Beatrice explained. "He is ex-military, and spent years as a professional bodyguard in the Middle East. I have instructed him to focus specifically on Juliet and the other humans on this trip." She gave me a wry little smile. "If it comes down to them or you, he will save them."

I had to doubt that. Besides, an ex-military bodyguard, around the clock? "Jesus, how much did that cost you?" I muttered under my breath. Dashiell and Beatrice both gave me a blank look. I sighed. Vampires. They genuinely didn't understand how people worried about money.

I was quickly losing ground in this argument. "What about my job *here?*" I said, a last-ditch attempt. "Who's going to handle any messes that come up while I'm gone?" Yeah, things had been slow, but it wasn't like we could schedule crises in advance. I never knew when I might be needed.

Beatrice cut her eyes over to Dashiell, who gave me a smile that was just a little too classy to be called smug. "I spoke to Mr. Cruz on the phone a few minutes ago," he informed me. "He has agreed to be on call for Old World emergencies in your place. All three leaders will assist him, along with Corry, who is able to take care of Shadow."

Dashiell had been busy. I was kind of surprised that Jesse had agreed to clean up crime scenes in my place, but then again, he'd changed a lot since getting divorced. He wasn't seeing things as quite so black-and-white anymore.

I got up from my visitor's chair and paced the back of the room for a minute, a habit I'd picked up from my ex-boyfriend, Eli. I didn't like this. I didn't like anything about it. And I really, really didn't want to go back to Las Vegas. But I couldn't help but think of Margaret, the vampire who was presumed dead because she had gone to investigate in my place. And Jameson—was he okay? What the hell was he doing in Vegas? I swallowed, my mouth dry. Dammit, I wanted to know what was going on.

But Juliet . . .

"Scarlett," Beatrice said softly, "if Juliet was allowed to know about the Old World, and you told her that this bachelorette weekend could be dangerous, but it could help keep you safe, do you think she'd still want to go?"

My shoulders slumped. "Of course."

"Then why are we still talking about this?" she said in a reasonable tone. "I have planned a wonderful weekend for all of you. You'll see a show, you'll have fun, and you'll come back on Monday with a full report about the Holmwoods. What is the problem?"

Wait, what? There was a gleam in Beatrice's eyes that I definitely didn't like. It was the same look Molly got when she wanted to dress me up in fancy clothes just for fun.

"Beatrice," I said suspiciously, "when you say you've planned a great weekend, what exactly do you mean?"

Her eyes brightened, like she'd been *dying* for me to ask. Well, so to speak. "I spoke at length to Juliet's matron of honor, and we chose activities that were both personalized for Juliet and in line with common bachelorette activities in Las Vegas."

Beatrice and Bethany, teaming up? That was ominous. I had the sudden feeling that I was on a train careening downhill with no brakes. There was no way to jump off without causing an equal amount of death.

Dropping the subject for the moment, I turned to Dashiell, squaring my shoulders. "The deal that we made," I said in a low voice, "was for me to be an equal partner in this city, on the same level as Kirsten and Will. Are you backing out of it?"

He gave me an insulted look. "Of course not. We have been most satisfied with your work, especially the way you handled the unfortunate incident with"—he waved a hand—"the deaths at USC."

I suppressed a snort. *The deaths at USC.* An insane, misogynistic vampire had framed Molly for the apparent murder of twelve college students, and tried to depose Dashiell himself, but the only way Dashiell could describe it was by the possible political ramifications.

I reminded myself to stay on topic. "And would you pull this kind of shit on Will or Kirsten?" I demanded, crossing my arms over my chest. "Would you put Kirsten's daughter in danger just to get some answers you wanted?"

Dashiell's dark eyes glittered at me. Before he could speak, Beatrice laid a hand on his forearm. "Scarlett," she said softly, "it's true that we resolve issues in a different way with the others, but that doesn't mean we're putting your family in danger. Hayne assures me that he's sending his best man. And for more reasons than one, you're the only person who can do this."

That brought me up short for a second. I studied Beatrice. Like all the vampires I'd met, she was an expert at keeping her thoughts off her face . . . as a vampire. Keeping your guard up is much harder when you've been suddenly thrust back into humanity. There was an edge of something in her eyes. Something desperate.

"What do you suspect?" I said, dropping back onto the edge of the chair. My eyes slid over to Dashiell, but he spent more time around me than Beatrice did, and his poker face didn't waver.

"We're not sure," he said stiffly. "Rumors have followed the Holmwoods for decades. There's something . . . off . . . about them. No one is willing to look into it, though, because they are always moving from one territory to another."

I sighed. Sometimes I forgot that Dashiell was sort of a maverick in supernatural society. Most vampires acquired power slowly as they aged, but every once in a while one of them was reborn with a great big chunk of it, and that was Dashiell. Hell, on paper, he was still too young to control *any* city, let alone one as big and diverse as LA had become.

Because he was younger than most of the vampires in his position, Dashiell had a lot of funny ideas about things like sharing power and giving people second chances—and investigating Old World situations even if they didn't directly affect him yet. It was amusing—and kind of scary—to remember that my authoritarian, rigid boss was a James Dean–level rebel among his peers. And I hadn't forgotten about Carlos.

Maybe Dashiell felt some personal responsibility for the current situation in Las Vegas, whatever it was.

But he was right about one thing: if there was a problem in Las Vegas, no one else would interfere, even if the Holmwoods were killing humans.

It was a blow to my pride, but I spat out the words anyway. "Fine. We'll do it your way, including the stipend you promised. But if, God forbid, something happens to Juliet, you will personally be buying both those kids a first-class college education. *Anywhere* they want." It sounded cold even as I said it, but Beatrice was right. Juliet would have agreed to the trip if she knew about the danger. At least this way I was securing the kids' future. "I'm talking Ivy League, PhDs, whatever."

"Fine," Dashiell said, his face unreadable.

"*And*," I went on, "I want your word that you will never again involve Jack or his family in your affairs without speaking to me first. Outside the purview of Jack's mundane human job, of course."

Beatrice looked at her husband expectantly, but he just stared at me with the same opaque expression. I didn't look away. I was the only sort-of human who could meet his eyes without fear, and I wasn't above reminding him of that. The staring contest continued for what was probably one minute but felt like much longer. Finally, Beatrice laid a hand on Dashiell's shoulder. "Consider it a gesture of trust," she said softly.

Dashiell paused for one more moment, then gave me a curt nod. "I give you my word."

Chapter 6

Which was how, a few days later, I found myself arranging a ride to Vegas with a stranger named Cliff.

Juliet and two of her other bridesmaids were going to fly, but I wanted to bring my throwing knives, and the bodyguard/driver that Dashiell was sending needed to bring God knew how many guns. A trip through airport security wasn't really a viable option for us.

Cliff was picking me up at seven in the morning—we were hoping to avoid the worst of the rush-hour traffic out of town—but Jesse came by at six thirty to say goodbye. He was also picking up my van, the White Whale, which was tricked out for handling Old World emergencies. Because he knows how I feel about mornings, he arrived with an enormous cup of coffee in hand.

"Mmm," I said by way of thank you, taking a big sniff of the coffee and opening the door wide. "Okay, you can come in."

Jesse stepped inside and immediately crouched down to pet Shadow, who was frantically waving her oddly clubbed-off tail. She liked Jesse nearly as much as she liked me. "Is Corry already here?" he asked, looking up at me. "I forgot to get her a coffee."

"Yeah, I got in last night," came Corry's voice from the direction of Molly's room. My vampire roommate had gone up to San Francisco for a few days, although she would be back Saturday evening, at which point Corry would move over to my room. Corry wandered into the little entryway, yawning. She was pretty and wholesome-looking, and with her dark blonde hair mussed and a knee-length pajama shirt, she looked more like a fourteen-year-old than a college freshman. "Hey, Jesse."

"Hi, kid," he said affectionately. He raised his arm and gave her a casual but affectionate side hug. Corry had been molested by a teacher four years earlier, and I'd noticed Jesse was always conscientious about how he touched her. He was good like that.

"Are you sure you're going to be okay here by yourself?" I asked her, trying to keep the concern off my face. "I mean, Molly will be back tomorrow night, but it might be late. You know, like, vampire-late."

"I'll be fine." Corry waved a hand. "We'll have fun, right Shadow?" She looked down at the bargest, who seemed less than enthusiastic. Shadow was no idiot. I had never been away from her for more than twelve hours since we'd first met, but she was supernaturally intelligent. She knew what the suitcase on my bed meant.

"Hmm, maybe I'll take her to the dog beach," Corry added playfully, and Shadow's tail began wagging frantically. I winked at Corry, who, like me, suspected that Shadow's big dream in life was to take down a shark. Corry smiled back and sniffed, eyeing my coffee.

"You want some?" I asked, hoping she'd say no.

"Nah." She flapped a hand toward the kitchen and mumbled, "Imma go make some more."

When she was gone, Jesse stepped toward me, close enough for me to smell his aftershave. I fought the blush that threatened to creep up my neck. He and I are just friends, but Jesse happens to be the best-looking human person I've ever seen in my life, and sometimes my body just kind of chemically reacts to that. Especially in a small room. Especially when I hadn't "been with" anyone in—

"Are you sure you're up for this?" Jesse said in a low voice. I just cocked an eyebrow at him. "I mean," he amended, "how have you been feeling?"

"Fine," I said honestly. "No more vertigo or anything."

A few weeks earlier, I'd "cured" a close acquaintance of vampirism. This was the third time I'd permanently removed someone's magic, and the first two times had been hard on me physically. But this time had been better. I didn't know if it was because Hayne hadn't been a vampire for very long or if my abilities were genuinely getting stronger, but instead of lapsing into a coma, I spent a few days in bed feeling weak and disoriented, like the way you feel when you're just getting over a bad flu. After that, I was fine.

I was anxious to do it again, with Molly's friends who had been turned into vampires against their will. But Dashiell had put his foot down, insisting I wait at least three months in between "cures," to make sure my health recovered. I also had to get a complete physical before each attempt, too, which was a pain in the ass. It would be another month before I could try again.

Jesse must have decided I was telling the truth, because he finally nodded, accepting my answer. "What about protection?" he asked.

"You mean like condoms?" I said brightly.

Jesse rolled his eyes. "Do you have your knives?"

"Duh. And my knife belt, for when I can't wear the boots. I even threw in my bulletproof vest, just to make you, Jesse, personally happy."

"Good." He gave me a speculative look. "Are you sure I can't talk you into taking something with a little more firepower?"

Jesse's mission in life was to get me to carry a handgun. I could shoot—he'd made sure of that—but the thought of carrying a weapon like that out in the world scared the bejesus out of me. "For the hundredth time, no. I'm not bringing a gun."

We'd had this argument too many times for him to push me further. "I should let you get moving, then." He held out his hand. "Keys?"

I reached into my hoodie pocket for the van keys, but then I hesitated, suddenly nervous.

"Scarlett," he said in a gentle voice, "it's gonna be fine. I'll keep an eye on Corry and Shadow."

That wasn't really what was bothering me. I knew Jesse could handle my job for a few days, and Corry and Shadow got along like gangbusters. But I couldn't tell him that I was scared for myself, or that going on this little mission made me feel outclassed in at least three ways. You just don't say that kind of thing out loud.

So I nodded and dropped the keys into his hand.

Jesse left, and Corry decided to turn on the Nature Channel for Shadow, who gave my face one last lick and settled on her Volkswagen-sized dog bed in the living room. I dragged my suitcase outside just as a big black SUV barreled into the driveway, right on time. The driver parked in front of the guest cottage door and climbed out.

I think I was sort of expecting Cliff to be a stereotype: a big, extravagantly muscled guy who had to turn sideways to fit through doors, kind of like Hayne. But the man who stepped out of the SUV was maybe five ten, with an olive complexion that made his heritage a mystery. He was in his mid or late thirties, and probably did have muscle, but it was hidden under his cargo pants and denim jacket. As he closed the SUV door and moved toward the house, I could see that he moved gracefully, like a ballet dancer or a fencer. Interesting.

I stepped off the tiny front porch to meet him halfway. "You must be Hayne's guy," I said. The man nodded, his hands hanging loose at his sides. No effort to shake my hand. "Do you mind if I see some ID?" I asked.

He pulled out a wallet and handed me a California state driver's license that said *Augustin Wesley Clifford*. That name was too weird to be anything but real.

I handed the ID back. "What do you want me to call you?" I asked, just to make him respond.

"Cliff."

The part of my brain that expected stereotypes had also figured he was the kind of guy who mostly grunted his words. But that "Cliff" was clear and matter-of-fact. He *could* talk, he just didn't want to.

And we were about to spend the next five hours in a car together. Goody.

Cliff opened the back so I could toss in my small suitcase, and we climbed into the SUV. It looked just like the vehicles that Dashiell kept for his security team, but from the personal touches—a couple of receipts on the floor, one of those organizers on the back of the visor, etc.—I had the feeling we were in Cliff's personal vehicle. Which made sense, given that this was supposed to be an under-the-radar mission.

As I'd expected, he was silent as we got on the street and skated the freeways out of town. I spent some time playing games on my cell phone, but when we were fully out of LA County and I lost the signal, I couldn't stand the silence anymore.

"So what's your story, Cliff?"

He just glanced at me, raising an eyebrow. "You know who I am, right?" I added.

"Yes, Miss Bernard."

Ouch. So it was going to be like that. "Call me Scarlett. Do you know about our real mission this weekend?"

"Yes, Miss Bernard."

"*Scarlett*," I said again. "If you know all that, and if Dashiell sent you along, you're not just a human security grunt. You know about the Old World. There are only a handful of humans in the city who know about the Old World but aren't connected to it in some way, and you're not one of them. So. What's your story?"

He was silent for a long moment, but I waited him out. Beatrice had said that this guy used to be a bodyguard in the Middle East, and he also reminded me of Jesse's friend Lex, who was ex-military. Which meant he was probably weighing my need to know. I gave him a minute to reach his conclusion.

Finally, he said, "My ex was a werewolf."

"Oh," was all I managed to come up with. Only ten or fifteen years ago, most werewolf alphas didn't let their pack members marry humans—or if they did, the human would have to become a werewolf, too. I didn't know how it worked in other places now, but in LA, Will let his wolves marry whomever they wanted, and he also allowed them to tell their spouses the truth. It had been a point of contention between him and Dashiell, but it was one of the few times Will had put his foot down against the city's cardinal vampire. All that had been before my time, though.

"Does she live in LA?" I asked, and then his words caught up with me. He had said his ex *was* a werewolf. Shit. She had died.

"No ma'am," was all he said, and I let the matter drop. I'd been working with Dashiell, in one way or another, for about eight years, and I couldn't think of any werewolves who'd died in that time who could be Cliff's ex. So this had to have been before my time, too. If Cliff had worked as a bodyguard in the Middle East after her death, it would be just like Dashiell to offer him a job when he got back. Dashiell liked to keep humans in the know as close as possible.

At any rate, I was relieved that Cliff already knew about the Old World. This weekend would have been way too hard if I'd had to keep secrets from him, too.

"Beatrice told me your job is to protect the human women on this trip," I offered. "Is that true?"

He glanced at me quickly, then back at the road. "Yes, Miss Bernard."

"Scarlett. Do you ever smile?"

"Yes, Miss Bernard," we said in unison, and despite himself, the corner of Cliff's mouth quirked, just a little bit.

Encouraged, I tried asking, "Do you like working for Dashiell?"

His eyes flicked over, trying to read me. "I work for Theo Hayne," he said finally.

Interesting. It didn't necessarily worry me—Cliff was loyal to Hayne, and Hayne was loyal to Dashiell, completely. In this situation, at least, their orders would be one and the same. But why did Cliff feel the need to make the distinction?

I didn't really think he was going to tell me, so I didn't ask. Who says I'm not growing as a person?

After a few more fidgety minutes of dead silence and desert views, I said, "Do you have any music?"

Cliff let me connect my phone's Bluetooth and serve as the in-car DJ for the rest of the trip. I assumed it was mostly just to get me to shut up, but that was fine. I played what I felt like hearing, and whenever I had a signal, I looked online for more information about *Demeter*.

It didn't surprise me to learn that in addition to big sites like Yelp and TripAdvisor, there were a whole bunch of websites devoted to reviewing the big casino shows. It also didn't surprise me to learn that *Demeter* was receiving excellent reviews.

But although I found dozens of evaluations for the show, I couldn't find a single one that was more than two sentences long. It was like they'd all been written by marketing interns. "This show is wonderful, you should go to it." "Way better than any other stage show in Vegas." Like that. At least none of them said, "Now I'm pretty sure vampires are real."

We stopped in Barstow for gas and a bathroom break, and by the time the SUV was on the road again, my initial caffeine rush was wearing off and I was starting to nod off. The next thing I knew, the SUV was slowing to a halt. Starting awake, I squinted against the sunshine and pulled sunglasses out of my bag so I could look around. We were at a red light, about to turn onto Las Vegas Boulevard. Damn.

It was a little after noon on a Friday, and the sidewalks were already getting crowded with tourists, but the traffic was still reasonably light. I found myself craning my head around to take in the sights on the Strip. Juliet was right: a lot had changed since I'd been there last. We cruised past the Luxor, the Excalibur, the MGM Grand—properties that had seemed so fun and innovative a decade earlier, and now appeared to be overshadowed by the adjacent shopping options. Teenage Scarlett had thought New York-New York was the coolest hotel on the Strip, but now it seemed kind of . . . tacky. Obvious.

A little farther north, there were a bunch of casinos that hadn't been there on my last visit: the Mandarin Oriental, the Cosmopolitan, the . . . LINQ? What did that even mean? Caesars Palace was even bigger than I remembered, and then suddenly we were pulling up to a sand-colored tower with the word *Venetian* running down the front in simple carved letters.

Cliff put the SUV in park and hit a button to unlock the doors. "I'll let you out here, go around, and park," he explained, which was the most words I'd heard him string together yet. "Lunch is at one, yeah?"

"Um, yes. Right."

"Here." He handed me a card with a phone number on it. "In case of emergencies. Dashiell already gave me your number."

"Thanks." I pocketed the card, resolving to program the number into my phone as soon as I reached my room. Then I got my suitcase out of the back and dragged it forward onto the sidewalk. Behind me, I heard the SUV pulling away again, and I craned my head back to look at the massive building, feeling a little claustrophobic. I lived in Los Angeles, which wasn't exactly a small town, but I rarely went into the downtown district. The rest of the city sprawled out, rather than up. I wasn't used to being around all this . . . size. Everything was so *big*, and the sidewalks were packed with people, which we also don't do much in LA.

On my left, man-made canals sparkled in the sunshine, and I could hear laughter and shouting from the handful of tourists lined up to take a ride. Beside them, a crowd seemed to be winding into the Venetian's entrance, so I pushed out a breath and followed them.

Here we go.

Chapter 7

Inside, I was immediately disoriented. I'd sort of prepared myself for beeping, flashing slot machines, but instead I was in some sort of opulent atrium, with statues scattered all over the pretty marble flooring. I could see the casino ahead, yes, but where the hell was check-in? How was I ever going to find my way around? I looked for signs, but they seemed to be mostly for towers and different sections of the casino, plus different sections of the connecting casino, the Palazzo.

Someone jostled me, making me stumble forward, and when I turned around to look it was two laughing teenagers, who apologized—I think—in a language I didn't recognize. I waved them on, chewing on my lip as more people pressed against me. God, I hated Vegas.

"Can I help you find something, miss?" came a voice from my right. I turned, and was relieved to see a competent-looking young woman in a black blazer. Her gold name tag said *Alyssa*.

"Um, check-in?" I managed to say. "Rooms? I have no idea where . . ."

Alyssa clucked sympathetically and held out an arm. "Why don't I walk you?" she suggested. "And we'll get you a map right away."

"Alyssa, will you marry me?"

She smiled. "You know, I get that a lot."

After checking in, I eventually managed to get on the right elevator and walk down the right hallway to the room where I would be staying. It was a few doors down from the other girls, who were rooming together. Beatrice had told Bethany that I would need my own space because I would be "conducting some business for Dashiell," which sounded vague and flimsy to me, but apparently Bethany hadn't questioned it. It was possible that they had made plans in person, where Beatrice could press her to accept whatever she wanted, but it seemed just as likely that Bethany had been secretly relieved. My absence would make it so much easier for the bridal party to discuss the important things in life, like getting your kids into private school and the perfect stretchy leggings.

After dropping off my suitcase, I exchanged the hoodie for a light jacket, shoved my wallet and phone into the pockets, and headed down to lunch with the casino map in hand. After a few false starts, I managed to find the entrance to the Grand Lux Cafe, one of the restaurants just off the casino.

I had been expecting . . . well, a *cafe*, with an order counter and cheap tables that hadn't been wiped properly, but no, this was a full-on, rather decadent-looking restaurant, done in low, warm shades of glowing gold and brown. I automatically glanced down at my clothes. Jeans, boots with hidden knife holsters, and a V-neck tee shirt. Should I have changed?

"Scarlett!" a familiar voice cried. I turned my head and spotted Juliet, waving at me from a crowded table. I recognized two of the women with her as fellow bridesmaids: Bethany, and a pale, shy woman in her midtwenties, Tara (pronounced TAR-uh, "like the sticky stuff they use on asphalt," she'd told me, almost apologetically). The last bridesmaid, Amber, was missing, and I didn't recognize the fourth woman at the table, a Caucasian woman about Juliet's age, midthirties. She had gorgeous, flame-red hair in a chin-length bob, but her beige sundress was frumpy and unflattering.

As I moved closer, I almost stumbled. Not from clumsiness—this time—but because I hadn't been paying attention to my radius. At home I was used to supernatural beings moving in and out of it at all times, but I hadn't been prepared for Juliet's third friend to be a witch.

Of the three Old World factions, witches are the most common, probably because they're born into their powers. Well, sort of: witchblood is hereditary, but every witch has a window of time near puberty when they need to activate their magic, if they're going to use it at all. If you miss the window, your capacity for magic goes dormant, and you spend the rest of your life as just another human.

I can't feel dormant witchblood, which means that whenever I sense a witch in my radius, I'm with an actual magic-user. I get a sense of how strong they are when it comes to magic, and the red-haired woman wasn't particularly powerful—nowhere near the level of, say, Kirsten or Lex. But she was an active witch all the same, which made this weekend even more complicated. If she tried to use any magic at all in my presence, she was going to figure out what I was real quick.

They were all staring at me, probably because I was standing next to the table gaping like a moron. I went to Juliet and accepted a warm hug. "Hey, ladies," I said over her shoulder, turning on my brightest smile. It wasn't really all that bright. "Good to see you all."

"Here, you're by me," Juliet said, removing her purse from the chair next to her. My sister-in-law looked so happy and excited that I felt a stab of guilt over the whole undercover ruse thing. She gestured toward the stranger. "And I don't think you've met Laurel, my best friend from college. She couldn't make it to the wedding, but she actually lives here in Vegas, so this works out great."

Laurel half-stood so she could reach across the table and shake my hand. "Nice to meet you," I said. The witches I know tend to accessorize a lot—they love amulets and protective charms, all that stereotypical crap—but Laurel's arms and neck were bare except for a wristwatch and an antique-looking necklace. It was a chunk of silver, carved in the form of what looked kind of like an ocean wave. Laurel didn't strike me as a big-time surfer, but what did I know?

There were a few minutes of small talk about their flight and my drive, and what everyone wanted to eat. The waiter brought out some warm bread that was so good that I basically forgot my own name for a few minutes, and by the time I finished my second slice, I'd missed a question from Laurel. "Sorry, what?"

"I was just curious about your job," she said pleasantly. "Juliet says you clean houses?"

I nodded. "And a few offices for a handful of clients, kind of a word-of-mouth thing." I didn't mention that I was also now licensed to clean up actual human crime scenes. We had set this up with the police as a precaution for when I needed to hide a supernatural incident. "I also help clients get their homes set up for parties and events, so I work a lot of nights."

"Did you go to school for that?" Bethany asked sweetly.

"No, I dropped out of college when my parents died," I said in as pleasant a voice as I could manage.

There was a moment of awkward silence, then Tara asked, "Did you ever think about going back to school? I mean, that's probably not the kind of job you want to stick with forever . . . right?" She immediately looked flustered.

I fought the urge to roll my eyes. They meant well—at least, I thought Tara did—but I'd run into this before. Educated white people just could *not* believe that a white kid from the suburbs would want to clean houses as a career. They were equally shocked that I'd gotten into a perfectly good college and didn't want to go back for a degree. So then I was expected to defend what I saw as a perfectly reasonable career choice—except it wasn't actually my career. It was my cover. The whole situation was just weird.

Luckily, Juliet jumped in to save me. "Scarlett started her own business when she was just twenty," she said proudly, "and now she has *employees*. She's doing just fine."

I had to smile at that. It was cute to hear her bragging about me, even if it was about my human cover. "Just one or two," I said. "I had a regular part-timer, but she went off to college. I keep meaning to hire someone else, but I've just been calling in freelancers." This was more or less true, if you counted Jesse, who I did not actually pay. He didn't need the money.

"What do you do?" I asked Laurel, mostly to get the conversation off my job. As far as I knew, my cover story was bulletproof, but there was no reason to test it.

"Well, I used to design fountains for some of the casinos," Laurel replied, "but now I run a nonprofit devoted to preserving Las Vegas's history. We had our big gala event the same weekend as Juliet's wedding, unfortunately." She shot Juliet an apologetic look, which Jules brushed off with a smile.

Fountain designer? That was a real job? I filed that thought under Things Not to Say Out Loud.

"Tara, honey, are you all right?" Juliet asked, looking across the table with concern. Sure enough, Tara had turned a little green.

"I thought I was past the morning sickness," she said with a shaky smile, rising from the table. "Excuse me." When she stood up, I saw the baby bump and remembered how at the wedding, she'd been talking about finishing her first trimester. Right.

She speed-walked toward the bathroom, and as my eyes followed the movement I spotted a familiar face hanging out at a table for one. Cliff, sipping from a glass of water, holding a book. He had changed into a charcoal suit with no tie. I tried to smile at him, but he ignored me.

Tara returned a few minutes later, looking much better. The others began chatting about pregnancy, so I pulled out my phone and surreptitiously sent Cliff a text. *Do you want to come meet everyone? You are the "driver."*

When you're all done, he sent back. *I want to make sure no one is watching you.*

I shrugged and went back to the conversation, at least as much as I could. I didn't know anything about pregnancy, or babies, for that matter. Nulls couldn't have kids, so there had never been any reason to learn. But Bethany had two teenagers, and Laurel's wife was apparently eight months pregnant with their second. Laurel turned to me. "Do you have any kids, Scarlett?" she asked.

Juliet shot me a sympathetic look. She opened her mouth, probably to stick up for me, but I answered before she could. "Nope."

"There's still time," Bethany said, in a voice that sounded sympathetic on the surface, but was really just bitchy. Tara, who was maybe a *year* younger than me, nodded encouragingly.

"Actually, I'm totally barren," I said, keeping my voice pleasant. "Pass the bread, please."

That was the end of *that* conversation.

When everyone was finished eating, Cliff came up to the table, as though he'd just wandered in from the casino. The suit wasn't flashy or particularly expensive-looking, but it had been beautifully tailored. If I hadn't known Cliff was carrying a gun, I'd never have suspected it.

I introduced everyone—the others knew that we'd driven together, although I'd claimed it was because I got airsick—and he gave each of the women a polite smile. In that moment he reminded me of Lex, and Jesse when I'd first met him. All three of them had that cop thing where they were completely polite—friendly, even—while remaining so guarded that you never quite trusted their authenticity. *Intense*, that was the word. Intense people freaked me right the hell out.

"Where are we heading this afternoon, ladies?" he asked after the introductions.

Bethany frowned. "Didn't Beatrice give you a copy of the itinerary?" she asked, in a tone that I recognized. It was the same voice LA women used when they addressed landscapers who spoke poor English.

Cliff's smile never wavered. "Yes, ma'am. As I recall, the next few hours are blocked off for shopping. Is that correct?"

Bethany settled back, pacified. "Yes."

I fought the urge to wrinkle my nose. Personally, I'd glanced at the itinerary that Bethany had *messengered to my house*, like we were rich people in Manhattan or something, and then tossed it in the general direction of my suitcase. I hadn't thought to take it out since.

Juliet was looking at me, and I reminded myself that this weekend was supposed to be about her. Or at least, I was supposed to be pretending it was about her. Undercover was so confusing.

But there were only, what, five hours until we had to be at the theater? How bad could this be? I put on a cheerful smile. "Sounds fun," I said, in what I hoped was a bright voice. "What are we shopping for?"

All four women chuckled, like I'd told a mildly amusing joke.

Uh-oh.

Chapter 8

Four interminable hours later, I staggered into my room, feeling like I'd just done back-to-back training sessions with Marko. Groaning, I fell face-first on the hotel bed, trying to summon the strength to kick off my boots. I wore boots pretty much whenever I wasn't training or out for a run, but for the first time ever, my feet were aching. I'd been betrayed by my own Fryes.

The other women were doing a quick change and then getting drinks and appetizers in one of the restaurants on the Venetian's shopping level, but I wanted to be away from people for a while more than I wanted food. There had just been so. Much. Shopping. The other four women had spent the whole time trying on clothes and giving one another opinions about the "cuteness" of each outfit. Molly liked to do that too. When had "cute" become the preeminent term to gauge the attractiveness of adult female clothing?

Still, it'd been nice watching Juliet have so much fun. She didn't buy much—I suspected this was because she and Jack were always saving money to put toward the hospital debt—but she was a good shopping buddy. She gave opinions in a way that was really sweet and supportive, gently nudging Laurel, Bethany, and even Tara away from unflattering choices. She'd encouraged me to try on a few things, too, but when it became clear that I was sick of it, she playfully recruited me to the opinion team. The whole thing was girly as hell, and I'd rather have been doing just about anything else, but . . . yeah. Juliet had clearly had a blast, and that was what mattered.

A light knock on the door interrupted my thoughts, and I would have probably jumped if I weren't too tired. "Who is it?" I mumbled into the pillow. No one answered, because no one would have been able to hear that. I extended my radius to reach the door.

Witch.

"Scarlett? It's Laurel. Can we talk?"

Oh. I didn't know what she wanted, but I wasn't really surprised, either. It was obviously that kind of day. I went to the door and looked through the peephole. The redheaded witch looked nervous, fiddling with her wave necklace, but she didn't give off an "I'm going to murder you" vibe, so I shrugged to myself and let her in.

Laurel stepped forward without waiting for an invitation. She glanced around the room. "Nice digs."

"Uh, thanks?" My room at the Venetian was palatial: an upper level with a king-size bed, and beyond it a whole lower level with a sitting area and windows overlooking the pool. Each separate area had its own television, and there was a third TV in the bathroom. A *third* television. Three. The whole thing was ostentatious to the point of discomfort, so I was trying to ignore it. "Um, do you want to sit?" I pointed down to the lower level.

Laurel followed me past the bed and down to the sitting area, dropping onto the loveseat. "That was a lot of shopping, right?" she said with a slight smile.

"For me, yes." I shrugged. "But you didn't come here to recap the day."

"No. I want to know why you're really here."

I just raised an eyebrow. Laurel sighed. "You're a null. I know you're a null. I've heard about you—"

"Wait, from who?" I broke in. This was so surreal, this merging of my identities. I'd just spent four hours shopping and making polite small talk with this woman, and now she was here talking about our mutual hidden lives.

"Does it matter?"

I didn't reply. She watched me for a moment, then nodded. It mattered to me. "Someone in my clan knows someone in the LA clan."

"They don't really call themselves that," I said automatically. Outside of LA, most witches organize themselves by family. Each clan contains all the witch members of an extended family, plus a few others who live in the same town and know the family members. Los Angeles, on the other hand, doesn't have a central family, so the witches organize themselves loosely under Kirsten in a sort of union or co-op.

"You know what I mean," Laurel said. "My clan is aware of the powerful Los Angeles null. I just never connected *that* Scarlett with Juliet's new sister-in-law."

I watched her carefully, but I didn't think she was lying. I was always sensitive about someone using my family to get to me—hence my fury at Dashiell—but Juliet had been friends with Laurel for years, well before she'd even met my brother. Of all the Old World factions, witches were probably the largest population, and they spent the most time with regular humans. So I didn't doubt Laurel's story . . . but I didn't really trust her, either.

"I'm here for Juliet's bachelorette party," I insisted. "It's a real thing."

Her eyes narrowed just a little. "I'm sure that it is," she replied, sounding just as careful as I had. "But from what Juliet says, it came together last-minute, less than a week after two famous vampires opened a show at the Bellagio. That can't be a coincidence."

Okay, now I was getting nervous. Laurel wouldn't tell Juliet anything—how could she?—but she could blow my bachelorette-party cover within the Old World, which would put Juliet and her friends at risk. So instead of answering the veiled accusation, I tried to throw her off-balance a little. "Who controls the Las Vegas Old World?"

She reared back, just an inch. "The vampires." She paused, reconsidering. "Well, sort of. The Strip and most of downtown belong to the vampires, and we don't interfere. We do all our magic in the real Las Vegas, the actual city where regular people live and work. We leave them alone, and they leave us alone."

"Do they?" I was genuinely curious. In most of the vampire-controlled cities I knew of, the undead were pretty hands-on. Werewolf packs and witch clans had to pay dues, run errands, and generally serve the vampire ruling class. Not everyone held the reins as tightly as, say, Malcolm, but they all held them.

Laurel shrugged. "It wasn't always like this, but in the past five or six years, the vampires have been infighting. They haven't had time to mess around with us when they're so busy trying to topple each other. But things are changing now." Her eyes sought mine, and something clicked: She wasn't here to figure me out. She was here to ask me for something.

But it also seemed like she was being straight with me. The least I could do was reciprocate. "Dashiell, our cardinal vampire, encouraged me to see *Demeter* while I'm here," I said, choosing my words with care. "He is concerned that the show is too revealing."

"Is that all?"

"Has something else been happening?"

Laurel pushed out a breath. "You don't know?"

Okay, that was enough. I was not the person you called for diplomacy and subterfuge. I was tired of playing games. "Not to overdo the Vegas puns here, but let's put all our cards on the table, okay? Yes, Dashiell threw this bachelorette weekend together as a sort of cover story for me to come check out the show. And if you tell anyone that, or do anything whatsoever to put my sister in danger, I will shove a four-inch knife through your left eye socket." I waved a hand. "Now you go."

Laurel's eyes widened, and for the first time I felt her magic flare as she instinctively tried a spell against me. She was pretty weak, but she probably could have thrown someone into a wall if she really pushed it.

Not me, though. Nothing happened.

Having her magic fail unnerved her, and Laurel jumped up, looking almost dazed. "Wow. So that's . . . real."

"Yeah. I am," I said matter-of-factly. "Now, what did you really come here to ask me?"

She blinked hard for a moment, easing herself back down onto the couch. "My clan has a good relationship with two of the vampires," she said after a moment. "A married couple. They're not particularly old or powerful, but they were close to my great-great-grandparents, and they've stayed connected to our family in a friendly way. I would call them allies, but they don't really do anything for us. We just . . ." She paused, searching for the right words to explain the relationship, but came up empty and shrugged. "We like them. They come to some of the family events, and they spoil our kids rotten. Sort of like godparents."

"Okay . . ."

"Last week, one of them, Ellen, went missing. Wyatt—that's her husband—was frantic. The vampires are always struggling for power, but Ellen and Wyatt are so weak that nobody ever bothered them before. Now Ellen has just . . . vanished."

"And you think the Holmwoods are connected?" I guessed.

She held her hands out, palms up. "I don't know. But Wyatt says that Ellen isn't the first vampire to have vanished in the last few weeks, or the last. Something like thirty vampires have gone missing."

"*Thirty?*" I blurted. "Well . . . shit." I thought of Margaret, the vampire whom Dashiell had sent to check out the show before me. Was it possible that she hadn't been killed because she worked for Dashiell? What if she'd just been killed for being a vampire? Or maybe that was jumping to conclusions. They could have been kidnapped or some-thing, but why would anyone want a . . . gaggle of vampires? Coven of vampires? Murder of vampires? How had I gone this long without looking up the group name for vampires?

"When I figured out who you are, I sort of thought you were here to figure out what's happening to the vampires," Laurel said, and I forced my attention back to her.

"Well, who's the cardinal vampire in Vegas right now? Shouldn't he or she do something?"

Laurel shrugged. "There isn't one, as far as I know. The last I heard a couple of vampires were fighting over it, but neither was really powerful enough to win."

Uh-oh. That was bad all on its own. No cardinal vampire meant a whole bunch of invisible killers were running around the city without any oversight. Crap. "Does this Wyatt have a theory?" I asked instead.

Laurel nodded. "He thinks there are skinners in town." At my confusion, she added, "Hunters? Human assassins who kill vampires and werewolves for money." Her face darkened. "Some of them even hunt us, although they usually restrict themselves to boundary witches."

Skinners. The idea rang a bell, even if the specific term did not. Years earlier, I had spoken to a very bad man who had hinted about something like this. I'd never heard about any of these skinners in Los Angeles, though. "Why are they called—" I began, then held up a hand. "No, wait, I don't want to know. Look, all of this is interesting, and I'm sorry about your friend, but I'm not sure what you want me to do about it."

Laurel chewed on her lower lip for a moment. "I thought . . . I thought you might be here to help. Maybe that was naive."

I had to hold in a sigh. "I'm not *not* here to help, but I'm just the scout. My assignment is to see tonight's show, assess the situation, and tell my boss what I learn. If I happen to get information about your missing vampires, I'm happy to pass it on to you, but that's not exactly my mission." *Mission?* Great, I was starting to sound like Lex.

"Fine." Laurel stood up, looking a little pissy. "I haven't seen the show, either. Maybe it'll give both of us some insight."

Now why did that sound so ominous?

After I closed the door behind Laurel, I started pacing my enormous room. I felt like I'd handled the confrontation more or less okay, but the news about the missing vampires troubled me. And I was also a little weirded out that Laurel saw me as someone who could do something about it. Most of the time I felt like the best I could do was project an image of competence—and I never did a particularly good job of it.

I checked my watch. The vampires would be waking up for the night in fifteen minutes. Surely Dashiell would know what to do. I would call and run all of this by him.

I took a quick shower to get rid of the signature Las Vegas smell: cigarette smoke and consumerism. Then I put on a green jersey dress and my black boots, complete with holsters for two of my throwing knives. The very tips of my knife handles were visible when I wore a dress, but you'd have to be looking for them. And there was no way I was going out in the city unarmed.

When I was as ready as I would get, I made the call to Dashiell, who didn't answer. I resisted the urge to swear on his voice mail, and instead left a message explaining Laurel's visit and the missing vampires. I told him I'd call again after the show, or at midnight if I got held up.

While I was at it, I called Corry to check in on Shadow, who was doing fine—although she'd shredded my comforter to protest my absence. I just shook my head at that. Shadow was so weird. And, of course, the reason why I can't have nice things.

A little after six, I was alone in the elevator, heading downstairs to meet Juliet and her friends. I tried to give myself a pep talk about being normal and human, not just for my sister-in-law, but also in case anyone else from the Las Vegas Old World figured out what I was. Laurel had been onto me pretty quickly. I would need to be ready to convince people that my being here was just a coincidence.

In any other city, this probably wouldn't have worked—Dashiell would have needed to contact the established cardinal vampire and inform him that a null would be traveling through town. But since Vegas didn't have a confirmed cardinal, at least not one that we knew of, there was no one for Dashiell to call. It was a loophole, but I was gonna cling to it.

Chapter 9

I was supposed to meet Juliet and her friends on the second floor of the Venetian, in the shopping area where the indoor gondolas turned around. It was crowded with people on their way to restaurants and shows, and as I walked out of the elevator bank and joined the throng, I actually staggered, needing to grab the canal railing to steady myself.

There were vampires *everywhere*.

It wasn't that there were thousands of them in my immediate vicinity, but as soon as one passed through my radius, another seemed to follow from a different direction, and then two more, and so on. It was disorienting, like being invisible in a crowd of moving people. I had a knife in each boot and a third in the small black clutch I'd borrowed from Molly, but I still felt practically naked with the need to protect myself.

The vampires were beginning to look around, too, because they felt themselves switching in and out of humanity. Nulls are rare, but at least Las Vegas did have another null hanging around. Hopefully these guys were looking for Jameson. I didn't want to blow my cover this soon, so I concentrated on shrinking my radius down to about two feet around me. I retreated to a less-crowded area a few feet away and tried to look innocuous.

"Hey, Scar!" Juliet's voice came ringing down the hall. I turned to see her walk up with the others—and immediately felt like a heel.

Juliet was wearing a tight white sheath that made her olive skin seem to glow. A bright pink sash that read *The Bride* was draped across her front. Tara, Bethany, and even Laurel were wearing black dresses that only made Juliet stand out more. All of them had on high-heeled pumps in bright colors—Juliet's were royal blue, and the others varied from red to purple. Even Tara tottered on four-inch spikes, one hand on her belly. They all looked so together, so coordinated. So . . . bridesmaidy. Hashtag squad goals.

With an effort, I did not glance down at my own casual dress and knee-high boots, which had seemed fine back in the room. "Hi," I said, accepting Juliet's light hug. "You look amazing." I glanced at Bethany. "Did I miss a memo or something?"

Bethany's thin lips were pursed with disapproval. I was starting to think that was just her go-to face. "I guess you didn't read through the itinerary," she sniffed.

My sister-in-law pulled me forward, steering us down the hall-way. "I know it's dorky," Juliet said in a low voice. "But Bethany really wanted to, and I couldn't say no. You look great, by the way."

"I could go back up and change . . ." I said distractedly. I was still trying to keep my radius tight around me, a difficult task that only got harder with someone talking to me.

"No, no. Don't even worry about it. I'm just happy you're here." She gave me a little squeeze and released me, which nearly made me stumble.

"You okay?" Juliet said, looking worried.

I summoned a smile. "I'm great. I had a drink at the bar on the way here, and I think it was just stronger than I anticipated. It'll wear off."

She shot me a grin. "Well, I'm glad you're enjoying Vegas."

Oh, yeah. I was having the *best* time.

• • •

I don't remember much of the walk to the car, because I was too focused on getting there with my radius contracted as much as possible. I had it down to about a foot around me, which was smaller than I'd ever managed before, but holding it there was straining my concentration to the breaking point. Normally my null abilities don't tire me out at all—it doesn't work like that—but the mental effort required to suppress my radius was like flexing a muscle and holding it that way. It made my brain tired.

Laurel must have figured out what I was doing, because after a few minutes she sidled up to me and took my arm to keep me steady. She even managed to make it look like she needed me to help her stay balanced on her high heels. I couldn't spare the concentration to form actual words, but I shot her a grateful smile. I didn't even care if she was just kissing my ass so I'd help her with her friend.

I was able to relax a little inside the SUV, since none of the people in the car were bothered by my radius. Sweat had broken out on my forehead, and Juliet shot me several concerned looks. I noticed Cliff glancing at me a couple of times in the rearview mirror, a slight question in his eyes. I smiled brightly and made an effort to join in the small talk during the short ride, though sometimes it felt like Bethany was deliberately steering the conversation toward things I knew nothing about. As soon as we got out, though, I had to clamp down on my radius, and Laurel took my arm again.

After what felt like hours, we made it into the Bellagio, through the slot machine gauntlet, and into the theater, where Laurel asked if we could take the small elevator so she wouldn't have to climb the stairs in heels. I shot her another grateful look, since our group would fill the elevator and I could relax for another moment.

I felt plenty of vampires while we moved through the theater, but after we found our seats, I loosened my grip on my ability as slowly as I could, and was relieved to find that there were no vampires seated within my radius. I slumped with relief and looked around. I was at the end of a row, with Juliet on my left and Laurel on her other side, followed by Tara and Bethany. Our seats were perfect: the first row of the balcony, where I could easily see the whole thing, but wouldn't be able to actually short out any of the performers' magic, at least not without a huge effort on my part. Nothing would scream "playing it cool" like me accidentally forcing one of the vampires to turn human and fall to his death or something.

There were another ten minutes before the actual start time, but on the front of the closed curtain, they were projecting a little movie, made with some kind of flat, papery animation. It took a moment for me to realize it was the basic story of *Dracula*. A man dressed in business clothes goes to a faraway land and meets a creepy old guy in a long black cloak. The cloaked guy tries to kill the businessman and then sails far away, to the businessman's homeland. He meets a beautiful and coquettish blonde woman with several suitors—Lucy—and takes a shine to her. The foreigner—Dracula, of course—bites her neck, and she grows ill. Eventually she dies in bed.

At that point, the suitors, along with another man dressed in strange clothes, probably Van Helsing, go to her grave site and find her alive. So to speak.

In the novel they stake her, but in this version of the story events unfold just as Dashiell described: Van Helsing leaves Arthur Holmwood to destroy Lucy's corpse, but he can't do it. Instead, Arthur returns later and throws himself down on his knees in front of her. Lucy takes his hand, pulls him to his feet, and bites his neck.

I knew that the novel went on quite a while after this, becoming a story about Jonathan Harker's attempts to thwart Dracula, along with his young fiancée and the other suitors. (Harker and the Suitors should be the name of a goth band somewhere.) But the animated recap ended after Lucy bites Arthur, probably to make the point that this wasn't Dracula's story or Harker's story. This was the Holmwoods' tale, and them becoming vampires together *was* the happy ending.

"Do you want a mint?" whispered a voice next to me. I jumped, and Juliet let out a surprised chuckle. She was holding out an open tin of Altoids. I took a mint.

"You okay?" she asked. "You look a little out of it. Don't tell me you're scared of Dracula."

"Dracula's not real," I said absently. Then I realized that she was staring at me, so I pulled together a wan smile. "Sorry, I was just . . . thinking about work."

Juliet still looked a little puzzled, but before she could say anything else, the lights switched off and the curtain began to open.

The stage was an enormous semicircle—no, nearly a full circle, going deep behind the curtain. At the far end of the stage there was an almost life-size wooden ship, battered and blackened from an imaginary wreck. The edge of the stage was rounded, and the surface had been painted here and there with thick, glossy red lacquer to resemble heavy puddles of blood. Charming. There was no orchestra section—music and lights were obviously being run from booths on either side of the heavy curtain—and the first row of seats seemed shockingly close to the stage itself.

The stage was completely empty, and then *thwick*—a spotlight snapped on, and suddenly a woman was standing in the center of the stage. Her skirts were still swaying a little from the movement. It was vampire speed, I knew, but the audience just saw another Las Vegas trick. They gasped and applauded. The woman, a small blonde in an immaculate Victorian gown, smiled at the applause for a moment, then held up a hand. The crowd went silent, staring at her. Her long hair tumbled down her shoulders in thick, shining curls. Even at this distance, she was exquisite, like a human doll.

"Good evening, my darlings," she said. "Welcome to *Demeter*. My name is Lucy, and I'm sure you know my story." She gave a coquettish smile, eerily similar to the animated version from the preamble, which wasn't an accident. She held her hands folded behind her back, a girlish, demure gesture that just happened to push her breasts out. Lucy made a show of looking down at herself.

"Of course, this is how I am always depicted, isn't it? In the films, the stage shows, the copycat novels." Her smile turned wry. "If, that is, I am not written out entirely or turned into a vapid whore." She sighed, one hand reaching up to play with a perfect corkscrew of blonde hair. "But this Lucy is only a facade. A perfect, useless representation with no thoughts, no agency."

The hand at her hair ripped viciously downward, faster than I could follow the movement. Suddenly Lucy was standing there in a skintight black sheath dress, holding up the ripped-away Victorian garb in one hand. There was a chunk of blonde wig attached to it, and when I squinted I could see that her real hair was cut in a sleek bob, angled so the points just brushed her shoulders on either side. Black high heels, at least six inches tall, were strapped to her feet. "*I am not a story,*" she said, in a voice so fervent it was hypnotic. "Not a doll, not a prize. Not anymore. I am *vampire.*"

Nerves churned my stomach. Dashiell was definitely not going to like this, but couldn't it be pretty much written off? Sure, she was telling the truth, but no one would think it was anything but a trick. Right?

Lucy began to move, prowling soundlessly around the stage in her obscenely high heels. Hell, just moving around in those shoes looked supernatural to me. I would have fallen and broken my jaw for sure. "Tonight I will show you otherworldly feats of hypnotism, agility, and speed." She paused, still in the center of the stage, only a few feet from the lacquer blood. She made a show of looking around the cavernous empty space. "But first, my darlings, first. I must show you the truth. Show you"—her lip curled, and her voice took on a terrible power— "what we are."

She raised her bare, pale arms into a *V*, and four additional spot-lights snapped on behind her, two on either side. From my angle in the balcony I could see the openings in the stage ceiling, where four men stood waiting in identical black slacks and ribbed tank tops that showed off arms corded with muscle. Before my brain could even guess at what would happen, they all dove from their perches. They spun through the air like Olympic divers, twisting and somersaulting before landing on the stage, each in a perfect crouch.

There was a moment of suspended silence as every single member of the audience realized the same thing: There were no safety harnesses. No nets, no ropes of any kind. As one, the four men held up their hands and turned in a slow circle, showing that they had no protective gear. The man closest to Lucy stepped forward to put his arm around her waist, claiming her. Arthur Holmwood. Together, the two of them thrust their free entwined hands in the air, and the audience exploded into applause. And I felt my stomach drop through the floor of the balcony.

Okay, yeah. Dashiell was going to be *pissed*.

Chapter 10

For the next ninety minutes, the Holmwoods—plus a cast of six more, by my count—showed off every vampire trick I could think of, and a few I hadn't even known about. They ran and danced onstage at superhuman speeds. Arthur wheeled out a tank of water for one of those old-fashioned magician tricks, where someone unlocks themselves from chains underwater—only this time, the vampire extra inside the tank simply tore apart the chains and settled down on the bottom of the tank, pretending to be bored. He even began flipping through a waterlogged magazine, getting a laugh from the audience. Vampires do breathe, partly from habit, partly to keep blood pumping through their bodies, and partly so they can speak—but they can go a long time without if they want to. After a few minutes with the magazine, an assistant ran out and pushed the tank to one side, where it would remain until the end of the show, to prove the vampire inside didn't need air.

After that, Lucy and Arthur did a bit where Lucy came out with a bow and arrow, and Arthur put an apple on his head. He made jokes about how his wife had terrible aim, and at the last second she lowered the arrow, which flashed across the stage and buried itself in Arthur's stomach. His white shirt instantly bloomed red. The audience screamed—beside me, Juliet practically jumped out of her chair—but

Arthur simply tore out the arrow with a rueful grimace and tossed it aside. "See what I mean?" he called, mugging for the crowd. "Terrible shot."

"What are you talking about?" Lucy retorted. "It went right where I wanted it."

The audience applauded and chuckled, and after an elaborate bow, Arthur walked offstage to change his shirt.

Before and after each of these bits, the vampires brought volunteers onstage—a short Asian man, a middle-aged white couple, a teen dressed in black clothes and black lipstick who looked downright worshipful when Arthur took her hand. Each human volunteer was then pressed to do something silly: the Asian man had to quack like a duck, the couple drenched their formalwear with buckets of water, and so on. Still, the audience members continued to raise their hands to volunteer. Next to me, Juliet nudged me and whispered, "Glad we didn't sit any closer. Tara would have volunteered for sure."

I let out a quiet snort, leaning forward so I could see past Laurel to Tara. She was actually sitting on her hands, her eyes wide, like she was afraid she would be suddenly teleported down to the stage and forced to participate.

I was keeping track of the number of volunteers, but it took me until the sixth one to wonder why they weren't immediately taken back to their seats when the trick was finished. Instead, each one was led into the wings. With volunteer number seven, the vampire escort didn't move quite as far offstage, and I watched as he took both her hands in his, looking into her eyes and whispering intently. Then something flashed from his hand to hers.

They were pressing the volunteers again, but why? Was it just so they wouldn't remember what had happened onstage? Or was something else going on? I decided I needed to find one of those humans.

The show ended with the enormous ship moving slowly forward to the front of the stage. Lucy did a little introduction for it and then asked us if anyone in the audience worked in construction. No hands went up, and she let out a dainty giggle. "Don't worry, I won't make you quack," she promised. "But surely someone here has some experience with . . . erections?" She batted her eyes theatrically, and the audience laughed. A couple of hands went up, and Lucy pointed at one. A lackey trotted out from the wings to guide the volunteer onstage. As they approached Lucy, I saw that he was a white guy in his early sixties, short and stocky, looking uncomfortable in his suit, though it fit perfectly well. Lucy smiled gaily and held her arm out to someone offstage. Light glinted in the air, and she was suddenly holding a silver microphone, which she handed to the older man.

"Hello," she said, in the same flirtatious tone she'd used all night. "Can you tell me your name, and where you work?"

"I-I'm Stuart. Stu," the man said nervously. "I've been a foreman at D&S Construction in Boise for thirty years."

"Wonderful," Lucy purred. She snapped her fingers, and three vampires jogged out of the wings, each pushing a wooden pallet on wheels. They'd been loaded up with stacks of wood and five-gallon buckets. "Stu," Lucy continued, "can you look at these materials and tell me if they've been tampered with?"

"T-tampered with?"

"Yes, my darling," she said, unfazed. "Are they real? Or simply fake Vegas props?"

Stu bobbed his head, handed her the microphone, and ambled over to the nearest pallet. He began running his hands over the supplies, knocking on the wood, digging through the buckets. His shoulders relaxed, and he looked comfortable for the first time since he'd stood up.

Lucy waited patiently while Stu investigated all three pallets, each one loaded as high as Stu's forehead. To keep the audience entertained, the vampire in the tank of water on the side of the stage began to stretch and yawn, pantomiming hunger and boredom. The crowd tittered.

Finally, Stu returned and held out his hand for the microphone, looking more confident than before. "As far as I can tell," he said seriously, "these are good quality, real materials."

"No fakes?" Lucy asked lightly.

"No fakes."

"Thank you, Stu," she said, kissing his cheek. The older man blushed, turning to walk away. "Wait just a moment, my darling," Lucy said, and the old foreman turned around. "Would you mind doing one more tiny favor?"

He gave her a guarded look. "Do I have to moon anyone?"

Lucy threw back her head and laughed. "No, no." She held up one leg, perfectly balanced on a single high heel, and rested her ankle on one of Stu's folded arms. "Would you mind taking these off me?"

Stu shifted a little, as though his pants had suddenly shrunk a couple of sizes. His big fingers fumbled at the straps on the shoe, while Lucy winked at the audience but didn't wobble. When Stu was finally holding both of the stilettos, she said, "Thank you, my darling. Be a dear and hold those, won't you?" Without waiting for his response, she turned to the audience, reaching one hand out toward the wings. Suddenly Arthur was there, holding her hand. No gasps this time—the audience had gotten used to vampire speed. "And now," Arthur announced, "we present . . . the *Demeter!*"

There was a flash of strobe lighting, and suddenly the pallets were moving, pushed by the five remaining vampire extras. They zipped back toward the ship, and the supplies began to fly off the top as the eight vampires began repairing the ship at their top speeds.

It was like watching time-lapse photography. The ship started out rather decrepit-looking, like a starved, broken animal, but it began to fill out, expanding with new boards and sails, even some paint. It was astonishing, and although several minutes ticked by, I couldn't look away.

Finally, the vampires sped to either side of the stage in a line, holding out their arms to show off the ship. Lucy Holmwood made the construction foreman go walk around on top, and his look of utter amazement couldn't have been more convincing. The ship had been transformed, like magic. Actually, scratch that: it *was* magic. I glanced at Laurel, who was looking at me behind Juliet. She looked as troubled as I felt.

What the hell were the Holmwoods doing?

Chapter 11

There was a standing ovation from the stunned crowd, and finally the lights came up. Juliet and her friends started collecting purses and jackets, turning toward me, since I was on the end.

Tara was actually the first one to stand up, giving me a pleading look. "I really have to pee," she said, embarrassed. I started moving us toward the balcony steps. "But wasn't that amazing, you guys?" she continued. "How on earth did they do that with the ship? Or the guy in the tank?"

"Vegas tricks," Bethany said dismissively, looking to Laurel for confirmation.

"Some of the best stage magicians in the world live in Vegas," Laurel said, noncommittal.

"I'm hungry," Bethany announced. "Shall we hit the buffet here? Or we could go somewhere a little less expensive?" She gave me a pitying glance. I ignored her. I had no time for Bethany nonsense.

"I could eat," Tara said, one hand on her stomach bulge. "Ooh, after I pee."

"What did you think?" I said to Juliet. Her brow was a little furrowed. "It was incredible," she answered, looking a little perplexed. "But I'm with Tara. How could they do that stuff?"

It was mostly rhetorical, but I pretended to feel my phone buzz in my clutch. "Oh, hang on." I pulled it out and looked at the screen. "Uh-oh. I've got to go, Jules. The manager of Dashiell's new building wants to meet over drinks."

"Now?" she said, and the disappointment in her voice cut at me. "Isn't it kind of late for business?"

I shrugged. "Everything happens at night in Las Vegas." I kissed her cheek. "See you in the morning, okay?"

"Don't be late to the spa," Bethany called after me. I rolled my eyes and kept going, clamping down on my radius.

I needed to find at least one of those volunteers. Fighting against the departing crowd, I threaded my way into the lower doors, ignoring the curious looks of the ushers, who made no attempt to stop me from moving toward the front of the theater. There were a handful of other audience members doing the same thing, in order to take pictures in front of the massive stage. I held my phone up, pretending to frame a selfie, while I looked around for any of the dozen people who'd been chosen as volunteers. I already wished I'd paid better attention to how they looked, but I'd been a little far from the stage.

It would have been smart to wander the aisles a little, but I had to concentrate so hard on keeping in my radius that it was all I could do to stand there smiling at my phone as I pivoted around, scanning the crowd. Just as I was beginning to despair, I recognized a bright fuchsia dress, walking away from me. That woman and her companion had been two of the volunteers.

I hurried after them as they walked through the theater's exit doors and into the lobby, which joined up with the rest of the casino. When I got close, I felt the tiny *zing* of two presses breaking.

To my relief, it felt like any other vampire press: just a simple little mind charm. Breaking the press doesn't usually affect the human, but this time the two of them paused simultaneously, looking at each other. I stepped a little closer, pretending to dig for something in my little bag.

"Do we even really want to go to this thing?" the woman said doubtfully. "I'd honestly rather just go out to dinner. Or head back to the room. I'm sick of these heels."

The man was looking down at something, and when I took a tiny step sideways I could see that he was holding what looked like two flyers, each about a quarter the size of a piece of paper. "You know, I don't even really care," he said slowly, like he was surprised. "Let's skip it."

"Awesome." The woman gave him a peck on the cheek, and the guy strode over to a trash can and tossed the flyers inside. He held out his arm, and the woman took it, leaning in to tell him something that made him laugh.

It was a weird time for me to feel a pang of loneliness. They were just so couple-y. It was obnoxiously cute. I pushed the thought aside, wandering over to the same garbage can. When I was sure the couple was out of sight, I pretended to reach into my mouth for a nonexistent piece of gum. I mimed putting it into the bin, but quickly pushed my whole arm inside, grimacing, until my fingers brushed against the edge of what felt like pieces of card stock. I pulled them out, glancing around to make sure no one was watching me. Then I looked down at the top flyer.

It was thick, glossy card stock, with an old-timey font that communicated class and mystique. *Thank you for participating in* Demeter, it read. *You are cordially invited to socialize with the cast during this evening's Volunteer Reception. Please bring this pass to ensure entry.*

Below that was today's date and the name of one of the ballrooms, probably in the Bellagio's conference center.

I leaned my back against the wall to think. I had the answer that Dashiell had been looking for—the Holmwoods were definitely giving away their vampire status, although that didn't mean anyone would believe them, especially in Las Vegas. At this point, I could consider my job finished. As soon as I updated Dashiell, I could go back to the bachelorette party and collect a fat paycheck for my trouble.

But I still didn't know what was going on with Jameson. Why was he working for the Holmwoods? Was he okay? And dammit, the disappearances bothered me. Vampires don't always report their comings and goings, even in a city that does have a strong cardinal vampire. But Margaret wouldn't have vanished without telling Dashiell, and Laurel had seemed convinced that Ellen wouldn't disappear, either. If there really were these vampire hunters or whatever in town, was anyone doing anything about it?

I tapped the end of the card against my palm, weighing my options. Technically, my work here was done, but I'd been sent here to observe and report. Surely it wouldn't hurt to make a quick stop at this party for a little more observing?

I would need to work hard on controlling my radius, though, which meant it would be good to have someone at my back. And I did have two tickets. Unfortunately, there was really only one person I could think to ask, and bringing him meant leaving Juliet unprotected, at least for a little while.

But it couldn't be helped. I pulled out my phone and called Cliff.

Thirty minutes later, the two of us were walking through the promenade of shops, on our way to the Bellagio's Renaissance-themed conference rooms. Or at least I hoped we were. I'd gotten lost twice trying to meet Cliff, so at this point it was anybody's guess.

I was holding on to his arm in what I hoped looked like a romantic, old-fashioned way, and not at all like I would probably walk straight into a wall without it. He was still wearing the suit from earlier, but he'd added a tie. "Are you sure they'll really stay put?" I said distractedly. I'd already asked this at least twice, but it was hard to concentrate on his answer when I was so focused on reining in my radius.

"As I said, Miss Bernard," he said patiently, "Miss Nash persuaded them to order pizzas and head back to their suite for an old-fashioned slumber party." Miss Nash was Laurel. I'd told Cliff that she was clued into the Old World, and he'd asked her to help keep the others corralled for the night. I didn't think anyone was aware that I was in town—yet—but I didn't want to take any chances while I was keeping their bodyguard with me. "She was very helpful," he added.

Of course she was. I was heading into a vampire den to get the answers she wanted.

We stopped—or, rather, Cliff stopped, and I stumbled for a foot before catching myself. "I think this is it," he said, looking from the invitation in his hand to the ballroom in front of us. I'd almost walked right by it, which did not escape my companion. He glanced down at me. "You sure about this?"

I nodded tightly. "We stay at least two feet away from everyone, do a quick circuit of the room, and get out of there. If we see Jameson, I need to talk to him." Although I hadn't worked out exactly what I was going to say.

Cliff's face was expressionless, but there was something in his body language that seemed . . . defiant. I glanced down at his hands. They were twitching, like he was trying to pull an imaginary trigger.

I pulled him down the hallway a ways, past the door and toward the bathrooms, which was one place where vampires did not hang out. I risked releasing my radius again so I could scrutinize him. "Can you handle this?" I asked.

"Of course, Miss Bernard."

"Cut the shit," I snapped. "You seem . . . I don't know, something. Scared. Do we have a problem?"

If anything, his face became more guarded. "No, ma'am. I am here on Theo Hayne's orders to protect a group of human women, and as a secondary subject, you."

"Are you aware that your right hand is resting on the butt of your gun?" I said, a little snide.

He jerked his hand away, smoothing down the jacket of his suit. "I apologize, Miss Bernard."

I studied him. Something felt wrong here. "What is it you usually do for Dashiell?"

"I protect the mansion," he said immediately. "I assess security threats, patrol, maintain the grounds. When Miss Beatrice's assistant needs to run errands, I drive her. I also maintain Hayne's weapons and vehicles. Ma'am."

"And you do all that during the day, right? Only during the day?"

"Yes, Miss Bernard."

I rolled my eyes and stepped forward, all the way into his personal space, and said very softly, "If you call me ma'am, or Miss Bernard, or anything at all besides Scarlett, *one* more time, I am going to call Hayne and tell him I need someone else, because your insistence on formality is threatening my cover story. Or would you *prefer* that I ask for someone else?"

"No, m—" He cleared his throat. "Scarlett."

"Thank you. Tell me the truth. Are you afraid of vampires?"

He bristled. "That's the wrong word," he said after a measured pause. "I am not afraid of sharks, as a concept, but that doesn't mean I'm going to carve a few gashes in my skin and jump into the Pacific."

I shot him a skeptical look. "Yeah, but in this analogy, you *work* for the shark."

"I told you, I—"

"Yeah, yeah." I held up a hand. "You work for Hayne. So why did he send you, if you're skittish around the Old World?"

"Because he trusts me," Cliff said simply.

That actually made more sense than just about anything else he might have said. Hayne owed me; I had saved his humanity. He wouldn't send anyone he didn't trust completely. "And because he doesn't know that the vampires . . . concern me," Cliff went on, looking a little sheepish. "It hasn't come up, with me working only the day shift."

Great. My backup was afraid of what he was supposed to be protecting me from. I pushed out a breath. I would have to make the best of it. "Well, you're with me. There *are no vampires* within a few feet of me, okay? We go in, we look, we get out. As long as you stay close, anything that comes at us can die."

He nodded, his impassive expression suddenly looking just the tiniest bit relieved. "I'm left-handed," he offered. "Stay on my right, so I can shoot."

I linked arms with him again, tugging him toward the ballroom. "Attaboy."

Chapter 12

The Donatello ballroom—named after the Renaissance painter, not the Ninja Turtle, sadly—had been cordoned off with those retractable walls, so the first room we entered was fairly small. It was obviously a party, with music and chill lighting. There were twenty or so people clustered around some of those stand-up "conversation" tables. I hate those tables, mostly because I am fundamentally very lazy and I want to sit down.

Scanning the crowd, I recognized a couple of the volunteers, mostly from their clothes, but there were way more people in the room than there had been volunteers on the stage. Then again, the Holmwoods could be handing out invitations on the street, for all I knew. I did recognize Stu from Boise, the contractor who had verified the building supplies. He was chatting and laughing with the way-too-beautiful woman at his elbow, and he looked comfortable as hell. Oh, yeah, she'd pressed him *hard*.

I spotted a burly guy with an intricate goatee, guarding the door that separated us from the next ballroom. That would be where the vampires took the humans. Just inside the main entrance, a rectangular table near the wall held glasses of wine and champagne, plus open bottles of what was probably fancy beer. Uniformed caterers circled through the volunteers, offering fancy miniature foods. A few people didn't seem to be eating or drinking, and I figured they were probably vampires, left out here to keep the crowd calm and happy. As long as I stayed well away from them, I could relax my radius a little.

I went to the table and picked up a glass of champagne and a bottle of beer, handing the beer to Cliff. "Hold it, don't drink it," I murmured. I wouldn't put it past the vampires to roofie the drinks. Cliff nodded and took the beer with his right hand. "You see the door in the corner?" I said, trying to look casual. "I need to get a look inside. Then we'll circle back toward the exit. Okay?"

He nodded again. I got a firm grip on his right elbow and pasted a big smile on my face. Then I reined in my radius as much as I could. "Smile," I reminded him. "We're at a party. We're a little drunk and having a great time."

One-second pause, and then Cliff's face broke out in a warm grin. It was so unlike what I was used to getting from his mouth that I almost told him to stop.

I made aimless small talk about the show as we sort of promenaded around the edges of the room, skirting the tables with the chatting vampires. One or two of them glanced at us a little uncertainly—who do *they* belong to?—but they seemed to relax when they noticed our full drinks, maybe figuring us for humans in the know.

The guy with the fancy goatee didn't move as we approached. *Please be human, please be human, please be human,* I thought at him, but I stayed a couple of feet away just in case.

"Hi, there," I said brightly, giving him a wink. I fanned myself a little with my entrance ticket. I didn't want to overdo the pretending-to-be-drunk thing, but I did allow myself to stumble a little. "Listen. I *really* liked the . . . um, the backup dancer? He was like, kind of tall—"

"Well, ish," Cliff put in, picking up the game. "I'd say tallish."

"Right, yes, thank you." I patted him on the chest and turned back to Goatee. "Anyway. He was tallish and hot and stood next to the chick vampire? On her left, I think." I held up my hands like I was reorienting myself. "Or would that be stage left? I can never remember."

"Yeah," Cliff said, nodding emphatically. "Right."

"No, left," I corrected, and looked at the guard again. The Goateed One was starting to look uncertain. "Anyway, could you see if he's free and if he, like, wants my number? Or maybe just a little, um, conversation, right here?"

Goatee looked back and forth between Cliff and me. "Aren't you guys a couple?"

"Oh, he likes to watch," I said brightly, putting an arm around Cliff. I didn't dare look up at his face. "We're both very . . . willing. So can we see him?"

Goatee's eyes narrowed, though I couldn't tell if he was suspicious or just unsure about what to do. After a long moment, he said, "Uh, hang on." He pushed open the door, then paused. "Just stay *right* there, okay?"

I nodded with my eyes big, but I was already looking past him to the room beyond. When the guard disappeared, I waited until the door had nearly swung shut before I stopped it with my foot. Leaning forward, I peered through the crack.

From what I could see, the second ballroom was identical to the first in size, but there was a surprising amount of furniture: couches and armchairs grouped with coffee tables to form little conversation areas. The lights had been dimmed, and the music in there was quieter and subtler than in the first room: something smooth and sexy with lots of cellos. Every sitting area held one or two couples—each consisting of a dazed-looking human and a vampire. And the vampires were eating.

The movies often depict vampire feedings as this sexy thing, and maybe it is for the victim, if that's what they've been pressed to believe. But for vampires, feeding from humans is a transaction, cold and a little nasty. Sure, you'll sometimes get the connoisseur who savors his meal, just like with humans, but most of the feedings we could see lacked any sort of art or finesse. It was a simple matter of one person attached to the neck or wrist of another, sucking greedily. And sometimes noisily. The humans, for their part, looked lost and vacant and small. I didn't see Jameson.

My hand was still on Cliff's arm, and I could feel his whole body stiffen with anger. "We should shut this down," he murmured, his voice a low growl. "These people don't want this."

He was probably right, but I shook my head. "They came here of their own free will, and they're all walking out of here alive and reasonably unharmed. Besides, I've got no authority to stop this, even if I could." I did not mention that I was actually a little relieved. There was something so weird about the Holmwoods and their whole "let's put it all out there" vibe. Part of me had been afraid they were . . . I don't know, butchering tourists and hanging their entrails around like Christmas garlands. A roomful of feeding vampires wasn't easy to look at, but it was also pretty routine, and I had been doing this job for too long to be outraged.

"That's bullshit," Cliff grumbled, but he allowed me to push him gently back from the door. Before I let it swing shut, I saw that Goatee was on his way back, with two men in dark polo shirts behind him. They looked less like vampires and more like security. "Time to go," I said to Cliff, keeping the smile on my face as I grabbed his elbow and pulled him away from the door. The most direct route to the exit was through the cluster of standing tables, so I led him that way, taking long strides and hoping we weren't walking too fast.

And then I lost my grip on my radius.

I'd gotten tired, and the combination of checking the feeding room, concocting an escape route, and keeping my radius cinched in tight was too much to juggle in my brain. I just . . . slipped. Immediately, several vampires at the tables doubled over, struggling with the twin sensations of a beating heart and the need to breathe. I had about five seconds before they recovered and started looking around for the null.

It would have taken a moment of motionless concentration to gather the radius around me again, so I just walked faster, pulling Cliff along behind me. I was moving too quickly to stop and glance back at the vampires, but I heard urgent yelling behind us, and I could picture them standing up and beginning to follow us, closing off exit routes as we fled, like pack hunters in the wild. I was suddenly very aware of how vulnerable I was if they caught me. I still had my cell phone in Molly's clutch, but who would I even call for help? There was no one who could get here in time.

Nearly jogging now, Cliff and I turned out of the ballroom—the vampires popped back out of my radius—and hurried back down the long corridor to the main casino. Cliff took the lead, looking ready to dropkick anyone who got in our way. I could hear footsteps from the hallway we'd just left, getting closer and closer. "Come on," Cliff shouted over his shoulder, breaking into a run.

Then someone very big came up behind me, pushing me through an emergency exit door before I could so much as scream.

Chapter 13

I hadn't realized we were anywhere near an exterior wall of the building, but I suddenly found myself in a dim outdoor area, the dry desert breeze blowing loose hair in my eyes so I couldn't see where I was being forced to go. I stumbled but managed not to drop the clutch as I was pushed along. With a little fumbling, I got out my knife and whirled around with it raised above my head, more or less at the level of the guy's face. But the man caught my wrist and held my arm above my head. He was damned tall, and I was off-balance as he pushed me until my back slammed against the adobe wall behind me. He pinned my wrist to the wall, and when I tried to punch with my free hand, he caught it and pressed it into the building, too. Now strong hands were holding both my arms in place, and I felt my pulse jump.

"Dammit, Scarlett! Drop it!" the man hissed, still looming over me. Oh.

I didn't drop the knife, but my arm relaxed as, for the first time, I focused on my radius . . . and felt the familiar, bizarre sensation of another null. If you thought of my ability as a light that emitted from my body, being near a null was like shoving the light into a prism.

But I knew this particular prism.

"*Jameson?*" I tossed my head to get my hair out of my face. Jameson Thomas was looking down at me, his face in shadow. Both of us were breathing hard. We were in some kind of maintenance courtyard with dim emergency lighting. Behind Jameson I saw two rows of those massive heating/air conditioning things, each row nearly as tall as I was. I could hear street sounds to my left, where a little driveway led to the street, and there was a dark wall to my right. The wall behind me was still warm with the heat from earlier in the day.

Jameson had eased up the pressure on me, but he didn't let go. "Are you gonna drop the blade?" he said in a low voice.

"No." But I reversed the knife in my hand, so the sharp end pointed toward me. Jameson released my wrist, allowing me to take a slow, careful step sideways so the street lighting would land on his face. He looked at me with hooded, worried eyes. Familiar eyes.

Not much else about him was familiar, though. When I'd last seen the null from New York, he'd been thin and still a little gawky, a nineteen-year-old black kid in expensive sneakers who was half-convinced that everything he had was going to be ripped away from him, either by Malcolm's enemies or by Malcolm himself. More than three years later, the gawkiness and uncertainty were gone, replaced by lean muscle and a snazzy suit. He was still tall, though—around six four. I had to crane my neck to look in his eyes. "You look . . . different," I said stupidly.

He let out a low chuckle, which brought me instantly back to my month in New York, when we'd stayed up into the morning hours watching action movies and eating gourmet popcorn, the kind covered in white fudge and sprinkles. Jameson had always complained that it was a ridiculous food, but he'd always eaten more of it than I had. Now he flashed me a grin. "*I'm* different? Look at you. You're Lara Croft with a blade."

I felt a blush creep up my cheeks and hurried to change the subject. "What are you doing here? Why are you helping them?"

"I could ask you the same thing." There was a sharp rattle to my left, and I realized that Jameson had shoved something small into the emergency exit door, blocking it. Someone was trying to follow us out. "That's probably my backup," I said, pushing off the wall and reaching for the door.

"Don't!" He caught my wrist again, surprising me with his intensity. I reacted on muscle memory. Dropping the knife, I reached up, pulled his head under my arm, and pushed into his lower back with my other hand, forcing him to fall backward onto the ground. He let out a surprised grunt as he fell, and I took a step away, scooping up my knife and holding it ready. I hadn't hurt him, but if I'd made him mad enough he might come up swinging. I eyed the exit door, but I would have to step over Jameson to get to it. And of course, the way out to the street was behind him, too. Stupid Scarlett.

Jameson just lay there for a moment, and then he started to laugh, which made some of my tension fade. "Okay, that's fair. I shouldn't have grabbed you. Was that aikido?"

"Yes." I wasn't an expert or anything, but I'd drilled hard on a few key moves to get me out of trouble. He didn't need to know that, though.

Jameson got to his feet, brushing off his suit and rubbing the back of his neck. "I'm not going to hurt you, Letts."

I blinked for a second. I'd forgotten all about that nickname, the remnant of some in-joke we'd come up with during my trip. Jameson was the only person who'd ever called me Letts. "How can I know that?"

He shook his head. "I never did before, did I? Why would I start now?"

Okay, he did have a point there. Jameson had always been kind to me, even when his loyalty lay with Malcolm. He had never hurt me, and I didn't honestly think he would start now.

I looked around for the clutch, picked it up off the asphalt, and tucked the knife back into it. The exit door had stopped rattling. I took out my phone.

"What are you doing?" he asked, looking anxious.

"Texting my guy to tell him I'm fine," I said. It was the truth, but I eyed Jameson to see if he was going to try to stop me.

But he just nodded. "What I was *going* to say is that the person at the door might not be your guy. One of the Holmwoods' security guys was following you out of the ballroom, and he had vampires with him. I'll try to convince them it was just me, expanding my aura, but if the Holmwoods figure out what you are, or who you work for, they're gonna kill you."

Well, *that* seemed melodramatic. "What? Why?" I asked, putting the phone away. "Usually people at least get to know me first."

"You're a null. In Vegas," he said. His eyes slid away from me to check behind him for threats. "They'd probably assume that you came to stop *Demeter*. Isn't that what your boss wants you to do?"

I batted my eyes with great innocence. "What? No. I'm just here for . . . um . . . gambling and dressing slutty and stuff. Getting my drink on."

"Sure you are." He shook his head a little. "Seriously, what were you thinking, showing up at that party?"

I straightened up, raising my chin. "I was *thinking* that something fucked up is happening in Vegas and I wanted to know what it was. Also, I saw a picture of you working for the Holmwoods, and I wanted to make sure you weren't being held here against your will."

"Oh." Jameson sighed. "It's more complicated than that, but working for the Holmwoods was my choice."

"And Malcolm?" The New York cardinal vampire wasn't the type who would just let a resource like Jameson walk away unchallenged.

To my left, I heard laughing. I turned to see a group of young men walking past the delivery entrance to the maintenance courtyard, several of them stumbling. They didn't notice us, but we weren't exactly well hidden.

I turned back to Jameson, who was watching the young men with one hand resting on his hip in a gesture I'd seen many times from Jesse. I started. Why would Jameson need to carry a gun? He was a null, like me. Did the vampires in Las Vegas go around armed? I hadn't seen any suspicious gun-shaped bulges in the ballroom.

There was a "suspicious bulge" joke in there somewhere, but before I could follow that line of thought any further, Jameson held up a hand. "Look, we can't talk now. I gotta get back before Arthur realizes I wandered off without my bodyguard."

"Without your *what*?" I sputtered. In New York, Jameson served as *Malcolm's* bodyguard during daylight hours. He was good with a gun *or* in a brawl. Why would he need his own personal security?

Impulsively, I took a step toward him and put one hand flat on his chest. Jameson reflexively curled his fingers around my wrist, but he didn't push me away. I tilted my head back again to meet his eyes. "Why are you wearing a bulletproof vest?" I demanded. "What's really going on here?"

He shook his head, brushing off the questions. The lighting wasn't great, but in that moment he looked so . . . lonely. Nulls are rare, and by definition, we don't really fit in anywhere. We're human, but all our value lies in the Old World. We're submerged in the Old World, but we can only live there as humans. And there are so few of us that until the last decade or so, we never interacted with one another at all.

We are alone just by existing.

"You can talk to me," I said quietly.

Jameson's dark eyes were fixed on mine, but he remained silent, looking troubled and intense. Which were probably the two words I'd pick to describe him overall.

Impulsively, I reached up and laid my free hand flat against his cheek. He covered it with his own hand, closing his eyes for just a moment. Then he moved it so he was holding both of my hands at his chest. He squeezed them gently, and let go, easing away from me.

"Go home, Letts," he said in a low voice. "Please. I'm fine. Everything is fine."

I stepped back, remembering myself. "Oh yeah, you seem *real* fine," I said sarcastically. A new thought hit me, and I took a leap. "Hang on. Do skinners hunt nulls, too?"

Jameson flinched, and I knew I was getting warmer. "What do you know about the skinners?" I demanded.

"Dammit, Scarlett!" he barked, smacking the wall beside me. But it felt half-hearted, like he was following a script. "I told you, stay out of this!"

I just folded my arms across my chest, not backing down. If he wanted to unnerve me with a temper tantrum, he was going to have to try a lot harder than that. "I'm not afraid of you."

His shoulders sagged. "I don't want you to be." He stepped back, away from me, rubbing a hand absentmindedly over his collarbone. I'd seen Jameson without his shirt once, after a run, and I knew there was a four-inch scar there. He'd said it was part of his misspent youth, but he used it like a worry stone. "Please, Letts," he said softly. "Please, just stay out of this. Go home."

Was he trying to protect me from the skinners, or was there more to it? "I'm not going anywhere until you tell me what's happening," I told him. And I had an idea. "Or would you prefer that I go ask Arthur and Lucy?"

He grunted. "God, you're still just as stubborn, aren't you?"

"That's what everyone tells me, yeah."

He checked his watch. "I've been gone too long already. Can you meet me tomorrow morning?"

"I guess . . ." I wanted answers *now*, dammit. But I would take what I could get.

"Come on. We gotta get out of here." He took a step, paused. "Hang on." Jameson reached for the emergency exit lock, pulling out a small metal object that he'd slipped into what looked like old padlock holes. "In case there's a fire or something," he said with a little smile. Then he took my hand, very slowly, like he was afraid I would flip him again. I allowed him to lead me to the little driveway on the left, which led to the street.

"Where are you staying?" he asked.

"Uh, the Venetian."

A quick nod. "We can't be seen together, so when we hit the sidewalk, turn left and go to the corner. You should be able to get a cab back. I'll meet you underneath Vegas Vic tomorrow at eleven, okay?"

I had no idea what that meant, but we were almost at the sidewalk, and it sounded like something I could google. "Fine."

We reached the street. I turned to go left, more or less on autopilot, when I heard Jameson call, "Hey, Letts?"

I turned. He was walking backward away from me. "That guy you were with, your backup . . . are you guys together?"

Cliff? Hardly. "That's none of your business," I said sweetly.

Jameson just shot me a wide grin. "You really do look good," he said, and then he turned and jogged off.

I just stood there for a moment, my head spinning. I'd seen the show, and I'd found Jameson, all according to plan. So how was it possible that I was even more confused than before?

Chapter 14

It was only eleven o'clock when I dragged myself back into the hotel room, but it felt more like four a.m. I dropped the clutch on the table just inside the door and kicked off my boots so they landed on the closet floor. I walked down the hall—my hotel "room" was so huge it actually required a small *hallway*—and fell backward onto the bed, staring up at the gilded ceiling. It was probably a direct homage to some fancy-pants Italian painter or ceiling designer or whatever, but like everything else about this ostentatious hotel, the significance was lost on me.

I needed to call Dashiell and fill him in on the night's events, but I wanted to collect my thoughts first. Arthur and Lucy Holmwood were definitely putting on a show that exposed them as vampires. But I still wasn't sure they were violating Old World laws enough to be stopped, given that (a) this wasn't Dashiell's territory, and (b) no one believed anything they saw in Las Vegas. If David Copperfield could make the Eiffel Tower disappear every night, what was falling from a six-story ceiling unharmed?

Happily, gauging whether or not the Holmwoods were committing a crime against the Old World wasn't actually my problem. I was a glorified messenger. But I did care about Jameson, and something was happening with him. Something that required him to wear a bulletproof vest and have a bodyguard. What was *that* about?

I shook my head and rolled off the side of the bed toward my suitcase, where I dug around until I found Bethany's itinerary. Tomorrow morning we were supposed to be at the spa at eight thirty for massages, followed by a . . . burlesque dance lesson? Ugh. I wouldn't mind skipping that, if I could come up with a decent lie. Maybe I could blame my pretend seizure disorder. Or my very authentic clumsiness.

I didn't have the heart to even look at the rest of the bachelorette party events, so I dropped the itinerary on a table. I peeled off the dress and climbed into pajama pants and a soft tank top to sleep in. When I couldn't put it off any longer, I picked up the phone to call Dashiell.

And someone knocked on my door.

I blinked hard. Who the hell could *that* be? Jameson? Or maybe Juliet? Cautiously, I got up and went to the door to look. Before I made it all the way there, I registered a vampire in my radius. Oh, great. I peered through the peephole.

A man I didn't know stood in the hall with his hat in hand. I mean that literally—he had taken a step back, and I could see the cowboy-style hat he held by his waist, as well as his long, duster-style jacket and handlebar mustache. There was an actual red handkerchief tied around his neck, underneath a chin covered in five o'clock shadow. A vampire cowboy? Huh. We got some weird stuff in LA, but this was a first for me. He looked a little disoriented, the way most vampires look when they're suddenly forced to breathe or die. What can I say, I have that effect on people.

The door had a sort of elongated bolt instead of a chain, so I cracked it open with the bolt still flipped. "Who are you?" I blurted.

The man held up his hat with one hand so it covered his chest. "Ma'am, my name is Wyatt."

Oh. "Laurel's Wyatt?"

A genuine smile lit the man's face under the big mustache. "Yes, ma'am. I've come to beg for your assistance. May I come in?"

Well, that was a new one. I looked him up and down, thinking of Jameson. "Are you carrying a gun?"

Surprised, he held his coat away from his body, displaying jeans and an untucked button-down that was cut slim to his body. "No, ma'am."

I shut the door, thought about it for a moment, then shrugged to myself. As long as he wasn't armed, I wasn't terribly concerned for my safety. Might as well hear him out. I put my hoodie back on and tucked a knife in a little holster in one of the pockets. Then I unbolted the door and opened it wide, gesturing toward the sitting area down the hall. "Come in."

Wyatt stepped forward. His eyes twitched slightly at the sight of my pajama pants, but he wisely chose not to comment. "Thank you, ma'am."

For some reason being called ma'am by this guy didn't grate on my nerves. Probably because he looked like he was on his way to the saloon for a card game with Doc Holliday.

Which was a scary thought, now that I considered it. "Wyatt as in Earp?" I asked him.

The vampire gave me a slight smile, showing tobacco-stained teeth that had never seen braces. I somehow got the impression that if he'd been wearing the hat, he would have tipped it. "No relation, I assure you."

"Fair enough." I pointed to the couch. "What can I do for you, Wyatt?"

The smile faded. He sat down. "Miss Laurel tells me you're here to investigate the vampire dealings in Las Vegas."

"That's probably stretching it. I was just supposed to go see the show tonight."

He lifted one heavy eyebrow. "And now that you have?"

"Now I go back to enjoying my trip," I said, not sure if I believed it. "I'm just sort of the spotter."

Wyatt studied me for a moment. He was leaning over, his elbows resting on his knees, fingers still kneading the hat brim. "But you're not the *first* spotter, are you?"

That got my attention. I sat up a little straighter. "No, I'm not. Do you know something about the woman who came here before me?"

"I know that she disappeared, just like my Ellen. And just like all the others."

"How?" I asked. "*How* did they disappear?"

He tossed the hat on the couch next to him and held out his empty hands. "I'm not sure. That's what's so goddamned frustrating. Ma'am."

I rubbed my eyes. "Okay, fine. First, call me Scarlett. Second, back up a little. When was the last time you saw Ellen?"

He nodded. "Just over a week ago. But for the last few months, Ellen had been doing a little work for the Holmwoods, like half the other vampires in town. She was helping organize publicity for the show by speaking to different groups of vampires in Vegas and the surrounding areas."

"Hang on." I held up a hand. Every once in a while I had an actual, detective-like thought. "Were all the vampires here okay with this show?"

"You're thinking someone may have been targeting the people involved with the show, like to get it shut down?" He shook his head. "It's a showbiz town, Miss Scarlett. The Las Vegas vampires were happy to roll out the red carpet for Arthur and Lucy Holmwood. It was about the first thing they'd all agreed on in ages," he added wryly.

Damn. But I did notice that Wyatt said *they* agreed to welcome the Holmwoods, rather than *we.*

"Did that include you and Ellen?" I asked, in case it was the other way around. Someone could have been targeting the people who were against the show.

But Wyatt said, "I just wanted to stay out of the whole thing. Ellen . . . she was a little worried about the show's exposure, but she did believe the Holmwoods might finally bring the Las Vegas vampires together. She wanted that so badly. Peace, I mean."

He paused, not meeting my eyes. "Ellen had mostly finished up in the week before the show opened. Then on opening night, Lucy and Arthur hosted a big reception. I didn't want to go. Didn't want to put on a suit and make nice with the vampire *celebrities*." He said this last word with great distaste. "But Ellen said she had to. Lucy had gotten word that a vampire from LA was driving out to see the show, and she wanted Ellen to make her feel welcome." He paused for a moment, and I realized that his eyes were wet. "That was the last I saw of her."

I gave him a moment before asking, "Do you know how Lucy found out about the LA vampire?" That part worried me. Dashiell had made it sound like Margaret was coming incognito, so how had the Holmwoods anticipated her?

"That, I don't know. I'm not even sure if Ellen made an appointment to meet with her, or if she was just supposed to keep an eye on her from a distance. Ellen had been working for the Holmwoods for a while by then without any issues, so I didn't think to ask many questions." His face darkened, and he looked at his empty hands. "And now she's dead."

"No offense, but how can you be sure Ellen didn't just . . . um . . ."

"Leave town?"

I nodded. It was still possible that the simplest explanation was the right one.

Wyatt raised his head, looking me square in the eye, and said, "Ellen and me, we've been together for a hundred and twenty-six years. If she'd wanted to end it for any reason, she would have told me so. And I can't think of a good reason for someone to capture vampires and imprison them somewhere long-term. Can you?"

"No," I admitted.

He nodded, resigned. "So the skinners killed my Ellen. Probably this Margaret, too."

The skinners again. I was really starting to hate that term. "Look," I said. "I really am sorry for your loss. But I'm not the one to help you with this. Does Las Vegas have a cardinal vampire? Laurel didn't know."

"In a way," he said, his reserved face twisting with sourness. "Before Arthur and Lucy Holmwood arrived, there were two vampires vying for control, Silvio and Minerva. They both wanted it bad, but the problem was that neither of them was really strong enough to hold a city like Vegas. Their little feud has been on autopilot for years, as though they were both just biding their time until one of them got more powerful with age." He gave me a wry smile. "Or like they were waiting for a real contender to show up and take over."

"And then the Holmwoods arrived," I mused. "When exactly did they get here?"

"Mid-January. And Minerva disappeared only a few days later, along with a few other folks."

I shook my head. This was getting ridiculous. "Wait, you're saying *Minerva* is one of these disappeared vampires?"

"Yeah. Though I don't rightly know if that was the skinners or the Holmwoods."

Huh. I sat back in my chair. I may have sucked at politics, but that didn't mean I couldn't follow his logic. "You think Silvio is working for Arthur and Lucy? That they're the real cardinal vampires?" It wouldn't be the first time someone in power installed a puppet to hide behind.

"I'm not sure I'd go that far," he admitted. "I don't get the impression that the Holmwoods give a shit about being in charge of the city. They're more interested in money and fame. But it was awfully suspicious that Minerva disappeared right after they arrived in town." He shrugged. "If I had to guess, I'd say Silvio cut himself a deal. Let Arthur and Lucy do their thing, no questions asked, and he gets the rest of the city."

It was possible. Then again, the skinners who had likely killed Ellen and Margaret might have taken out Minerva, too.

"What a mess," I muttered. It sounded like three things had happened more or less at the same time: the Holmwoods opened their show, the skinners came to town, and Silvio rose to power. How could I figure out how these things were connected, if they even were?

I told myself to focus on the problem at hand. Wyatt's problem. Which was not, in fact, *my* problem. "Still, if Silvio is your cardinal vampire, can't you go to him about the skinners and the missing vampires?"

Wyatt snorted. "I tried. His people told me to come back on the first Sunday of the month, when he'll be 'holding court.' I'll have to wait my turn in line, of course," he added sarcastically.

I just had to ask. "Did they really use the phrase 'holding court'?" Most of the vampires I knew didn't bother with vainglorious speaking patterns. They needed to blend in with humans, not sound like a reenactment from a special on the History Channel.

"Yep." Wyatt rubbed his face again. "I don't know if the man is just an imbecile, or if he doesn't want to look into these disappearances because he promised the Holmwoods not to make any big moves. Could be both, I reckon."

Ugh. I couldn't really blame Wyatt for being upset, or for wanting to find Ellen's killer some other way. The Holmwoods had come to Las Vegas with their big, attention-grabbing act, and in the process they'd more or less undermined the power of their puppet cardinal vampire. The skinners could be using that gap in authority to come in and kill a bunch of vampires. It was actually a pretty slick idea, from their perspective.

"What can you tell me about the skinners?" I asked Wyatt. It was like the third time I had asked that question today.

"Nothing I can prove. There are rumors that they're in town, that they're here to kill as many vampires as they can. But no one has any descriptions or names, nothing like that."

"Are they after the Holmwoods?"

He pursed his lips, his old-fashioned mustache pointing outward like bristles. "To kill them? I don't know. But I suspect all the publicity drew them here."

That was kind of what I was thinking, too, but Wyatt wasn't finished. "Miss Scarlett, you have to understand, vampires flock to Las Vegas because of the easy pickings. The tourist population, the homeless, the sad sacks who have lost all their money and are half-suicidal anyway. It's a goddamned buffet for us. Point is, there already *were* lots of vampires, and now that the Holmwoods are here, more and more will be coming to visit. Which makes *us* easy pickings for the skinners."

Goose bumps broke out on my bare arms. Even Molly had talked about coming to see the Holmwoods, and she couldn't be the only one. It certainly seemed possible that these skinners had followed the Holmwoods here, or been drawn by their extremely well-publicized vampire show. If your goal was to kill vampires, this was a great fish-in-a-barrel kind of setup.

"In that case, they'd *want* the Holmwoods to stay alive. As bait," I said, mostly to myself. Wyatt nodded.

Then I got it. If you were a skinner and your goal in life was to kill vampires, what would be the best possible tool in your arsenal? A null. Jeez, no wonder Jameson had a bodyguard. And maybe *that* was why he'd said the Holmwoods would kill me if they saw me. Nulls are rare enough that they might assume any other null in Vegas had to be with the skinners. Dammit, this was getting too complicated. Not to mention way above my pay grade.

"I'm sorry about your wife, Wyatt," I said, meaning it. I've never been a fan of the "all vampires are evil" mentality, mostly because around me, they were just people again. Often arrogant, out-of-touch people, but still. After meeting Wyatt, I had to agree with Laurel's assessment that he was a decent guy. "And I'll tell the cardinal vampire of Los

Angeles everything I've learned, so he can decide on further action. You have my word on that." I stood up, hoping he would take the hint.

But he didn't move. "That's not enough," he said firmly. "I want you to find the skinners who killed Ellen. The Holmwoods won't do it; they don't give a shit as long as they're making money. That means Silvio won't waste resources on it either, and I'm guessing Minerva is as dead as the rest of 'em. We need *you*."

Wait, *what?* "I'm sorry, I think you have the wrong idea," I said, sinking back into my seat and crossing my arms. "I'm not actually investigating this. I'm only here for the weekend."

"I made a few calls tonight, to friends in LA," he said, with a new glint in his eye. "They all said that Scarlett Bernard has a tendency to make things move. And that you've gotten involved in this kind of business before."

"In *my* town, on *my* turf, and with *my* own allies," I countered. "This is a very different situation."

But Wyatt went on like he hadn't heard me. "You also do jobs for hire. Freelance jobs."

I shook my head. This was getting away from me. "That's not why I'm here." Okay, it was *exactly* why I was here, but this guy didn't need to know that.

Wyatt frowned at me, and then he reached into both his coat pockets. I felt my fingers automatically stray toward the knife in my pocket, but he just pulled out two flat stacks of cash, each one maybe an inch thick. He slammed the stacks on the coffee table between us, hard enough to make me jump.

"That's a hundred thousand dollars," he said flatly. "That's our emergency money. I want you to use it to find Ellen's killer."

I sat there for several seconds with my mouth opening and closing like a hungry goldfish. Wyatt waited, looking resigned to my incredulity.

My head suddenly felt full of helium. The money on the table would pay off pretty much all of Jack and Juliet's hospital debts. Of course, that was assuming I could figure out how to launder it, which I knew nothing about. And then I'd have to turn it into an anonymous donation to Logan. Or maybe I could tell Juliet and Jack I'd won big at poker? No, Jack knew how bad I was at cards. An inheritance from a dead client? Then they were going to think I'd done a lot more for him than clean the floors.

Slow down, I told myself. Yeah, daydreaming about sudden riches was fun, but at the end of the day, it was just money. And all the money in the world wouldn't buy me any investigative competence in a city I didn't know. I was just a twentysomething from LA who could barely dress herself. I was not the person to handle this disaster of a situation. I took a deep breath in and let it out slowly. The money Dashiell was giving me for coming this far would clear up a chunk of Jack and Juliet's debt, too, and I'd keep saving.

"I'm not looking for more work," I said at last, tearing my eyes away from the cash. "But like I said, I will talk to Dashiell for you. He feels some responsibility for Las Vegas; I'm sure he'll help."

Wyatt sighed and added, "Look, I hear good things about this Dashiell, but he has his own interests, not to mention his own city to worry about, hundreds of miles away. He's not going to be able to move around in the daytime like you can. Plus, he won't be able to ask questions and poke around without risking a vampire war. You're a third party; you're not bound by our rules."

I had to admit, that was sort of true. If I was here on a freelance job, then my actions wouldn't reflect back on Dashiell or the LA Old World. At the same time, no one who knew about me would be anxious to hurt me, considering my day job was for the cardinal vampire of Los Angeles.

But that was assuming everyone would know my whole employment situation before they decided to try to kill me, which was a pretty big leap. And what about Juliet? If I gave up on the bachelorette party ruse, and someone learned that I had family in town, they could hurt her to get to me. It was an old, tired cliché, but only because it was so effective.

I shook my head. "Wyatt . . . I can't. And, honestly, even if I could, that's way too much money. I don't . . . that's *way* too much. I don't know who gave you null freelance rates, but he and I do not play in the same league."

Wyatt looked tired all of a sudden. He'd probably been in his early thirties when he was turned, but suddenly I could make out the cracks and fine lines in his face, a weariness born of too many years and too many unwanted experiences. He picked up his hat again, turning it over and over.

"This isn't just a freelance rate," he said, his voice catching a little. "Like I said, this was our emergency savings. After I kill whoever took Ellen away from me, I won't need it anymore. If you think it's too much, you can give it away, gamble it, save it, whatever. I don't give two shits what you do with it after I find Ellen's killer."

"Why not?"

"Because," he said, looking me square in the eye, "when this is over, I want you to kill me too."

Chapter 15

When you consider it objectively, it might seem like a pretty common request for a null—helping a vampire or werewolf commit suicide. But no one had ever asked me this before. I'd never even thought about it, and if I had, I would have assumed the request would come from one of the werewolves, who are constantly struggling against the ill-fitting magic that tears them into two shapes. Vampires have it good: super strength, speed, advanced healing, eternal youth, and the ability to control human minds. The only cost is being nocturnal and taking a blood donation every night or two. And unlike the werewolves, vampires almost always choose that existence, for one reason or another. Turning someone into a vampire is too much work for it to happen by accident very often.

"I've never met a suicidal vampire," I blurted. "Isn't that kind of at odds with your whole . . . everything?"

"I would appreciate if you did not make light of my situation," he said stiffly. "Ellen was my soul mate, Miss Bernard. I have no interest in spending eternity in a world without her."

"I apologize," I said. "I wasn't trying to mock you, I promise."

Wyatt went on as if I hadn't even spoken. "It's only been a few days, really, and I already feel like someone cut off one side of my body and left me to die. I'm not complete anymore. Ellen was . . . she was everything." I glanced down at his hands, which had been worrying at his hat again. It was practically a new shape by now.

Suddenly the idea of a cowboy vampire didn't seem like such a joke. For the first time, I looked past the vampire and his clothes and saw a man in serious pain. "Wyatt . . . I'm so sorry."

"Then *help* me," he said doggedly. "All I can think about is finding out who did this and killing them myself. After that, I want to be with my Ellen again."

"Even so, why would you need *me* to kill you?" I blurted. "Can't you just . . . like . . ."

"Wait for the dawn?" He looked amused. "I can, if it comes down to it. But I've no desire to burn. I'd rather eat a bullet. It's cleaner and simpler." Seeing my horrified expression, he added in a softer tone, "You wouldn't have to pull the trigger, Miss Scarlett. I just need you to be there." He gazed at me, his eyes pleading. "*Please.*"

"I gotta think," I said abruptly. I stood up and paced over to the window, resting my forehead against the cool glass. My room had come with a partial view of the Strip, and it was instantly mesmerizing. Lights didn't just shine in Las Vegas; they glittered and flashed and blinked in an always-moving, almost violent display of opulence and recklessness. Environment be damned! We've got neon!

Stop distracting yourself, Scarlett.

I usually prided myself on being more or less dead inside, but dammit, Wyatt had gotten to me. And it wasn't just because I'd recently broken up with Eli. That was too easy. Even if I wasn't in a romantic relationship, there were plenty of people I cared about: Jack and his family, and Molly, and Jesse too. I wasn't alone, not like Wyatt.

Or was I? Just a little while ago I'd been thinking about how being a null came with its own isolation. In a way, you were *always* alone, always different, whether you were in a group of humans or a group of supernaturals. Wyatt had had one person in all of time and space who got him, and for that, I envied him. And now that that person had been taken away . . . well, yeah. I could relate to not having anyone who truly saw you. Hell, I understood that a lot better than I understood healthy relationships.

Despite my better instincts, I wanted to help him. But how would I even start? I wasn't actually an investigator; that was Jesse's job. And I couldn't just ask him to come help me, because I needed him to be on call in LA. And to keep an eye on Corry and Shadow for me.

I thought about the little I knew about what was happening: the Holmwoods, *Demeter*, the missing vampires, Jameson, the skinners. It all seemed so big, like a huge piece of wallpaper plastered to a wall, and I couldn't figure out where to begin trying to scrape it off. There was no obvious loose corner I could get my fingernails under.

Yes there is, insisted my inner voice. Which sounded suspiciously like Jesse's.

It was the victim pool.

I turned around to face Wyatt again. "I would need to check with some people before I could agree to help you. Can you give me an hour or two?"

He nodded eagerly. "Anything you need."

"Okay. Meanwhile, if I *were* to help find Ellen's killer, I would need to know exactly who's gone missing. And," I added before he could speak, "not just who, but when, and from where. If we can figure out what they have in common, or how they're being chosen, we'll be a lot closer to stopping it."

Wyatt jumped to his feet, looking as excited as a laconic cowboy vampire probably gets. "I can get you a list," he said, his eyes bright. "I'll get started right now."

Wyatt left the room to make some calls of his own. I didn't know where he'd go to do that, but it didn't matter. As soon as he was through the door and out of my radius, I went back to my phone and called Dashiell.

The phone barely got through a single ring; he had been expecting my call. As quickly as I could, I explained what I'd learned that night: the missing vampires, the show, the Holmwoods' people-eating after-party. He listened in silence for most of it, although I could swear I heard him actually hiss when I described the rebuilding of the *Demeter*. And then I told him about Wyatt's offer of a freelance job.

Part of me was hoping he'd get all blustery and possessive, forbidding me to take the job in Vegas. Although if he'd actually reacted like that, I would probably have jumped to take Wyatt's offer, because I am naturally contrary.

Maybe Dashiell had come to the same conclusion, because at the end of all that he said, "My, Scarlett, you *have* been busy," in his usual dry tone. "You're right, the situation is more complicated than I had suspected. Are you calling for an extraction?"

"An extract—no," I said, confused. What was I, James Bond? "I want instructions."

"Ah," he said, more thoughtfully. There was a pause, and then he added, "In that case, as far as I am concerned, you have fulfilled the terms of our agreement. You went to Las Vegas, saw the show, and reported your findings to me. I release you of all further obligations to me this weekend."

Well, *that* didn't help. "But what should I *do*?"

"You're on your own time now, Scarlett," he said, and there was something in his voice that was hard to read. Smugness, maybe. "You can come home, or continue investigating. All I ask is that you come to the mansion on Monday night to debrief me. I can make further plans at that time."

And then he hung up.

He *hung up*?

"Dammit!" I yelled at the silent cell phone. Dashiell was supposed to tell me what to do. Now I felt more frustrated than ever, and images from the last twelve hours were spinning through my brain. Jameson's guarded, troubled expression. Laurel's plea for me to help Wyatt. Wyatt himself, looking so forlorn and lost.

Pacing the opulent suite, I called Jesse and ran *him* through the whole story. He was flabbergasted. And also extremely entertained.

"You know, for someone who claims her dream job is a professional couch potato, you find yourself in the most bizarre situations," he marveled. "Jesus, Scarlett, I don't even know where to start."

"What do I say to Wyatt?" I pleaded.

"What do you want to say?"

I fidgeted. "It's too much money, you know? And I don't know the city, and it's probably dangerous, and there are Juliet and her friends to consider. I should just come home, right? I mean, at this point I'm so far outside my job description—"

"Oh my God," Jesse said in a groan.

That brought me up short. "What?"

"Your *job* description? Are you frickin' serious right now? Or are you just fishing for compliments?"

I was genuinely perplexed. "Dude, I have no idea what you're talking about. I definitely don't need you to tell me I'm pretty or whatever."

I heard him take a deep breath, and I strongly suspected he was also counting to ten. "Scarlett. My friend," he said, in a slow, patient voice, like I was kind of an idiot. "You seem to be under the impression that you are not important. That you are a nobody who occasionally gets cornered into doing something big. I'm not sure where you got this stupid idea, but even if it was true once, it is now the *opposite* of true."

I blanched. "The hell does that mean?"

"Look around, dummy. You're the good guy. You are, in fact, a hero."

A tiny bit of hysterical-sounding laughter escaped my lips. "That's you. That's Lex. I'm not like that."

"You're more like Lex than you think."

I didn't answer, and he filled in the silence. "Scar, you didn't spend the last few years learning to throw knives, or check a car for explosives, or flip giant men on their asses because you were planning to sit out fights. And you didn't save Molly because you had no other alternative."

"What do you mean? That's *exactly* why I helped Molly."

"Oh my God, you stupid woman," he said affectionately. "You don't even see that there was a choice, do you? That's okay. It just means I'm right."

"I don't . . . I'm not . . ." I stopped pacing and sat on the edge of the couch, curling my knees to my chest. "I don't feel like that."

Jesse sighed audibly. "Listen, moron, because I'm only going to say this one time," he said in a sharper tone. "The Old World system is full of cracks. You are the champion of all the people who fall through those cracks. And that's *okay*, Scar. This is who you were always supposed to become, if you hadn't gotten sidetracked by that psycho Olivia. Even I can see that, and I'm supposedly on the outside of all this."

I just sat there, taken aback. I could not think of a single thing to make with my mouth words.

"Anyway," Jesse went on, "you can stop trying to find a reason not to do what we both know you want: to help this cowboy stop the skinners. Because it's the right thing to do, and because no one else will."

"I . . . I . . ."

"What?"

I swallowed the lump in the back of my throat. "I didn't know there was so much name-calling in motivational speeches."

"Not everyone does them as well as me," he said airily. "Do you want me to come out there and help?"

"No. I need you in LA. But Jesse . . ." I paused for a second, trying to figure out what it was that I was so afraid of. "If I come at this thing head-on, blow my cover, the skinners are going to come after me. They'll pretty much have to."

"You have allies there, right? The cowboy, the bodyguard, that witch—"

"You make them sound like a bad Village People cover band, but yeah. Probably." I thought of Jameson, but he had his own plans. I couldn't count on him to leave the Holmwoods and play for Team Scarlett.

"Then let the skinners come. Maybe that's how *you* find *them*. Just wear your bulletproof vest, okay?" he added hurriedly. "And call me every day, please."

There was a moment when I could have said . . . what? That I appreciated him? That he was important to me? That his pep talk had meant more to me than I could ever say? Instead, I just said a simple, "Thanks, Jesse."

"Anytime."

When I hung up the phone, I sat there for a long time, thinking about Jesse's words. No matter how I tried to shove the square peg in the round hole, I couldn't see myself as some kind of champion. Just the word "champion" kind of made me want to barf, like when you see a white dude who's made a man bun with his dreadlocks. The only heroes I'd ever met were scary badasses, like Lex. And I felt about as scary as the average Yorkshire terrier. The teacup kind.

But then, maybe I didn't need to see myself as a champion to the overlooked. Maybe it was enough that Jesse did. And Wyatt.

I thought that over for a long time, and then I swallowed my pride and called Dashiell back.

"Hello again, Scarlett," he said. He'd restricted himself to just a hint of smugness.

"I need a favor," I said without preamble. "Can you find out if vampires have disappeared in other cities the Holmwoods have visited?"

A beat, and then he said, "You're thinking the skinners are following them from town to town?"

"It's just a hunch at this point, but yeah."

"Hmm. I can make some calls to Europe, but I probably won't have answers until tomorrow evening, due to the time change."

"That's fine. Please just get me whatever information you can."

Wyatt didn't return for almost two hours, but when he knocked on my door again, he had a fistful of hotel stationery. "Is that the list?" I asked.

"Yes, ma'am. It was more than I'd thought." He handed over the papers, looking a little triumphant. I looked through them quickly. There were thirty-eight names on the list, and next to each one was the date and location from which the vampire had disappeared. A few of them didn't have the information filled in yet. "There may be some names missing, too. I've put in calls to learn more," he added.

"Okay, good. I can start with this."

"Does this mean you're going to take the job?"

"I have obligations during the day," I warned. "And I need to go back to LA on Monday. That's nonnegotiable."

"I understand." His eyes were practically dancing, damn him.

"If we can't find the skinners by then, I'll give you everything I've got and collect half of that." I nodded at the pile of money.

Carelessly, Wyatt collected all the cash, which was really four small stacks held together with rubber bands. He pocketed three of them and tossed one stack toward my midsection. I managed to catch it, although I found myself not really wanting to touch it. "You should have some walking-around money, in case you need to grease some wheels," he explained.

"Fine." The money felt weird in my hand, heavy and surreal. But I could lock most of it in the room's safe.

"What about the other thing?" he asked. "Helping me move on?"

I pushed out a breath. "Honestly? I'm not saying no, but . . . I need to think about it."

We negotiated for a little bit, and determined that I would keep fifty grand if I found Ellen's killer but *didn't* help Wyatt with his suicide. If I couldn't find the killer by the end of the weekend, I would keep the twenty-five grand I had now.

I walked Wyatt to the hotel room door, where he put his hat back on. "Where will you start?" he asked mildly.

I sighed. I needed a better idea of the power structure in Las Vegas before I started dicking around with it. "It's probably time to go introduce myself to Silvio."

Chapter 16

I was already tired as I pulled my jeans and boots back on. I was used to staying up until at least three or four—the by-product of working regularly with vampires—but between the long hours of shopping and spending most of the night trying to suppress my radius, it seemed like a week since I'd left Los Angeles, instead of only that morning.

Still, I couldn't get myself any deeper into the Vegas Old World without talking to the guy who was allegedly in charge. And, giant dickhead or not, Silvio needed to know that skinners were killing vampires in his town. I couldn't seek justice for Wyatt without giving the actual authority a chance to do his job.

Assuming he didn't know already. I found it hard to believe that he wouldn't have noticed thirty-odd missing vampires, but then again, there were thousands of vampires in Las Vegas, and Silvio had been in charge of them for only a few weeks. I could give him the benefit of the doubt, at least a little.

Wyatt had wanted to go see Silvio with me, but I'd refused to let him tag along. I didn't trust the cowboy to keep his cool if Silvio was as big of a tool as he sounded, and besides, the new cardinal vampire might not take kindly to being challenged by such a weak subject. He was also likely to be annoyed that one of his vampires had gone outside the fold for help. Silvio probably wouldn't kill *me* just for going to see him—there would be too many political ramifications, plus nulls are valuable. But I didn't want Wyatt anywhere near him right now.

Of course, going to see the cardinal vampire alone was not without its risks. Jameson had suggested the Holmwoods would kill me on sight, and there was a chance that they might be there. I decided to pull on my bulletproof vest, just to pacify Jesse's imaginary voice in my head.

But I wasn't too worried. If Silvio was the dim-witted figurehead he seemed to be, there was no reason for Arthur and Lucy to be randomly hanging out with him.

Besides, I was not without my own defenses.

I didn't bother to suppress my radius when I left my room. If anything, I let it blaze around me like a calling card. Introducing myself to Silvio would mean I was "coming out" as a null in Vegas, so there was no point in exhausting myself trying to hide it any longer.

Of course, as soon as I got off the elevator on the ground floor, vampires started trickling through my radius like flies bumping into a bug zapper. It was disorienting at first, but after a few minutes—and a lot of stares—I adjusted and kept moving, ignoring the men and women who had stopped dead in the middle of the casino floor, craning their heads to find the null. Let them look. I was moving too quickly for them to pinpoint me anyway.

According to Wyatt, Silvio had recently moved into a suite at the Mandarin Oriental, one of the newer big resorts on the Vegas Strip. It was easy enough to get a cab, but we had to fight through some of the Friday-night traffic. While I waited I looked up the Oriental on my phone. Apparently it was unique among the behemoth hotels in that it didn't actually have a casino floor, which meant it catered more to the deeply rich than to the usual gambling riffraff.

On the inside the Mandarin Oriental was decorated like a P.F. Chang's that had come into some money, covered with a sheen of Vegas gloss. Cardinal vampires always have security around, so as soon as I reached the center of the main lobby, I let my radius expand. Three vampire thugs appeared out of the crowd almost instantly, looking around like they might be able to actually sniff out the big bad null. I approached the nearest one and waved a hand. "Hi, I'm Scarlett," I said cheerfully. "I would like to see Silvio, please."

The thug—a beefy white guy with a hooked nose that must have been broken a lot when he was alive—did a double take, his eyes going so big that I had to fight not to smirk at him. "Who . . . I can't . . . but . . ." he sputtered, and I almost had to feel sorry for the guy.

Aw. He was so stupid it was cute. "It's okay," I assured him. "Just call Silvio on the phone and tell him that Scarlett Bernard, the null, is here to see him. I can wait."

The big eyes narrowed, but he could see the logic in the suggestion— or maybe he just couldn't think of a better one. At any rate, he made the call, and within ninety seconds he was escorting me through the hotel and toward a private elevator.

If you called Central Casting and asked them to send you a stereotypical Italian American gangster type, I'm fairly certain you'd get someone who looked exactly like Silvio. He was a short, stocky guy with olive skin, a suit with no tie—possibly because his neck was too thick— and an honest-to-goodness pinkie ring. He sat on a leather couch in the little seating area, with two vampire goons standing near the wall on either side.

I wasn't surprised to see the goons—although vampires are mostly loners, cardinal vampires need extra security in case another vampire decides to attack. If anything, I was a little surprised that Silvio didn't have *more* people. If the city had just settled a long-standing leadership dispute, he should have been more wary.

Unless he knew for a fact that no other vampires were going to challenge him.

All three vampires gasped a little when they hit my radius, but they recovered quickly. *Too* quickly for vampires who hadn't been human in centuries. I'd bet Wyatt's stack of cash that they'd been near Jameson recently. Interesting.

Silvio stood up as I approached, taking a deep breath and buttoning his suit jacket.

"Hello, Silvio," I said first, holding out a hand. This was on purpose. Older vampires don't often bother with handshakes, probably because they see themselves as above that kind of base human flesh-pressing. Nobody pets the cow before they eat the steak. But I had made Silvio human at the moment, and I wanted to remind him of it. Kind of a petty little power move, but I never said I was above that. "I'm Scarlett Bernard. I'm a null from Los Angeles."

Silvio allowed me to grasp his hand, though he put no effort into reciprocating. "I know who you are, Miss Bernard," he said, taking his hand back. He didn't actually wipe it on his nice pants, but I could practically see how much he wanted to. "I assume that Dashiell sent you here to check up on my city. Please inform him that—"

"Oh, on the contrary," I said cheerfully. Silvio's eyes widened. I had *interrupted* him? "I'm not here representing Dashiell at all. I just have a few questions for you about your missing vampires."

He made a show of looking elegantly baffled. "My missing . . . I don't understand."

"At least thirty-eight of your people have disappeared in the last few months. There is a rumor going around that there are skinners in town." Without waiting to be asked, I went to the grouping of plush furniture and plopped down on a couch.

Silvio's frown deepened, but he went to the adjoining armchair and lowered himself onto the edge. "Skinners? In Las Vegas?" he scoffed. "You've received bad information, Miss Bernard."

"Then how do you explain the missing vampires?"

Slowly, Silvio leaned back in his chair, squirming a little. He wasn't used to having to make a human body comfortable. "I'm not sure I understand. You're *not* here on behalf of your city's cardinal vampire?"

"Nope."

"And you don't work for any official Old World organization, because there isn't one anymore. So why are you asking about this?"

I had decided to tell part of the truth. "I happened to be in Las Vegas this weekend, purely for pleasure," I told him. "But I was approached by a local vampire, who is concerned about these disappearances. I do take a number of freelance ventures when I'm in Los Angeles, so I agreed to poke around a little." I gave him a sunny smile. "I wasn't aware you were Las Vegas's cardinal vampire when I took the job, but I assume you're all right with it. I'm sure you're just as anxious as I am to find out why your vampires keep disappearing."

He ignored the commentary and went right to, "Which vampire hired you?"

"I'd rather not say."

Silvio glanced at the men on either side of him. Why don't cardinal vampires ever have female bodyguards? Man, sexism really is eternal. "Leave us, please," he told them.

The thugs exchanged glances, but they did as they were told, disappearing through the same door we'd entered. Probably going to stand in the hallway with one hand crossed over the other.

Silvio shifted in his chair again, looking me up and down. I forced myself not to fidget.

"Ordinarily," he said at last, "I would have Domingo and Telly force the vampire's name out of you, just on general principle."

A wave of fear crested inside my stomach, but he couldn't smell it on me while he was human, and I made sure my expression didn't change. "However," Silvio went on, "you are in a unique position of being valuable to a man I'd like to stay on good terms with, so instead

I will just explain to you, Miss Bernard, that we do not have skinners in my city. *If* it is true that vampires are disappearing, I'm sure that is simply because they have chosen to do so." He spread his hands. "As you may have gathered, I came into this position fairly recently. There are always people who decide to leave when a new power rises." A self-satisfied smile broke over his face, which did not make it any friendlier.

"Do you even know how many vampires live here?" I asked. "Aren't you keeping track of their numbers to make sure there's no overfeeding? All of that is pretty standard in Los Angeles."

"*This is not Los Angeles*," he said through his teeth. "Now, as a courtesy to you and your boss, I will overlook the fact that you stormed in here demanding answers, and simply wish you a good evening." He stood, buttoning the damn jacket again. "The next time you are interested in coming to town, I am sure you'll have your cardinal vampire call for permission first."

I didn't move. "Seriously? You're just going to pretend like you don't have a problem?"

"Because I do not. Domingo! Telly!" he called toward the door.

The bodyguards reentered. I wondered if Silvio told them when to sit and stay, too. "Please escort Miss Bernard out of my building," he said to them, gesturing at me.

The two beefy guys advanced on me, popping back into my radius. I had learned all I was going to. I finally stood up. "I can find my own way out, thanks."

"I'd feel more comfortable," Silvio said evenly, "if you were to make sure Miss Bernard leaves the building, gentlemen."

The two big guys hadn't even broken their stride, and now they were both reaching for me, obviously intending to each take one of my arms.

Eh, fuck it. I wasn't making friends here anyway.

I had palmed my knives the moment Silvio diverted his attention to the guards, and now I flashed out my hands to throw both, burying one blade in each bodyguard's shoulder. I was weaker with my left hand, so whichever one of the thugs was on that side got his knife a little higher, but he still staggered back with a howl, as though I had ripped off one of his limbs.

Silvio's eyes looked like they were going to pop out of his head with rage. "How *dare* you—" he began, but I overrode him.

"What? Poke your bodyguards after you told them to put their hands on me? Don't be a baby. We both know they'll heal in ten minutes." *And if you didn't want me to stab them, you should have respected me enough to check for weapons.* I didn't say that part, but I'd like to think it was implied in my tone. I stepped over the coffee table and right between the two guards, who had both sat heavily on the floor, clutching at their wounds. They were going to have to take the blades out in order to heal anyway, so I bent down and plucked out both knives at the same time, prompting a new chorus of moans. The one on the right looked like he might cry, but they let me saunter past without further interference. I thought about saying something like "don't forget to tip your waitress" on the way out, just in the spirit of Vegas, but there's only so far even I can push my luck.

Chapter 17

"Miss? Miss!"

"Grkgne," I mumbled, or something very close to it. I made an effort to open my eyes as wide as possible. "What?" I managed to say. "Sorry, I think I drifted off there."

Of course I had. I was operating on five hours of sleep, I'd been putting a lot of effort into my radius, and someone had put me in a heated bed and rubbed my back.

It was my first time getting a massage, and I'd been a little shy about getting mostly naked and letting a complete stranger rub oil on me. But the process had been a lot less sexual and a lot more soothing than I'd thought. Of course, it didn't hurt that my masseuse was a benevolent woman in her early sixties.

"Our time is up, miss," she repeated patiently. "Shall I get you some water?"

I propped myself up on my elbows with the sheet pulled up to my shoulder blades. "Uh, sure. Water. Yes."

My masseuse nodded and slipped silently through the door. I blinked, trying to reorient myself.

The spa at the Venetian was as beautiful and opulent as the rest of the resort. There was everything you could imagine having in a spa, and a lot of things I had never thought of, like a giant climbing wall and a bunch of different "environments" that were supposed to detox your body of various . . . things. I was still a bit fuzzy on what I was detoxing *from*, but everyone made it sound very important.

As impressive as it was, the spa also shared the casino's commitment to spatial confusion, which meant someone had to guide you everywhere. After I dressed in the spa robe and opened the door, my masseuse was waiting for me with a cup of water. "Your friends are gathering in the igloo room," she said, smiling and gesturing for me to follow her.

"The igloo room?" *Please be a clever name*, I thought.

Nope. A few moments later I was opening the door to a freezing cold and very round chamber, where Juliet, Bethany, and Laurel were standing in a little circle in their robes, rubbing their hands together. "What the *what*?" I sputtered as the door swung closed behind me. "Why are we standing in the Arctic? People pay real human money for this?"

Juliet laughed. "It's part of their whole schtick. They alternate hot and cold, which is supposedly good for you . . . somehow."

"It's European," Bethany said airily. "They do this every winter in Scandinavia, with their saunas."

"Tara's back in the conservatory, because of the baby," Laurel added. She sounded a little wistful.

Bethany, meanwhile, was studying my face. "God, you look terrible. Was the massage that bad, or did you just stay out partying all night?"

"That's me, big party animal," I muttered. "But please don't call me God. I hate to reveal my lack of European sophistication, but can we get the hell out of here?"

Bethany opened her mouth to say something, but Juliet and Laurel were already moving toward the door. "Yes, please!" Juliet said, laughing a little.

We began to file out of the pointless torture that was the igloo, starting with Juliet and Bethany. Before I could follow, though, Laurel reached out and got a loose grip on my arm, giving me a meaningful look. Reluctantly, I let the igloo door swing closed and turned back to face her, shivering.

"Wyatt said he came to see you last night," Laurel began. She was watching my face with an intensity that made me nervous. The cold didn't seem to bother her anymore.

"Yeah."

"And that you agreed to help him find Ellen's killer."

"Try," I corrected. "I said I would *try* to find Ellen's killer, while I'm here."

Her eyes narrowed. "He also said you were going to help him die."

Ah. That was what this was about. I held up a hand. "Not sure about that last part. Assisted vampire suicide isn't exactly on my résumé."

"So don't do it."

I thought of the pain in Wyatt's face, his longing to be reunited with Ellen. "What do you care?" I asked.

Laurel's eyes hardened. "My daughter refers to him as 'Uncle Wyatt.' She's already lost Ellen. I don't want her to lose him, too."

"That might not be up to you," I said, edging toward the door. "Regardless of whether or not I get involved."

She put a hand on the glass door. "All I'm saying is, don't help him destroy himself. It's going to be hard enough to talk Wyatt out of it without you making it easy on him."

I set my jaw. Historically speaking, Scarlett did not like being told what to do, but I was trying to see things from Laurel's perspective. Go, me. "I'm not going to do anything until we find the skinners, but I'll tell you what: *if* I decide to help Wyatt die, I promise to give you a call beforehand so you can try to talk him out of it."

She pursed her lips, thinking that over. Juliet chose that moment to poke her head back into the freezing room. "Everything okay, guys?" she said, looking back and forth between us.

"Great," I said. "I was just asking Laurel for a restaurant recommendation." I herded her out of the room as I talked, and Laurel lagged behind us. "I didn't get a chance to tell you, I have to work again today."

"Oh no!" Juliet said, crestfallen. "Did drinks last night go badly?" She pointed down one of the short, labyrinthine halls, directing me. We entered a room with several large stone lounge chairs, sort of like the adjustable kind you see at the pool. There was a small hot tub in the center of the room, which smelled pleasantly of eucalyptus. Bethany and a beaming Tara were already sitting in the stone chairs.

"Hi, Scarlett!" Tara chirped.

"Hey, Tara," I replied, happy for a way out of the conversation with Juliet. "How's the baby this morning?"

She put both hands flat on her stomach. "Oh, wonderful. No nausea at all."

But Juliet wouldn't be deterred. "You met with the building manager, right?" she continued, sitting down at the side of the hot tub and dangling her legs in.

"Yes, and it was fine." I followed her lead, sitting on the other side. The water felt deliciously warm as it hit my feet, which were still a little sore from all the walking yesterday. Between that and my recently unkinked back muscles, I was going to have a hard time staying upright through this conversation. They didn't hand out caffeinated beverages at the spa, unless you counted unsweetened green tea, which I most certainly did not. "But he wants me to help him interview cleaning companies after we're done here," I said in my most regretful tone. I'd come up with this particular lie on the cab ride back to the Venetian the previous night.

I checked my watch, which I'd insisted on keeping even during my massage. I needed to get going if I was going to meet Jameson. "I'm afraid I'm going to miss dance class, and possibly more than that." I hung my head, trying to look contrite.

The others all voiced their sympathy, even Bethany, who was obviously faking it. "Are you sure you need to?" Juliet said anxiously. "I feel terrible that we're having so much fun, and you're stuck at work."

Oops. Maybe I'd overdone it a little. I gave her a smile. "Don't worry, Jules. I'm sure he'll take me out to a nice brunch, and although I'd much rather be with you guys"—not exactly the truth—"it won't be so bad."

"Well, it's great that Dashiell trusts you so much," Juliet replied, looking more or less pacified. "Will you call me when you're done, so we know when to expect you?"

I agreed to do so, and fled the relaxing utopia for something more familiar.

Chapter 18

Vegas Vic, as it turned out, was a massive neon sign in the shape of a waving cowboy, which currently presided over a souvenir shop on Fremont Street in downtown Vegas.

When I'd come with my family, years earlier, we hadn't actually gone to the downtown area, but I'd gotten the impression that it was pretty seedy—not the kind of place tourists would want to visit. Either I had been wrong or something had changed, because when my cab dropped me off at the corner nearest Vic, I saw that part of Fremont Street had been blocked off into a perfectly nice outdoor mall area, but instead of stores there were casinos, bars, and restaurants. Some enterprising committee had also decided to hang an enormous, circus-tent-like tarp over the whole plaza, providing much-needed shade from the Nevada sun.

It must have still been fairly early for Vegas, because as I walked down the sidewalk there were very few people out there with me, and most of them looked like they'd been out all night. I hadn't been totally wrong about the seedy factor: there was nothing overtly trashy, but an element of glitzy sleaze lingered in the air, as though the whole place had just been power-washed after an all-night orgy.

Jameson was already at Vegas Vic, leaning against the side of the building, just below the sign. He had on jeans and a black tee shirt, and despite the shade overhead, his eyes were hidden behind wraparound sunglasses. The part of his face that I could see seemed frozen in an inscrutable expression, and overall he looked like the world's scariest bouncer, inexplicably hired to guard a garish souvenir shop.

When he saw me coming, he pushed off the wall and gestured toward the pedestrian mall. "Come on, let's walk. There's a good coffee shop a couple of blocks down."

Good morning to you too, I thought, but I followed his lead. The two of us began strolling on the pedestrian mall, where we had to circle around a couple of different families taking photos with the dreaded selfie sticks.

"A few years back there was a major push to revitalize the downtown district," Jameson told me. "They installed *that*"—he pointed to the blocks-wide shade above our heads—"and tried to pull the area together with the Neon Museum, the Mob Museum, and so on."

"You sound like a tour guide," I remarked.

He shrugged. "This is my town now. It's important to know the place where you live."

It was hard to read his expression, but he seemed . . . troubled. I tried to figure out a place to start, and settled on, "So I met Silvio. He seems like kind of a joke."

Jameson didn't deny it, just said, "He serves a purpose."

"Leaving the Holmwoods alone? That purpose?"

He gave me the side-eye. "Something like that. How did you meet him?"

Wondering if he already knew the answer, I said, "I went to see him last night. I wasn't impressed. I don't think he's up to stopping the skinners."

"I'm not even convinced there *are* skinners in town," Jameson contended. "There's not much evidence. Sure, vampires are missing, but it's not like we're finding any bodies. If ancient bones had been discovered in the city limits, I'm sure we would have seen something about it on the news."

When a vampire dies, the magic leaves their body, and their remains revert back to whatever age they would have been if they'd never become a vampire. So very old vampires do, in fact, turn into dust, but younger vampires might leave behind a skeleton or even a desiccated corpse. Unless they died in the presence of a null, in which case they would look like any other recently deceased. Jameson didn't do the same kind of cleanup work I did, but he knew this as well as I did.

"Yeah, because *no one* has ever made a body disappear in the desert outside Vegas before," I said sarcastically. "What about your bosses? Don't Lucy and Arthur care that someone is killing vampires in their town?" Jameson didn't respond. "Don't *you*?"

"Scarlett . . ." His voice was weary. "Please go home. There's nothing you can do here."

This again. "I'm pretty frickin' sick of you saying that," I said, letting the frustration leak into my voice. "I can at least find the skinners." *And get justice for Wyatt* was the unspoken part of that thought, but I wasn't going to mention him. Or the fact that I wasn't really sure *I* was up for this kind of work.

When he didn't relent, I added, "Look, how about we speak hypothetically for a second?"

"Okay . . ." He looked wary.

"Hypothetically, *if* skinners really are in town killing vampires, what's their endgame? What's the point?"

He shrugged, uncomfortable. "Hypothetically, they would probably be here on a species bounty. Someone pays them to kill a certain number of vampires, and when they hit the goal they go back to where they came from. This would be the easiest hunting ground in the US."

"Is that seriously a thing that happens?"

"Sure. If you're rich and you've got a grudge against vampires, you can pay to thin the herd. Which means that even if you stop *these* hunters, more will just take their place."

I threw up my hands in frustration. "I still don't get it. Who *are* these people? Humans who kill vampires and werewolves, fine, but are they, like, a union? A club? One family with a serious grudge and excellent fertility rates?"

He smiled. Finally. "Nothing that dramatic. Killing the supernatural isn't a full-time gig, like in the movies. Generally, skinners are private security guys who have found out about the Old World somehow and are put to use. They're run through a firm that takes the occasional 'specialty' job."

"So they're mercenaries," I said, not really as a question.

"You could say that," he agreed. "Malcolm uses a company in New York, for when he needs to kill someone outside the five boroughs."

Of course he did. God, Malcolm was a tool. "Why don't we have them in LA?"

"Because until recently, LA was a podunk town in the Old World," Jameson replied. "You probably do have the occasional contractor here and there, but they don't do enough damage for anyone to notice."

Touché.

Then I stopped dead. "Wait. If the skinners are just killers for hire . . . who's paying them?"

He stopped, too, turning to point at me. "Now *that* is a great question, but I don't know how you'd find the answer, short of capturing one of the skinners alive and torturing him for information."

"So we should just, what? Let it happen?"

"This city just avoided one war, Scarlett. Nobody wants to start another one."

Jameson started walking again, and I reluctantly trotted after him. "Wait. You didn't answer me. Don't Lucy and Arthur care that they probably drew the skinners here?"

He glanced at me, eyebrows raised.

"All that fucking publicity?" I said. Jameson paused for a moment, just gazing at me. "You hadn't thought of that," I concluded.

"No, I didn't get that far. But you're probably right." He rubbed his eyes with the heel of one hand, looking tired. Jameson had really great hands, I couldn't help but notice. "Look, do you have any idea how much work goes into a show like *Demeter*? I don't mean the funding and the rehearsals and all the PR, but just the actual, day-to-day work of putting on that kind of production?"

"No."

"Lucy and Arthur do care about other vampires, especially if the skinners came to town because of them. But they are focused on what they came here to do."

"Tell the world about vampires?"

He gave me an exasperated look. "Put on a show. These two aren't like any of the others, Scarlett. They're performers. Their interests are pretty centralized."

"So they're vapid," I suggested.

He shrugged, unperturbed. "But they pay well."

It shouldn't have stung, but I couldn't help picturing Wyatt's broken expression. I stopped walking. Jameson realized I wasn't keeping up and turned to look down at me. "And that's all that matters, right?" I said. "Jesus, Jameson, what happened to you?"

His face went so hard it might as well have been chiseled. "I *survived*," he ground out, meeting my glare with his own. "Just like always."

Just like always? What the hell did that mean? "Why did you leave Malcolm?" I asked, hands on my hips.

He glared down at me without answering. We stood there for nearly a full minute, but I held my ground. Finally, he said, "Look, when you were visiting, there was a lot I didn't tell you about Malcolm and his business. *Couldn't* tell you. And I shouldn't now, either. Malcolm guards his secrets very closely."

I blinked. In New York, there had been times when Jameson had sent me sightseeing or told me to stay in the apartment, with a sense of urgency that had unnerved me even then. I began to suspect it was because Malcolm was making him do something really bad. Hurting people, or worse. And Jameson had always looked so tired. So resigned.

He pointed ahead, and I saw a sign for a coffee shop that looked like it might double as an old-fashioned record store. We resumed walking again.

"When did you really start working for him?" I asked quietly. "How old were you?"

Jameson flinched, and I knew I'd poked a sore spot. Nulls are always valuable, but you can get the most out of us if you start training—or brainwashing—us when we're young, as Olivia had tried to do with me. The last time I'd seen Jameson I had asked him how long he had been with Malcolm, and he'd just said, "a long time." But he'd only been nineteen.

"I was twelve," he said in a low voice. "But don't ask me about that time, Scarlett. Please." The words started out rough, but his voice faltered at the end.

And I finally thought I understood why Jameson was in Las Vegas. Very few people would have the balls to offer Malcolm's personal null a job right under the cardinal vampire's nose, but the Holmwoods sure as hell did, judging by what I'd seen at their show. And they could get away with it, too, because they were big-time celebrities.

Jameson had probably taken the gig as his way out of Malcolm's service. Maybe his *only* way out. And now I was yelling at him about it. I touched his arm. "I'm sorry."

He just looked at me, and I could see so much anger and frustration and sadness in his face. Jameson was three and a half years younger than me, but in that moment he looked ancient. And I felt like a fool.

We were at the corner of Fremont and Sixth Street, near the doorway of the coffee shop. People—humans—walked right by us, in and out with their mugs, but Jameson ignored them, stepping closer to me until we were toe to toe. He bent his head to look at me, and it was like he was creating a private space just for us. He took one of my hands. "Listen, Letts," he said huskily. "There are things that I can't—"

Then a gunshot rang out over the morning, and Jameson collapsed.

Chapter 19

The shot hit him in the back, and he stumbled into me, half-falling, half-pulling me down with him. I managed to land in a sort of crouch and looked around wildly. We were at an intersection, but judging from the angle, the shooter had to be up Sixth Street. I scooted around the coffee shop door and back onto Fremont, pulling Jameson along with me, his long legs scrabbling at the pavement, trying to help. I yelped once when I felt another shot hum past my face, close enough to shift my hair. He was moving okay, all things considered, and I realized that he'd been wearing his vest. *Thank God.*

We made it into the alley just as another bullet hit the asphalt right next to Jameson's leg, spitting up dust. He rolled the rest of the way behind the wall, trying to stay between me and the opening. He groaned, leaning his back carefully against the building.

"You okay?" I asked.

He nodded. "Just give me a minute. Did you see where he was?"

"No, but if I were him, I'd be walking up to this alley right about now." I tugged a knife from each of my boots, wishing like hell that Jesse were here. Or that I'd thought to wear my own bulletproof vest to this meeting. As soon as I got back to the hotel, I was putting it on for the duration.

Assuming we lived that long.

"What do we do now?" I asked Jameson. The shooter had gone silent, and I imagined him bursting around the corner to gun us down. I was fast with the knife, but not that fast.

Carefully, Jameson ducked his head out, peeking around the corner. He pulled his head back quickly, cursing. "There are two of them, coming this way fast."

On either side of the mall, passersby were screaming and ducking, cowering against the buildings or running down side streets. "Three," I breathed, and Jameson whipped his head around to look. Over his shoulder, I had spotted a big guy marching determinedly toward us. He wore a knee-length jacket and black pants, way too warm for the weather, and everything about his body language and detached expression screamed "paramilitary." Especially the rifle he was pulling out from under the jacket.

"Skinners," Jameson hissed.

Oh, God. Until that second, I realized, part of me hadn't really believed there was such a thing as skinners. Now they were way, way too real. And they were closing in.

Jameson struggled to his feet, eyes filled with panic. "Run!" he shouted, grabbing my hand.

We raced across the Sixth Street opening and farther down Fremont, where there were plenty of pedestrians and mall paraphernalia to provide at least a little cover. I heard two more shots from behind us, but I didn't dare slow down enough to look. A voice way in the back of my head was bursting with questions: Who were they? Were they after me or Jameson? Could the skinners have a bounty on nulls, too? Anything was possible, but I wasn't about to go back there and ask them.

We ran out of the outdoor mall and onto a couple of generic-looking city streets. I didn't know the area, so I let Jameson pull me along. I was suddenly incredibly thankful for all the mind-numbingly dull hours of running I'd put in over the years, which gave me the stamina to keep up.

Jameson didn't slow down until we approached some kind of massive metal sculpture. "Turn in here," he shouted over his shoulder. We ducked underneath an enormous sign that said *Container Park*.

Jameson slowed to a walk, not letting go of my hand. He was obviously trying to look calm, but I felt too flustered to fake it. We were in some kind of shopping center, but it was built out of what looked like those giant metal shipping containers they have at the Port of Los Angeles. A whole bunch of them had been fused together and stacked up, forming a U-shaped retail area with a playground in the middle. We'd just run into the mouth of the U.

And I didn't see any other exits. "Jameson—" I began uncertainly, but he was already turning to face me.

"Pick a store and wait inside," he ordered. "I'll go back out and lead them away from here."

"You can't just—"

"I've got the vest and the gun; I sure as hell can," he said firmly. "Wait here as long as you can stand it, okay? Then go back to the Strip."

I started to argue, because even in life-or-death situations, I am me. "What if they—"

Jameson bent his head down and kissed me.

The kiss was forceful and intense, like he—we—were trying to fit something a lot bigger into fifteen seconds. My arms went around his neck, and I felt him wrap one arm around my waist, pulling me tight for better access.

Then he was stepping away, moving back toward the entrance. "I'll find you, Letts," he promised, and he turned on his heel and was gone.

For a moment, I thought about following him. What if the three men we'd seen had *wanted* us to run in this direction? What if they were herding Jameson into a trap? I needed to think, so I ducked into the first business I saw, a gourmet hot dog joint. It was too early for lunch, and the place was empty except for a grouchy-looking clerk refilling the napkin container. There were windows on two connecting sides, and I could see the entrance to the container park.

So I had a great view of the paramilitary guy I'd seen on Fremont Street, as he looked up at the sign and decided to step inside. The rifle was gone, probably hidden under his jacket, but his right hand was in his pocket, and I would bet money there was a handgun in there.

"Shit!" I said out loud. I shrank back, lining up my body with the supporting beam in the corner, between the two windows. Of *course* one of the skinners would stop and search the container park. There were enough of them that they didn't need to all follow Jameson.

"Hey. Lady."

Startled, I turned and saw the bored-looking middle-aged clerk eyeing me. Without realizing it, I had drawn a knife from my boot, though it was still hidden behind my body. "What can I get you?" she said pointedly, motioning toward the menu. "Or you meetin' someone?"

"Um, you could say that. My ex is out there, and he looks pissed."

"Oh." Her face softened a little. "You need me to call the cops?"

"That's probably not a bad idea," I said in a voice that came out more like a squeak. I had literally brought a knife to a gunfight, and Jesse wasn't here to back me up.

The clerk picked up a phone, but then her eyes widened. "The brother in the long coat? That your ex?"

"Yeah. And I think he's got a gun. You see him?"

"He's looking around the park." She sounded scared. Smart woman.

"Don't talk to me," I warned her. "Don't look at him. Just act like there's no one in here and everything's normal."

She chewed on her lip but started fussing with the condiments, lining them up by color. I looked around the store, which really was just a frickin' shipping container: a long rectangle with tables on one end and a little partition behind the clerk. That had to be the kitchen, although it couldn't be much of one; the whole place was tiny. "You got a back exit?" I asked her. "If you do, move the ketchup."

She leaned over and shifted the ketchup closer to the mustard. Her hands trembled.

The exit had to be behind the partition that was at her back, which meant I couldn't get to it without crossing one of the giant windows. "Calm as you can, turn around and walk out the exit," I instructed her, "like you are going for a smoke break or something. When you're safe, call nine-one-one."

"What about you?" she murmured, trying not to move her lips.

"I'll be fine. Please, go."

The woman turned around and darted toward the partition separating the counter from the kitchen. As she went, though, she accidentally knocked the metal napkin dispenser off the counter. It fell to the floor with an enormous clang. If the skinner was still standing in the mouth of the container park, there was no way he hadn't heard that.

I cursed and squatted down so I was more or less hidden from the door by a small table. I pulled a second knife from my other boot, listening intently. There was a little bit of muted conversation, probably from the container next to this one, and a few screams of children in the playground area. The air smelled of sausage and charcoal. I waited, afraid to pop my head up to look out the window. Afraid to do anything, really.

Then the tiny bell over the door jingled.

Fuck. Why hadn't I told the woman to lock the door before she left? But it was too late now.

A heavy, booted foot stepped onto the hardwood floor. "Hello?" a deep male voice called. "Anybody here?" A little bell rang on the counter.

Which meant he was facing away from me. I snapped my body up, knife in position, but it had been a trap: the guy was standing with his gun pointed right at me.

His pockmarked cheeks split in a grin. "I can't believe you fell for that."

"Yeah, well, me neither," I muttered.

"Drop the knives," he said, advancing on me. "Do it now." I let them clatter to the floor. He smiled. "Look, we don't want you, princess. We're lookin' for that fella you were with. Tell me where I can find him, and I'll be on my way."

Had to doubt that. This guy had proved he was willing to kill, and there was no reason to leave me, a witness, alive.

"The fella I was with?" I said, feigning confusion. "You mean last night? Or two Thursdays ago, that guy? Because he was—"

"Cut the shit," he said in a growl, and I had to fight off panic. He was nearly within arm's reach.

"I don't know where he was going, really," I said. "He just wanted to lead you guys away from me."

"Why?"

That was actually kind of a good question.

"I don't know!" I wailed, dredging up some tears. "I just met him last night, and we . . . you know . . . and now he like doesn't want me to get hurt, but I don't know who you are or what's happening!"

Without warning, he drew back his arm and cracked me across the face with the gun. I felt the blow reverberate through my cheekbone and into my skull as I fell to the ground.

He'd actually fucking pistol-whipped me.

"Don't lie to me, bitch," he said conversationally.

God, that hurt. Apparently my acting skills were not as impressive as I'd hoped.

My knives were on the floor somewhere, but I couldn't organize my thoughts enough to look for them.

From outside the container, I heard the sudden crack of gunfire. Had the skinners caught Jameson? I flinched, but when I looked up the thug was swearing and holding his shoulder, his attention fixed on the window as he ducked in between the panes. I automatically followed his gaze and saw a bullet hole in the window.

"Who the fuck is *that*?" he snapped, not turning to look at me.

That confused me—it *wasn't* Jameson? The skinner raised his gun and squeezed off two shots, infinitely loud in the small metal space. The window splintered with the first shot and shattered with the next.

This might be my only chance, so I ignored my throbbing head and scooped up one knife by its handle. The guy realized his mistake and swung the barrel of the gun back around at me, but he was too late. I flung up an arm and threw the knife straight into his neck.

He dropped the gun, gurgling, and brought both hands up to his neck, trying to hold in the blood that was spurting from the artery. "I can't believe you fell for that," I said sarcastically, but he didn't hear me. He was already dropping to the ground.

I looked out the empty window frame for Jameson, but he wasn't there. Instead, I saw Cliff lying on the ground, surrounded by a rapidly expanding pool of blood. And I heard the sirens.

Oh, *shit*.

Chapter 20

Please don't let him be dead.

I pulled my knife out of the dead guy and raced outside, dropping to my knees beside Cliff. When I rolled him onto his back, he gasped in pain, and something in my chest loosened.

The whole front of Cliff's dark shirt was wet and sticky with blood, but I didn't exactly want to start poking at it to find the wound. "Where did he get you?!" I yelled. Too loud, but my ears were still ringing from the gunshot.

"My side," Cliff muttered. "I think it went through."

It must have, judging by the amount of blood on his back. "Can you walk?"

I helped him up, and we stumbled out of the container park. Cliff had parked his SUV right around the corner, and I took a second to thank the gods of Las Vegas parking, who were really quite generous once you got off the Strip.

"You were supposed to stay with Juliet," I cried as I helped him into the passenger seat. "How did you even find me?"

"Tracked your phone," he said in a strained voice. "Dashiell's orders. Last night."

Goddammit, Dashiell! He'd told Cliff to stay with me instead of the other women, who were out there unprotected right now. Then again, I couldn't deny that Cliff had probably saved my life back there.

But now I had to keep him from losing his. It felt weird to abandon the skinner's dead body—my whole job was avoiding things like that—but I didn't have a choice, and besides, he had two friends with him. If they were the hunters I thought they were, they would get his body out of there.

Cliff's SUV still had my Bluetooth programmed in, so while I sped away from Container Park, he tapped in Laurel's phone number for me.

"Hello, this is Laurel," she said in a businesslike singsong.

"It's Scarlett!" I yelled. Too loud, too fast. I forced myself to take a deep breath. "I need help."

There was a moment's pause, and then, "Hang on a second, Jules, this is work calling." A little rustling, and then Laurel's voice said urgently, "What happened?"

"Cliff, who was supposed to *stay with you guys* this morning"—I glared across the seat—"got shot. In the side. He needs a doctor, but we can't go to a hospital. Can anyone in your clan help?"

Cliff grunted in surprise, and I realized he hadn't known about Laurel being a witch. Oops.

There was a silence, lasting long enough for me to say, "Laurel? Can you still hear me?"

"Yeah. I just . . . no, none of my clan witches are doctors or nurses or anything . . ."

"But?" I prompted, hearing it in her voice.

"But when I worked at the Flamingo there was this woman we called sometimes, when one of the guests got hurt and we couldn't call the cops. Turns out she's an outclan witch." She said the phrase with disgust, the way people in Bel Air would say "homeless." "She's on retainer to all the big casinos," Laurel added. "She specializes in thaumaturge magic. Healing."

"Do you still have her number?"

"Yeah, they made us memorize it."

I got the number, thanked Laurel, and hung up. Then I called the thaumaturge witch.

Sashi Brighton answered her phone on the first ring, saying "Hello," with an English accent. I quickly gave her my name and explained the problem. There was a long pause.

"I know I'm not with the casinos," I added in a rush, glancing at Cliff. He was terribly pale, and his eyes were starting to glaze over. "But I'm Old World and I've got money. Please."

"It's not that," she said faintly. "Just . . . Scarlett Bernard from Los Angeles? The null?"

"You've . . . *heard* of me?" What the hell? I could see Laurel or Silvio recognizing my name, because they were both deep in the Old World and had ties to LA. But I'd never heard of this woman, and she was outclan. It made no sense.

"We've a mutual acquaintance," she said. "Look, I'll text you my home address. Just get him here as quickly as you can."

"Who—" I started, but she had hung up.

I glanced over at Cliff, as though he might explain what the hell had just happened. His eyes were closed. *Crap.*

"Cliff?" I pulled over and checked his pulse. Thready and weak, but there. His eyelids fluttered for a moment, but then he closed them again. "Hang on," I muttered. I entered Sashi's address into my phone's GPS and peeled off as fast as I dared.

Sashi Brighton lived in one of the suburban areas off the Strip. It seemed like a nice enough area, but I was barely paying attention to anything beyond the GPS and the labored breathing coming from Cliff's seat. By the time we reached her house, Cliff was completely unconscious. She opened the garage door the minute I pulled into the driveway, motioning for me to park next to the lone vehicle, a late-model Prius. As soon as I did, she started closing the door again.

Sashi was a stunning Indian woman in her mid to late thirties, with long shiny hair in a fishtail braid down her back, expensive jeans, and a canvas apron over a light sleeveless sweater. My mouth dropped open in surprise as she stepped into my radius. She was as powerful as Kirsten, or damned close.

"Help me get him inside," she said in the same urgent-but-calm tone you hear from ER doctors everywhere.

She propped Cliff up under his good arm, and I sort of deadlifted his lower body, and between the two of us we managed to get him around the car and up the little steps leading into a clean mudroom. It opened directly into a kitchen, where Sashi had laid a pallet on the floor, along with a large and extensive first-aid kit. More of a first-aid suitcase, really.

She pulled out scissors and began cutting away Cliff's shirt. "You have to move away from him," she ordered. "My room is at the end of the hall. Get cleaned up and grab some of my clothes to put on."

I looked down at myself. Cliff's blood was smeared all over my jeans and tee shirt. "Really?" I said stupidly. She was just going to let me, a stranger, go into her personal space and raid her closet?

"Go!" Sashi barked. A little softer, she added, "Trust me. This is what I do."

I kicked off my boots on the linoleum floor, where they wouldn't make a mess, and bolted toward the bedroom in my socks.

Sashi's bedroom was beautiful: clean and sunny, with yellow curtains and an Indian-print bedspread that was a welcome explosion of color in the otherwise minimalist decor. Walking a little stiff-legged from the drying blood, I made my way into the adjoining bathroom and surveyed myself in the mirror. The blood hadn't gotten in my hair, but it had soaked through my shirt and the side of my pants where I'd helped haul Cliff, and run down my leg under the jeans. I considered it for a moment and decided that taking a quick shower would be less of a violation than accidentally smearing someone's blood all over Sashi's house. I opened cabinet doors until I found a clean, fluffy towel, and then I got under the hot spray, trying to calm myself down. My radius had expanded a little when I was panicking about Cliff, and I needed to pull myself together so I didn't turn Sashi into a human when Cliff needed her magic.

When I was sure I was reasonably okay, I got out, put on my own bra and underwear, and dressed in the first clothes I found: yoga pants and a workout tank. I saw the labels as I pulled them on, and almost took them off again. The top and pants combined probably cost more than a night at my hotel. But they were clean, and I had the feeling that if I kept digging through Sashi's clothes I wasn't going to find anything cheaper anyway.

When I was dressed, I wasn't sure what to do next. I had my cell phone, since it had been in my jeans pocket, but I was effectively trapped in the bedroom until Sashi helped Cliff. *If* she could help him. I didn't know anything about thaumaturge magic.

I took my phone out of my jeans pocket, intending to fold the bloody clothes. A wad of paper fell out of the pocket, too. The list of missing vampires, with their last known locations. Right.

Relief flooded through me: I couldn't help Cliff now, and I didn't even have a way of contacting Jameson. But this was something I *could* do. I left the pile of stained clothes on top of a magazine and carried the list to a small armchair in Sashi's bedroom. I'd glanced over the list earlier, but I hadn't taken the time to actually study it yet. I sat on the floor with my back against the chair and spread the list out on the carpet in front of me, studying the names of the missing vampires.

I didn't recognize anyone, and I wasn't familiar with a lot of the locations, either, so I started googling, using a pen from Sashi's dresser to make little notes. I kept an ear out, but although I could hear movement in the kitchen, I didn't want to risk getting any closer, even just by peeking my head out of the doorway. The thaumaturge witch had shown me a lot of trust by letting me into her house like this; it seemed only fair that I try to trust her with Cliff.

When I'd gone through the whole list, I saw that of the thirty-eight vampires who had gone missing, fifteen had last been seen on the Strip. Thirteen had vanished from downtown, and three from apartment buildings in the residential districts. The rest of the locations were unknown, at least in the little time Wyatt had had to investigate. He had said he would dig into it some more when he woke up that night.

I leaned back against the chair, thinking it over. The locations made sense, since Laurel had told me that the vampires in Las Vegas pretty much stuck to downtown and the Strip, but knowing that wasn't particularly helpful, as far as I could see. I turned my attention to the dates, opening up the calendar on my phone so I could get a sense of any pattern.

Minerva, the vampire who had been fighting Silvio for control of the city, had disappeared January 19, along with three others. The following week, four vampires had disappeared, then four more, then five, then seven, always on a Friday or Saturday. The numbers might be slowly escalating, but it was hard to tell with the amount of data I had.

I pulled up the *Demeter* performance schedule to see if there was any correlation, but the show was on two times every night except Tuesday, so I couldn't see how it was related. But why did the vampires always disappear in multiples? And why on the weekends?

When I couldn't really see any big shiny clues in the information, I decided to call Jesse for a consultation.

"Hello!" he said in a shout. Loud eighties rock was playing in the background.

"Whoa, hi. Everything okay?"

"Hang on." There was some fumbling of the phone, and I could clearly hear him saying to someone else, "Look, man, don't let him rile you up like that, okay? . . . I *know* what he said, but violence is never the answer. I gotta take this."

Another moment, and the music died down. "Hey, Scarlett," he said, a little breathless.

"Werewolf fight at the bar?"

"Yep."

This wasn't surprising. Half my job consisted of cleaning up after a bar fight went too far at Hair of the Dog. I'd had to get rid of fingers, toes, arms—and once, seven rabbit corpses. Don't ask.

"And your solution was 'violence is never the answer'?" I said, amused.

"Well, it isn't," he said defensively.

"Unless the question is, 'What is never the answer?'" I pointed out.

There was a pause, and then Jesse said, "Did you actually need something?"

I explained the list of missing vampires, and told him the little I knew about their disappearances, including Ellen and Margaret.

When I was finished, Jesse said, "Hmm. The locations, is that where you know for a fact they were, or where they were last spotted?"

"Uh . . ." I thought over what Wyatt had told me. "Last *known* locations, so where they said they were going, or where the last person to see them alive saw them."

"Okay, look. I'm not there, and I don't have all the details, but my guess would be that each of these missing vampires got a phone call to come to a party."

I blinked. "Why a party?"

"Because that's what happens on Friday and Saturday nights," he said sensibly. "And because of the whole Vegas culture. If someone said you could go to an exclusive party or a new club opening or whatever, but you had to keep it a total secret, wouldn't you go?"

"*Hell* no," I said. "I'd laugh and put on my jammie pants."

"Well, yeah, but that's *you*. To the average Vegas resident, an invitation like that would be irresistible."

I thought that over for a moment. "Wyatt didn't say anything about Ellen going to a party . . . except for the big public reception that the Holmwoods held on opening night, but the skinners wouldn't have killed her right there in public."

"Maybe not, but if one of Ellen's friends pulled her aside at the reception and invited her to come to a post-show after-party, would she have told her husband about it beforehand?"

Huh. "I'm not sure," I admitted. "I never met Ellen, so I'm just going from what Wyatt told me, but I got the impression that he's sort of the curmudgeonly homebody, and she was the social butterfly. They've been together forever, and vampires stay up all night. She might not have felt like she needed to tell him exactly where she was going after the show."

"Especially if they're from a time before cell phones," Jesse pointed out. "Not all couples feel the need to know where their spouses are at all times."

"Okay, I can buy that. But who lured her to the after-party?"

"Say you're a skinner, and you want to kill a whole bunch of vampires," Jesse went on. "You find the names of one or two, maybe by asking around at the show. You call that vampire and say, 'Hey, I've got this great club opening just for your kind. We're doing an exclusive party in two hours, and we want you to come.'"

"Wouldn't that seem awfully suspicious?"

"If you knew the skinners were in town, maybe. But what if the person on the phone said you could bring a friend? Or two friends? I bet if you dig deeper, you'll find that most of the people who disappeared knew at least one other person who vanished on the same night. People think there's safety in numbers, and I would imagine vampires already see themselves as bulletproof."

"Huh." Based on what I knew about the Old World . . . he had a point. The vampires in question would probably have felt comfortable enough to let their guards down, confident that no one would try to take on two or three of them at once. "Damn," I said, half-admiringly. "That's a hell of a trap."

"Can you get the phone records for the missing vampires?" Jesse asked. "If we're right about this, they would probably point you right at the skinners."

Could I? I didn't see how. Silvio might have access, but even if I hadn't stabbed two of his bodyguards, he'd made it clear that he wasn't going to admit to a problem.

Wait. I could probably get Ellen's records from Wyatt, when he woke up. And before that . . .

"Scarlett?" came Sashi's voice from the kitchen. "You can come out now."

She sounded tired, but otherwise I couldn't read her tone. Was Cliff better? Worse? Dead? "Okay," I called. Into the phone, I said, "Jesse, I've got to go, but I need a favor. Can you call Abby and see if she can get the phone records for the vampire that Dashiell sent, Margaret?"

"Yeah, I'm on it."

We hung up, and I hurried into the kitchen.

Chapter 21

Cliff was still spread out on the floor, with a large white bandage covering his abdomen. Sashi was sitting on the floor next to him, her back leaning against the cupboard. Neither of them moved as I approached, which brought me up short. "Is he . . ."

She gave me a weak smile. "He's going to be fine. You got him here just in time." She gestured to the piles of bloody towels on the floor all around them, like wounded soldiers after a battle. "He really should have a transfusion, but if he rests a lot and gets plenty of iron and sugar, he can recover without it." She raised an eyebrow at me. "Unless you happen to be O positive?"

"Actually," I said, surprised, "I am." It wasn't the world's rarest blood type or anything, but still. Every once in a while, things do just kind of work out. It was sort of encouraging to be reminded.

"Brilliant!" Sashi said, turning to dig in her first-aid case.

"But how do you know that's Cliff's blood type?"

"He woke up for a few minutes, from the pain. I asked him then," she said, pulling out some tubes and needles. "Here, let's get a transfusion going, shall we?"

● ● ●

A few minutes later, I was settled on the other side of Cliff's prone body, watching the red fluid flow out of my arm and into his.

"Better," Sashi said, looking at him with satisfaction. "Thank you."

"Thank *you*," I said earnestly. I was a little amazed. In LA we had a human doctor who catered to supernatural clients, but he didn't have actual magic on his side. I wasn't sure Cliff would have survived even in a regular hospital. "How soon can I get him out of here?"

She checked her watch. "Let's give him at least another hour, just so I can make sure the stitches stay closed."

"He has stitches?" I said without thinking.

She smiled. "Yes. I spent most of my time on the internal bleeding, and encouraging his body to regulate his blood pressure. His skin can heal from the puncture without any trouble, so there was no need to use magic for that. I try to give the body a chance to heal naturally when it's not life-threatening."

I nodded. She stood up, wobbling just a tiny bit but steadying herself on the counter. "If you want to stay with him for a moment, I'll go get cleaned up."

I was limited in how far I could move with the tube in my arm, but I did what I could to pile up the bloody towels and pick up the trash from the bandage packets while Sashi was in the shower. She'd only used the supplies in the suitcase, which suggested to me that Sashi usually treated her patients somewhere else. She had made a special exception for me.

I was grateful, but also . . . why? Why would she allow me into her home, much less into her bedroom and her clothes?

When Sashi came padding back into the living room, still rubbing her damp hair with a towel, I finally asked the question that had been bugging me. "You said we had a mutual acquaintance."

Sashi grinned—not the well-bred, polite smile I'd seen earlier, but a full-on, amused grin with teeth that were just a little crooked. It made me like her more. "Allison Luther is a friend of mine," she explained.

"*Lex?*" I said, stupidly. "How did you meet Lex?"

"Through mutual witch acquaintances, same as you. The witch clans dislike me, but they can't deny my usefulness. I've picked up something of a reputation. I even—" She cut herself off, as though she'd changed her mind about adding to that. "Anyway. I've known Lex for years."

"And she told you about me?"

Sashi's face grew somber. "She mentioned you when she told me about her sister's death. And again later, when Katia came to live with her. Lex says you're a magnet for trouble."

"Yeah, she doesn't think much of me," I admitted.

Sashi looked surprised. "That's not the impression I received at all. I think you . . ." She paused, her eyes going out of focus for a moment as she looked for the right words. "You worry her. Because of Charlotte."

"Lex's niece?" I'd never actually met the little girl, who had to be four or five by now, but apparently she was a null, like me.

Sashi nodded. "When Lex looks at you, she sees Charlie's future. And since every time you see her you're destroying a body or in mortal danger . . ." She spread her hands. "Look, Lex and her niece are under the protection of probably the oldest vampire on the planet, and there have still been a couple of kidnapping attempts, from people who wanted to take Charlie and use her to do bad things. I think Lex worries that even as an adult, the threats won't stop."

Oh. I hadn't really thought of it like that. I kind of wanted to think that over when I was alone, but for right now I was ready for a change in subject.

"I saw the pictures in your living room, and on the fridge." I tilted my head toward the studio shot of Sashi posing with a young woman, around Corry's age. "Is that your sister?"

"My daughter," she corrected. "Grace." A darker look spread over her face for a second, and then she said carefully, "I had her rather young. She's away at college now." Sashi glanced at the fridge photo, a little wistful. "She's studying at the University of Colorado in Boulder, so now Lex sees her more than I do. But I visit."

Sashi seemed to remember herself, and her face shut down, closing me out. And then I saw it.

The accent, the dark hair, the way her brow furrowed, the mask she used to hide her true self. "Holy shit," I blurted. Sashi's eyes flew to me. "You look just like her." How had I not seen it earlier?

"Who? Grace?" Sashi asked, but her eyes told me she suspected exactly what I was going to say.

"Stephanie Noring, from Minnesota. You're Dr. Noring's daughter, aren't you? Or at least her niece or something." Noring was the physician who had come to LA to take care of me after I'd cured a werewolf and twisted my knee in the resulting seizure. Because I was a null, she had never used anything other than conventional human medicine on me, but still, I should have seen it.

Sashi's face had gone glacial. "Her daughter."

"Damn, I'm an idiot. Dashiell said there was a whole specialty in healing magic, but Dr. Noring acted like what she did was kind of different from that, and I only now put it together," I babbled. "You're much stronger than her, though."

"Yes. I was bred to be," Sashi said coolly. "My mother and I don't speak. We haven't for many years now." She nodded to the transfusion equipment. "That's enough, I should think. Let's get you unhooked."

Expertly, Sashi pulled out the tubes and attached Band-Aids to my arm and Cliff's. His color had improved dramatically, and she looked pleased. "He could wake up anytime now," she said, looking up at me. "How do you feel?"

"A little light-headed, but nothing major." I should have picked up on her obviously intentional subject change, but I was too intrigued by my own discovery. Because I'm actually quite dense. "Hey, do you know why Noring has a feud going with our alpha werewolf?" I asked eagerly. "His name is Will, and they've got this weird frenemy vibe, but neither of them would tell me why, and I've never had anyone else to ask until now . . . Sashi?" The witch had gone pale, and I could see the muscles jumping in her cheek from her clenched jaw.

Then her eyes jumped back to the fridge, and I turned to see that she had glanced at the photo of Grace again. Without speaking, I stood up and walked over to it, examining the girl more carefully. "Oh, wow," I said softly. Grace looked so much like Sashi—but her skin and hair were lighter, and there was something about her stance and the way she squared her shoulders. Something I had seen so many times before.

Will had a daughter.

Chapter 22

I turned around. "I am so, so sorry," I blurted. Sashi just sat there, pale and frozen, as though I'd just pulled down her pants in a crowded church. "I wasn't trying . . . I mean, I'm sorry to have brought it up . . ." I flailed my hands helplessly.

"It's all right," she said in a soft voice, but her eyes were filled with tears. "I know you didn't do it on purpose."

This explained so much, on one level, but I also had a thousand questions. Most of them were way too personal, and it wasn't my business. But there was one that I *had* to ask her. I sat back down and said, "Does Will know?"

"No," she whispered. Her eyes had filled with tears. "It was so long ago. When I found out about the pregnancy, he had just been changed, and he was so violent . . ." She shook her head, like she was banishing a bad memory. "I was young, and frightened, and I didn't think I could trust him."

I felt compelled to defend Will, who was truly a good guy, and the best alpha werewolf I'd ever heard of. "Did you know he's alpha now?" I said anxiously. "He owns his own bar, where the wolves hang out. And he's never taken a mate." I wasn't sure why I'd added that last part, but it sent the tears falling down her cheeks. "I'm sorry!" I said, horrified.

"I'm really bad at knowing the right thing to say, ask anyone. Please don't cry. I promise I'll shut up now."

She shot me a quick smile through the tears, and we sat there in silence for a few minutes while she composed herself. I watched Cliff's chest rise and fall, waiting and feeling generally miserable. I had made a nice lady cry.

When Sashi finally did speak, it was in a whisper. "I never took a mate, either. I . . . I came close, once, but . . ." She didn't finish.

And my heart broke for her. "It's not too late," I said urgently. "You could go to LA, or—"

But she was already shaking her head. "I don't . . . react well to werewolves," she said, looking ashamed. And for about the fifteenth time in the last three minutes, I felt like a moron.

The three species within the Old World do not inter-date. In fact, something about their various magics causes them to be repulsed by each other, like trying to connect magnets at the wrong ends. When Sashi said she didn't react well to werewolves, she meant physically.

Then a new thought struck me, an important one. "Wait—if you could become fully human and go be with him, would you?"

She blinked, surprised. "What did you just say?"

I had accidentally dragged her massive secret into the light, so it seemed only fair that I give her one of my own. "I can make someone human again. I mean, I've only done it with vampires and werewolves, but I think it would work for a witch, too," I rushed out. "I would offer to turn Will into a human, but honestly, that would be terrible for so many people. He's a really great leader. He takes good care of his pack. And it would be effectively asking him to choose between you and them."

"I wouldn't want to do that," she said, looking dazed. "You . . . you're saying you can, what, *cure* magic?"

"Yes. I can't do it very often because it takes a lot out of me, but . . . yes."

"I've never heard of that." For just the briefest moment, her face glowed with hope. I could practically see her imagining a happily-ever-after with Will. But then the light abruptly died and she shook her head. "He's a werewolf," she said. "He's violent, dangerous."

Before I could protest, she added, "And even if he wasn't . . . I'm rather needed here." She glanced down at Cliff. His color was a little better, though still much paler than it should be. "You have no idea how many idiots hurt each other or themselves at the big hotels. Many of them would die without intervention, and the casinos don't like hospitals, not when it could tarnish their reputation with tourists."

"So let them get a shady hotel doctor like everyone else!" I said indignantly.

She smiled a little. "You are very young." Her eyes were suddenly so sad. "It's just not that simple."

She was, what, maybe fifteen years older than me? At the most? Then again, I couldn't imagine what it must have been like to raise a daughter as a single parent, especially in Las Vegas. And she'd done it without her own mother. It must have been so hard.

No wonder Will and Dr. Noring had their contentious connection. Will had told me once that Noring used to be *his* doctor, meaning his oncologist. If Sashi and Will had been in love, and then Will had been changed in order to survive cancer . . . what a mess.

Some of these thoughts must have played out on my face, because Sashi's eyes narrowed a little. "Are you going to tell him about Gracie?"

I shook my head. "It's not my place. But will you at least think about contacting him and telling him yourself? I promise, he's got control of his wolf side. He's the best werewolf I've ever known."

"Bernard?" Cliff's eyes fluttered open, his gaze fastening onto my face. He took in the room, and the beautiful woman on the other side of him, and his brow furrowed. "The hell is going on?"

"Cliff, meet Sashi," I said. "She's a thaumaturge witch."

His hand strayed up to his midsection, encountering the bandage. "It barely even hurts," he said in awe. "What did you do?"

"Everything I could," Sashi said briskly. "And your friend here donated blood."

Cliff's eyes returned to me, and I gave a weak wave. "Thank you," he said.

Sashi's violet eyes were boring into me. "We should talk again, before you leave town." She pushed a strand of hair behind her ears and stood up. "If you can walk, Cliff, you can go."

"You'll think about it?" I pressed.

She gave me a short, tight nod. Cliff looked back and forth between us, bleary-eyed, and I could practically see him make the decision not to ask. Instead, he pushed himself up onto his elbows, wincing a little, then sat all the way up. "Where to, boss?" he said to me.

I glanced at his blood-soaked clothes. "Do you have a change of clothes in the SUV?"

He looked mildly insulted. "Of course."

"Excellent." I checked my watch. Midafternoon, and I realized I was starving. "First, food. Then—and I can't believe I'm saying this—we better get back to the bachelorette party."

If Cliff had been at full strength, I would have liked to push on for more answers for Wyatt. But Cliff needed food and rest, and anyway, I couldn't think of anything I could do at the moment, short of waking up some vampires and knocking their heads together. Doing that without permission was expressly taboo, and even if it wasn't, I didn't know where any of them spent their daytime hours. I would have to wait until sunset, when I could ask Wyatt for Ellen's phone records. Meanwhile, my top choice would have been to go back to the room for a nap, but we'd been away from the bachelorette party for too long—Cliff had told the other women he was driving me to my "meeting."

We stopped at the Las Vegas In-N-Out for lunch. I know—all the great restaurants in Vegas, and I go to an LA chain. What can I say, I like what I like, and I was in no mood to eat fancy, especially in workout clothes. No matter how expensive they were.

Cliff moved a little stiffly as we walked into the restaurant, but otherwise he seemed pretty okay. He kept touching the bandage, as if to assure himself that it was really there.

When we were finally seated with our burgers, I caught Cliff giving me a speculative look. "What?" I asked, suddenly self-conscious.

"You just dipped french fries in your soda."

I looked down and swore. "I forgot I didn't get a milkshake this time."

He watched me. "You're worried about your friend, aren't you? The big black guy?"

I raised my eyebrows at him. "Just how long were you following me? And were you . . . eavesdropping?"

He shrugged. "I couldn't hear your conversation, no. But it looked intense. You guys have a history?"

"Something like that."

I ate a few more fries, then blurted, "I don't have a way to find him, is all, at least not until the show tonight. And that guy who came after me today, the skinner you shot at . . . two more of them went after Jameson."

"He moved like he could handle himself," Cliff offered. "I'm sure he's fine. We can go look for him at the theater later, if you want."

"Thanks." Embarrassed, I tried to focus on my food, but I could feel Cliff still watching me. I looked down, but my fries were in ketchup this time and I hadn't managed to drip special sauce all over Sashi's clothes . . . yet. "Now what?" I asked.

"You donated blood," he said simply.

I shrugged. "We have the same blood type. Yay, us." But he was still looking at me. "Stop staring at me," I said, getting irritated. "You would have done the same for me."

"Yeah, but I'm a . . ." He stopped himself.

I pointed a finger at him, angry now. "Finish that sentence."

"A human," he said reluctantly.

"So am I."

"That's—" But he cut himself off again, shaking his head a little. "Sorry," he mumbled.

I put down the burger, which was a big deal because they're very hard to pick up again. "Is *that* why you've been so weird to me? Because I'm Old World and you're not?"

He shrugged, looking a little abashed. "I've dealt with plenty of vampires since I took this job, and more than a few werewolves before that."

"And *none* of them were nice to you?"

"None of them were selfless," he corrected. "The wolves put the needs of the pack before anything else, and the vampires don't do anything without getting something in return. They've all got Asperger's or something."

I stifled a smile, the anger draining out of me. I hadn't really looked at it that way, but from his perspective, he did kind of have a point. "They're transactional, yeah, because when you live forever, you've got a lot of time to accrue and spend favors. And when you have endless amounts of money, favors and power are the only currency worth caring about. As for the werewolves . . ." I shrugged. "Think of them as a particularly tight AA group."

He gave me a bitter smile. "That's not how my ex saw it. They were always . . . well, hounding him, excuse the pun. Calling to check on him, inviting him to things, *pushing* at him. He was always looking for a way out of it, but he kept getting dragged back in to help someone."

I blinked. It hadn't occurred to me that Cliff's ex was male, but I shouldn't have made assumptions. At any rate, that was a weird way to describe the werewolves. Most of the pack members I knew seemed to depend on the pack to stay sane, to help them maintain human-ish lives. Then again, maybe I was looking at it from Eli's perspective, since we'd been together so long. He saw the pack as a force for good, a tool to help everyone keep it together. It hadn't occurred to me that some members would feel differently. "What was his name?" I asked Cliff.

"Drew."

Oh. I put my burger down again, suddenly not hungry. I *had* known Cliff's ex. Drew Riddell had gotten sucked into helping a sketchy werewolf named Terrence try to broker a deal to take down Will. The plan had backfired, and Drew had been killed by the Luparii. Only they'd used Shadow to do it.

My bargest had killed Cliff's ex. What do you even say to that? *Small world?*

I decided not to mention it. Cliff probably knew—werewolves were nearly impossible to kill, unless you had a null or a magically spelled creature who'd been created for that singular purpose—but if he didn't, I had no reason to tell him.

"Anyway," Cliff said gruffly, trying to break the sudden silence. "The wolves are too insular, if you ask me. They're all about secrets and insider plans."

Yeah, I could see how that would be hard on a relationship. But I had a bizarre impulse to defend Will's people. "They're protective of each other, but they sort of have to be. Sometimes knowing you have support is the only thing that keeps you from losing your shit."

He raised an eyebrow. "Speaking from personal experience?"

Happily, my cell phone rang at just that moment. I glanced at the screen and saw Abby's number. "Hey," I said.

"Hey, yourself," she retorted. Abby is a little brusque. "I got the information you asked for about Margaret's cell phone."

"And?"

"She did receive a call shortly before her disappearance. The number is registered to an Ellen Jones."

"Damn," I said, disappointed. That had to be Wyatt's Ellen. Jesse had probably been right about vampires inviting each other into the trap, but this didn't really help me. "Okay, thanks, Abby."

"Hang on," she interrupted. "There's something else. One of your old cell phone numbers has been called three times in the last two hours."

Abby changes my number periodically for security purposes. And, okay, because I keep trashing cell phones. She takes care of forwarding the number or intercepting calls or whatever, because I am technologically uninclined. "Did you answer it?"

"Noooo," she said in a tone that reminded me that she was not an answering service. We'd actually come a long way: only a few months ago she would have barked this at me and hung up. "But here's the number."

She rattled off a stream of digits, but I didn't recognize it. I jotted it down on an In-N-Out napkin and studied the area code. "Six-four-six?" I said. "Where's that?"

"Midtown. New York," Abby said, and hung up the phone.

My heart leapt. Jameson.

Chapter 23

I called Jameson back as we left the restaurant and walked out to the parking lot. He sounded anxious but said he was fine, and we arranged to meet in person outside my hotel.

Cliff claimed he felt well enough to get back behind the wheel, but I insisted on driving us back to the hotel, letting him play navigator. When we got there, I tried to send him back to his room to rest, but of course he refused. After five minutes of bickering—and me reminding him that whatever Dashiell said, *Hayne's* orders were to stay with the other women—he agreed that he didn't need to follow me to meet Jameson. Instead, he would rejoin Juliet and friends as they went about their bachelorette activities.

Better him than me. What did it say about me that I was more comfortable having clandestine meetings with the supernatural than I was taking a dance lesson?

Jameson was waiting for me outside, at the lower entrance to the Venetian. He had a beauty of a black eye, and he was keeping one arm close to his body, like it hurt to move it. When he saw me walking toward him, he straightened up, looking concerned.

"Your face," he said, taking my chin in his hand and turning it to the side. "What the hell happened?"

"One of those guys followed me into the container park," I replied. "In related news, pistol-whipping is apparently still a thing."

"God, I'm sorry." He let go of me, looking remorseful. "I thought they'd stay with me."

I shrugged it off. "Anyway, I'm not the only one who looks like they lost a fight. What happened to your eye? Did they catch you?"

"Shh," he hissed, and I realized I'd been too loud. There were a lot of tourists around. "Come with me." Taking my hand, he led me to the end of a nearby line.

I craned my neck to see what we were waiting for. "The *gondolas*? Why?"

"So we can talk and stay in public at the same time."

I was about to ask why we needed to stay in public, but then I realized he was afraid we might be attacked again. Unlike the streets downtown, every casino is plastered with video cameras, which would make it hard for a gunman to get away with shooting us. Even the skinners didn't want to interfere with casino security.

When we reached the front, Jameson gave the attendant some money and then helped me climb down into one of the gondolas. The gondolier, a stout Hispanic woman in her midfifties, began to sing loudly in Italian. Actually, it could have been any number of languages, for all I knew, but it sounded pretty. Jameson scooted closer to me.

"This is so cheesy," I muttered, although in all honesty, I kind of liked it. The boats were beautiful, and the water was a very calming shade of blue. Plus it was nice just to be away from the constant crush of people.

"Okay, *now* can you tell me what happened?" I said, keeping my voice low.

"I lost one of the skinners, but another one cornered me in an alley," he murmured. "I ran out of ammunition, but I knocked the gun out of his hand and we fought. I won."

"That's it?" I said incredulously, when he didn't continue. "'*I won*'?"

"What else do you want to know?"

"The skinner who came after me said they wanted to know where *you* went."

Jameson nodded. "They want to kill me. What did you tell him?"

"Nothing. I killed him with a knife." Okay, technically I'd had help, but as a general rule, I'm used to playing my cards close to the vest. I didn't want to give away too much about Cliff, even to Jameson.

And, okay, maybe I was showing off a little.

Jameson's eyes practically bugged out. "Damn, Letts."

"How did *you* know that they're after you?"

"Because I recognized the guy I fought," he answered, looking grim. "He works for the same company Malcolm uses, in New York."

My jaw dropped. "*Malcolm* sent the skinners?"

"I can't prove it—I didn't get a chance to ask the guy any questions before I heard sirens—but that would be my guess." Jameson made a face. "I knew he was unhappy about me leaving, but I never thought he'd really send someone to *kill* me."

"You say that like he's sent people to *not* kill you," I remarked. It was a joke, but Jameson's expression flickered. I stared at him. "Wait, he's sent people before? To what, beat you up?"

Jameson nodded, then shrugged. He was absently rubbing at the scar on his collarbone again. "But that's just Malcolm being Malcolm. I thought he'd punish me with a couple of beatings and then let it go. Maybe I shouldn't have fought back."

What? "Let me see if I'm following here," I said in a voice that squeaked. "Your former boss sent people to beat the shit out of you, but you resisted. Now he's escalated to sending real shooters with actual guns, and your response is to wonder if you should have let the first guys kick your ass?"

He gave me a rueful grin. "That's pretty much it, yeah. The guys he sent before were just a couple of street assholes. Lackeys. I thought Malcolm was just trying to make a point." The smile faded. "I didn't think he'd actually have me killed."

I couldn't blame Jameson for that. Nulls are so rare that it usually gives us a kind of protected status in the Old World. It wouldn't have surprised me to hear Malcolm was trying to have Jameson kidnapped and dragged back to New York, but actual murder seemed . . . short-sighted? Wasteful?

Still, it was hard to argue with the very lethal bullets that had been flying our way. Malcolm had to be *really* pissed.

But that didn't explain everything that was going on. "I don't get it, though. I can totally see Malcolm sending skinners against you, but why would he pay them to kill vampires in Las Vegas?"

Jameson shrugged, looking uneasy. "Maybe to make the Holmwoods' show fail, so they'd have to fire me. Maybe out of spite. Or maybe vampires really are just leaving town because Silvio took over, and the skinners have nothing to do with it."

That didn't sound right to me. I believed Wyatt when he said Ellen wouldn't leave him without saying goodbye. There was no reason for him to lie about it, not when all he wanted to get out of it was revenge and a quick death.

But I wasn't going to be able to convince Jameson of that, at least not yet. "So what do we do?" I said instead.

All this time the gondolier had been singing loudly in maybe-Italian at the far end of the boat, but in the moment of silence following my question I realized she'd switched up the music, possibly to win back our attention. The new song began, "*Row, row, row your boat.*" Well played, lady.

"*You* do nothing," Jameson said firmly. "I don't know if the guy I fought lived or not, but at least one of them got away. Now that they're aware of our, um, connection, they'll come after you, too. And if they figure out who you really are . . ." He shook his head. "I don't know. Maybe they kill you, maybe they put you in a trunk and drive you back to LA. I'm not willing to risk it. You need to get the hell out of Vegas."

I glared at him. "It's cute how you think you get to be in charge of what I do."

"I'm serious, Letts. I want you out of this."

"Let's say I did leave," I said, though I had absolutely no intention of doing it. "Let's say I pack my shit and run back to LA. What exactly are *you* going to do?"

He hesitated, but only for a second. "I'll talk to the Holmwoods. They might be willing to intervene on my behalf."

"Bargain with Malcolm, you mean. For your life."

Jameson shrugged. *If that's what you want to call it.* Why wasn't he more upset about this? Why did he seem so resigned? "But you've helped them set up the show, and it's running now," I pointed out. "And this is the second time I've seen you today. So I'm guessing the Holmwoods don't need you so much anymore."

"They need me."

"For what?"

"Daytime stuff," he said vaguely.

That line of questioning wasn't getting me anywhere. "Look, Arthur and Lucy like money, right?" I countered. "Isn't it just as likely that they'd sell you out to Malcolm? Hell, it would probably smooth things over with him, after they poached you."

Jameson shook his head, looking frustrated. "They wouldn't. There are still things they need a null for, trust me."

"I trust *you*," I said, realizing it was true. "But do you trust *them*?"

He opened his mouth, closed it again. "Then I should stay," I insisted. "I'll watch your back."

The corner of his mouth quirked up, but I missed whatever he said next. Just past his shoulder, a familiar head of red hair caught my eyes. Laurel. She was winding through the crowd, with Juliet, Tara, and Bethany behind her. All of them were smiling and chatting.

They weren't looking this way—yet. "Shit," I said, ducking down below Jameson's shoulder. They were supposed to be going out for cocktails after their dance class. Maybe they'd come back to the hotel to shower first.

"What?" Jameson said, scanning the crowd urgently. Probably looking for a shooter.

"No, it's just . . . someone I know. I don't want them to see me." It was going to be pretty damn obvious that I wasn't working. Unless I could convince them that Jameson was the new building manager? No, even if I could get him to play along, that wouldn't really explain why I'd brought him back to the Venetian for a gondola ride.

"Oh." He relaxed. "Damn, you scared me. You owe them money or something?"

"Shh!" I kept ducking, trying to sort of maneuver myself awkwardly behind Jameson's body. He started to turn. "Don't look!"

Jameson just glanced down at me, amused. "This is adorable."

"I hate you." I yanked out my ponytail holder and hunched over so my hair would fall in my face, but the movement caused the gondola to rock slightly. The gondolier paused her song, then gamely resumed.

Jameson snickered. "You realize you're calling *more* attention to yourself, right?" he asked.

"You got a better idea, smartass?" I snapped.

"Yes." Jameson turned his body toward me, and I thought he was going to try to shield me. But then he slid his hands into my hair on either side of my face. He tilted my head up and kissed me.

And kissed me.

I wish I could say that I instantly forgot about being caught by Juliet, but covering shit up is what I do. There was a part of my brain that started instantly recalculating: if they did see me kissing someone, they would just assume I'd snuck off to see some guy I'd met. Not super flattering, but it was a narrative I could work with.

Then the tip of Jameson's tongue slid into my mouth, and I really did forget about my sister-in-law. And the skinners, and Malcolm, and the vampire disappearances. Piece by piece, it all dropped out of my awareness, until there was only Jameson's intensity meeting the heat of my body. It had been so long . . .

We finally broke apart when the gondolier cleared her throat dramatically. I opened my eyes and realized that we had returned to the gondola dock. And there was a line of people waiting. And some of them were catcalling us.

I didn't care.

Neither did Jameson, apparently. We climbed onto the dock—I saw Jameson give the gondolier a fat tip—and he took my hand and led me out of the throng of people, to the side of the building. When we had gotten some distance from the crowds he turned to face me, still breathing hard. "Your room?" he asked huskily. Then he winced, drawing back a little. "I mean, if that's not too . . . I don't know if you have a boyfriend or whatever. I kind of just sprang that on you. I know you probably don't want to rush . . ." He looked embarrassed. "Oh, hell. Stop me anytime here, Letts."

"But this is adorable," I said with a smile. It was probably the first time I'd ever seen Jameson flustered. I could feel that weird null sensation in my radius, and this time it almost felt like it was shimmering around us. For a second I even wondered if other people could see it. But we had sort of sidled over to the wall of the hotel building to get out of the path of the crowd, and no one was watching us.

"The truth is," he said, his tone suddenly very serious, "I want you. I've wanted you since that first night in New York. The time was just never right. Maybe now I could take you to dinner, or—"

I went up on my tiptoes so I could kiss him again, a chaste brush against his lips that ended up being sexier than I'd intended. Urgently, he wrapped his hands around my waist and picked me up, pressing my back against the sun-soaked wall so that our eyes met. It was maybe two thirty in the afternoon.

"Come to bed," I whispered.

Chapter 24

"Scarlett. Wake up, babe."

"Mmmf. Don't wanna."

"I need to go soon."

I cracked open an eye, instantly aware of Jameson in my radius. I was starting to really enjoy that feeling. He was sitting at the edge of the big king-size bed in my palatial hotel room. He'd already put his pants back on, which was just tragic. "I fell asleep?" I mumbled, stupidly. Of course I'd fallen asleep. "Time's it?"

He grinned, a flash of white teeth in the darkening hotel room. "Almost five. The sun's going down soon. I need to get to work."

I yawned and rolled over so I could reach for his arm. "Come back to bed. Be my friend."

He let me pull him until he was propped on one hand, right next to me. "I seem to recall already being your friend," he teased. "A couple of times."

"Shh. It's better for me when you don't talk."

Still smiling, he bent his head and kissed me. I yanked at his arms, forcing him to fall on top of me. He chuckled and let me roll us both over so I was on top. "I win!" I crowed.

"You wish." Jameson rolled me hard the other way, holding himself on his elbows so he could look down at me. "I accept your surrender," I said graciously.

"Oh, well, thank you." He kissed me again, then held up his head, looking at me intently.

After a moment, I got embarrassed. "What?" I said. "Is it my hair? It's my hair, isn't it?"

"Oh no," he said solemnly. "It's your best hair ever." He brushed his thumb against my eyebrow, tracing the lines. I had a hard time reading his expression in the fading light, but he looked almost . . . sad.

"Do you think this has ever happened before?" I asked without thinking.

His lips quirked. "Yes, Scarlett. My understanding is that interracial sex is a fairly everyday thing now."

I made a face at him. "I meant between two nulls, dummy."

"Oh." He tipped himself onto his side, holding his head up with one elbow. Damn. I didn't know the names for all the muscles in his upper arms and shoulders, but I could certainly see them just fine. "Probably not, now that you mention it. Before the Internet, or at least long-distance phone service, I'm not sure how two nulls could have ever met. Then getting two nulls who can travel to meet up, are within acceptable age ranges, and are attracted to each other—"

"Whoa, slow down, buddy," I objected. "I never said I was attracted to you."

Jameson wrapped one hand around my bare hip, drawing me close. He kissed me until I was breathless. When he finally pulled back, I was very much awake.

"I accept your surrender," he whispered.

I swatted him, and he started to roll off the bed. I touched his arm. "Wait," I said. "Don't go."

"I have to work, Letts."

"No, I mean, don't go *back*. At all."

Jameson reached over to turn on the bedside lamp. The sudden light made me flinch, but I resisted the urge to cover myself up. Jameson had already seen the show, what did it matter now? "If the skinners know you're working for the Holmwoods," I said, not bothering to keep the worry out of my voice, "they know right where to find you tonight."

"Maybe so, but I still have a job to do. You know what that's like."

I did, didn't I? It was strange, because Jameson and I sort of had the same skill set without having the same job. Oh, and our skill set wasn't really a skill at all, just something we could do. It was like we'd made completely different careers out of being able to juggle. Our lives were *so* weird.

"I know you gave your word . . . but I *also* know that Arthur and Lucy Holmwood are not worth your life." I reached up to touch his face. "Come back to LA with me," I pleaded. "I'll talk to Dashiell, maybe he can negotiate with Malcolm."

"Bargain for my life, you mean," Jameson said, echoing my words from earlier. "How is that any better?"

"I trust Dashiell. He would do this for me." At least, I was pretty sure. "And I can work off whatever he needs to pay Malcolm to get him off your back."

"So you want to get your rich white boss to buy a black man's life for you?" he said in a teasing voice. "That's pretty twisted, Letts."

"I'm serious."

He sighed. "I know you are. But Dashiell's still a vampire. He cares about blood and power, and that's it. He's just another monster. Like the rest of them."

"Well, that's not fair," I said, sitting up in bed. I pulled the sheets up over my chest, feeling self-conscious. "He loves Beatrice, and he cares about his community. Hell, if *I* were to be brutally murdered, I think he might even feel a twinge of displeasure. He can be a dick, but he's not a *monster*." At least, not any more so than the rest of the Old World. All of them—werewolves, witches, the undead—had the power to mess around with forces that humans probably shouldn't be allowed to touch. But that alone didn't make them evil.

"They're *all* monsters, Letts," Jameson said with surprising vehemence. He sat up, too. "Lucy and Arthur are at least up-front about it." His face had hardened, and my eyes dropped down to the thick line of light scar tissue on his collarbone. I didn't know much about his years with Malcolm, but I did know this was not an argument I would win.

"Look," I said, trying again, "those guys downtown, they didn't come here to give you a love tap. They're the real thing, and if they work for a whole company, there will be more of them. Come to LA with me." I leaned forward to kiss him again. Kissing Jameson was beginning to feel really . . . right.

He leaned his head forward so his forehead rested on mine. "I love that you want to save me," he said softly. "But I can handle things here. And I can handle Malcolm. I know how he operates, remember? I'll talk to Arthur and Lucy tonight; we'll figure something out."

"But you said yourself that you don't trust them!" I protested. I didn't really have another argument, or a better one. But going to Lucy and Arthur just *felt* wrong to me.

"I trust how much they want what they're doing here, and that they need me to do it," he reasoned. "I'll be fine."

"And . . . you and me?" I suddenly felt completely pathetic. Was I really sitting here begging him to . . . what? Go steady?

He smiled. There was a little sadness in it. "When things settle down with Malcolm, I'll come to LA for a weekend, okay? You can show me around. We can figure out what this is."

Why didn't that make me feel better? Was I being paranoid and weird, or was there something in his face like he didn't really believe it would ever happen?

He reached out to play with a strand of my hair. It tickled my shoulder, making me shiver. "Listen," he said, "I still want you to go home tonight. Back to LA."

"Oh, so I can't protect you, but you can protect me?" I said indignantly. "I'm gonna have to call bullshit on that one."

He tucked the wayward strand of hair behind my ear. "The difference is, this isn't your fight." His voice was firm. "It never was."

"But I can still help. I've got this idea—well, I had some help—about the phone records of the vampires who went missing. I think maybe the last or second-to-last person who called them might have been the skinners, or someone working for the skinners. And—"

"Stop." Jameson raised a hand, cutting off my protests. He said, "Scarlett, we've got this under control. You saw the show, you know that I'm fine. Your part in this is over."

I just looked at him, my arms crossed over my chest. Abruptly, he stood and picked the rest of his clothes up off the floor. He started yanking them on as he spoke. "Besides, now that you've gotten the skinners' attention, what do you think is going to happen to Juliet? And Bethany, and poor pregnant Tara? Not to mention the local witch, Laurel Nash."

I jerked back, stunned.

He knew. He'd known all along about my sister-in-law and her friends. I scooted to the far side of the bed, but that wasn't far enough away from him. I pushed off the bed, yanking the sheet around me, and stalked down to the seating area, trying to rein in my temper. I looked out the window and took a few deep breaths. Behind me, I could hear him putting on the rest of his clothes. Then the movements stopped.

"Scarlett . . ."

I spun around. "First," I said coldly, "it's TAR-uh, like the sticky stuff in parking lots. Second, how the fuck did you know about them?"

Jameson kept his voice perfectly calm, but he didn't exactly look repentant. "I told you, this is my town now. I've been here long enough to know people at all the casinos." He held up two fingers. "It took me two calls to the Venetian staff to figure out who you were here with, and why. Imagine how fast the skinners could find them. What were you thinking, coming here with civilians?"

I stared at him for a long moment. "You've been checking up on me?" He didn't say anything. He didn't need to. "For who? Yourself, or the Holmwoods?"

"They still don't know you're here," he said, his voice flat. "I've made sure of it."

"Oh, so you just . . . what? Didn't trust me?"

"It's been years, Scarlett," he answered. He had to sit on the bed to put his sneakers on. "You said it, too: we've both changed."

I couldn't help feeling betrayed. Had I been wrong to trust him? Had I been stupid to sleep with him? Probably and probably. I hugged my arms against my body. "Yeah, well, I think one of us changed more than the other."

"Don't be a child, Scarlett," he snapped, tying his shoes like he was hoping to hurt them. "Go home. Back to your nice little life. This is my problem, and there's no reason to get your humans caught up in it."

Anger and hurt boiled up in me, but I didn't trust those feelings, either. Was he pushing me away because he thought it would keep me safe, or did he actually think I was useless?"

Either way, the rational part of my brain knew that he was right: I'd taken a hell of a risk bringing Juliet and her friends here, especially after I'd agreed to take up Wyatt's cause.

"Okay, you win," I said flatly. "I'll shut down the bachelorette party. Today, now."

His shoulders sagged with relief. "Thank you," he said, looking surprisingly not smug.

I turned back to the window. After a few seconds, I heard the hotel room door open and shut.

Chapter 25

I sat on the couch for a long time after Jameson left, trying not to look at the clock. I was probably supposed to be somewhere right then, celebrating life and love with the rest of Juliet's friends. I knew my cell phone had buzzed a couple of times, probably Juliet wanting to know how my "meeting" had gone, or just to check up on me. She was really nice, my sister-in-law. A hell of a lot nicer than me.

Nice people probably don't sit around in bedsheets ignoring everyone while they stare at dark television screens. But I stayed that way for a long time, weighing my shitty options.

I'd made a promise to Wyatt. I wanted the money for Logan, but I also wanted the vampire to get the answers he needed. No one else was going to help him—not Silvio, not the Holmwoods. If they cared about the skinners, it was only in terms of protecting themselves. No one was looking out for the vampires of Las Vegas. And no matter what Jameson said, they weren't monsters, at least not all of them.

But Jameson *had* been right about one thing. It was time to stop risking Juliet and her friends. I hadn't lied when I'd told him I would shut down the bachelorette party. When I couldn't put it off any longer, I heaved a sigh and went to get my phone.

Molly answered on the first ring. "Wasssup," she drawled. "Remember those commercials? Weren't they annoying?"

"Molls, what time will you be back in LA tonight?"

She must have picked up on the urgency in my voice, because she dropped the goofy tone immediately. "Actually, I'm just passing Panorama City. I decided to drive as far as Bakersfield last night so I'd have time to hang out with Corry. What's wrong?"

The sun had only set forty-five minutes ago, and Bakersfield to Panorama City was usually an hour and a half, which tells you everything you need to know about Molly's driving habits. "I need a favor," I said. "A terrible, terrible favor."

"Name it," she said promptly, her voice immediately losing its mirth. "It's yours."

I felt sick with self-loathing, but I pushed past it. "Remember that time you pressed Jack for me?" I began.

When I'd hung up with Molly, I called Wyatt's cell phone. "Do you have access to Ellen's cell phone records?" I asked, and explained Jesse's theory about the missing vampires being invited to a secret event.

"We use prepaid cells," he said. "I think you can still look up the call history online, but I've never tried it. Give me a few minutes to figure it out and I'll call you back."

"Fine."

I took a long, hot shower, washing the smell of Jameson off me. I tried not to think too much about our last conversation. Then I got dressed in what I usually think of as my work clothes: jeans, tee shirt, boots. I'd already gotten Cliff's blood off the soles, thanks to way too much practice. I was still toweling my hair when the phone rang. It was Dashiell.

"I've heard from the cardinal vampires in several cities that the Holmwoods have visited," he began. "The results were mixed. A handful of vampires did go missing in Barcelona, Prague, and Rome, around the same time the Holmwoods appeared, but I'm not sure one could prove a connection. This was four or five vampires, not thirty. And we do move around."

I slumped on the bed. No leads there. "Okay, thank you."

"You are being careful, aren't you, Scarlett?" he asked.

You mean like having sex with untrustworthy men? "Sure I am."

A few minutes later, Juliet called. Cringing, I took a deep breath and answered the phone. I deserved this.

"Scarlett?" I could already hear the tears in her voice. "Jack just called. He's been in a car accident."

"Oh no!" I said, trying to sound appropriately shocked. "Is he okay? Were the kids in the car?"

"No, they were at after-school stuff, but Jack hit his head, they think, because he can't remember anything and the car is totaled and I've got to get back there," she said, sobbing. "Can I borrow Cliff's SUV? I don't have his number . . ."

"He'll drive you," I said promptly. "Bethany and Tara should go, too."

"No, you don't have to stop the party . . ."

"Jules, of course we do. We can't have a bachelorette party without the bachelorette."

"What about you? Aren't you coming?"

"If you need me, or if Jack's in serious danger, of course I'll come," I said, crossing my fingers that she wouldn't call the bluff. "But it'll be hard to pack us all into Cliff's car, and I'm supposed to sign the contracts for Dashiell tomorrow morning. I'll try to move them to tonight, and get the first flight out tomorrow. If that doesn't work, I'll rent a car. Is that okay?"

"Yeah, of course," she sniffed. Lucky for me, she was too upset to wonder why anyone would sign business contracts on a Sunday morning. We talked for a few more minutes about logistics, and I hung up hating myself. If I'd had more time, I would have tried to come up with a gentler way to get Juliet to rush back to LA, but with short notice I had few options.

Molly hadn't really hurt Jack, I knew, but he was in for a night of tests at the hospital, and Juliet was facing hours of worry—not to mention the hassle of dealing with a wrecked (but insured) car. And *all* of that was my fault. I had played with their lives to get us here, and now I was playing with them even more to dig my way out of it. As the weight of that washed over me, I wanted to curl up and hide from the shame.

But I couldn't. Dashiell had promised this was the last time we would drag my family into the Old World messes. It was a small consolation, but it was all I had. And one thing was for sure: I was not going to put my family through all this and not get a resolution. One way or another, I would finish this.

I was just gathering my things to leave when there was a knock at my door. I extended my radius and felt a single vampire, not particularly strong. I went to the peephole and saw Wyatt, in full cowboy getup, holding a handful of papers.

I opened the door. "Hi. You could have just called."

"Yeah, I could have," he said easily. "But then you might have made a move without me."

Okay, that did sound like something I'd do. I stepped aside so he could come in. "Does that mean you found something?"

Wyatt swept past me, the tails of his long coat brushing against my shins. "I'm not sure. Hoping you can help."

He raised an eyebrow at the unmade bed, which looked . . . well, it looked like I'd recently had sex with someone, but Wyatt didn't comment. He went straight past it to the sitting area and began spreading the three pages across the coffee table. They were lists of phone numbers, and Wyatt had highlighted many of the lines in yellow and a few in light blue. "Yellow are the numbers I know," he explained. "Me, Laurel, a couple of her family members, a few friends in other cities that we keep in touch with." He tapped a line of blue numbers. "The blue ones are numbers I was able to look up right quick, and they're all easily explained. A hair salon, the dry cleaners, that kind of thing."

"Okay." I turned the last page toward me. It had a lot of yellow lines and a couple of blue ones. The last three numbers had no highlights.

Seeing my gaze, Wyatt pointed to the bottom number, an outgoing call. "This is an LA area code. Could that be your friend Margaret?"

"We weren't really friends," I said, "but yeah, I think so. I know that the last call Margaret received was from Ellen's number."

"Which would make sense, if your theory is that Ellen invited Margaret somewhere with her. So the second to the last number—"

Ignoring him, I picked up the page and studied the number right above Margaret's. And I froze.

"I don't know the area code," Wyatt was saying. "Six-four-six? Where is that?"

"Manhattan," I heard my voice say. "Midtown."

Wyatt went on speaking to me, but suddenly it was like I was underwater. With shaking fingers, I grabbed my own phone and compared the phone number on the paper to the one Jameson had used to call me.

They were the same.

"No," I said out loud. "No, it can't be." But the pieces were slamming into place whether I wanted them to or not. Jameson's reluctance to talk to me about the situation. His insistence that I stay out of this mess and leave town.

Jameson, who I had trusted, who I had *slept with*, was working for the skinners.

Chapter 26

They're all monsters. That's what he had said.

When I reviewed every conversation we'd had in the last two days, I could see that he'd been putting me off the whole time, pushing me away from the conflict. He'd told me to go home, that there was nothing I could do, but I wouldn't listen. *God, you're still just as stubborn, aren't you?*

So he'd saved a trump card: Juliet and the others. He'd played on my guilt to get me away from all of this. I had thought he was protecting me. And maybe he was, a little, but really he was making sure I couldn't stop him.

"I'm such a fool," I whispered. I had *slept* with him. I was now every girl in every crime drama ever.

"*Scarlett*!" Wyatt was shaking my shoulder now, bringing me back to myself. "What is it?" he demanded. "What did you just figure out?"

I swallowed hard. "I think my friend Jameson may be working for the skinners. He's a null, too."

"Jameson?" he repeated. "Black guy? Really tall?"

I nodded. Wyatt dropped down onto the chair nearest me. "Hell, I met him," Wyatt said in a daze. "Ellen was helping him put together a list of local vampires so they could promote the show . . ."

His voice trailed off as we both realized the implications. That was how the skinners had found local vampires to kill. And if Ellen had unwittingly helped Jameson find vampires to destroy, it made sense that she'd end up on his list, too. "Did she trust him?" I asked quietly. "That is, if Jameson called Ellen and invited her to a party or meeting or something, would she have gone?"

Before he could respond, the room filled with the sound of an old-fashioned piano riff. Wyatt's cell phone. He reddened slightly, which was possible because he was still within my radius, and dug it out of the pocket of his duster. "One second," he said, frowning down at the screen. He turned away to answer it, pacing back toward the hotel room door.

As for me, I just sat there with my arms and legs collapsed around me, like a rag doll set on a shelf. In my entire life, I had never wanted to be wrong about anything as much as I wanted to be wrong about Jameson, but too many things fit: his hatred of vampires, born out of years of abuse by Malcolm, the way he'd insisted on keeping me separate from Arthur and Lucy, his evasiveness, his demands that I leave Las Vegas.

It all made sense . . . except for one thing. I had personally witnessed those skinners attack him, and that hadn't been faked. Those bullets were real.

Okay, I was calling it. This was officially above my pay grade.

Wyatt was still on the phone, so I picked up my own mobile and called Dashiell.

"Hello, Scarlett," came his smooth voice over the line. "I was just about to call you. What—"

"I need you to listen," I interrupted. That was a little disrespectful even for me, but this was too important. I explained my suspicion as quickly as I could, the words tumbling out of my mouth with an edge of hysteria attached. Dashiell, to his credit, listened quietly as I laid out my case against Jameson. It all seemed pretty circumstantial when I said it out loud, but the phone number thing was damning. "But there was a group of skinners who came after us, for real, so now I'm confused," I added. "Could there be two groups of skinners in town?"

"Yes and no," Dashiell replied heavily. "As I said, I was going to call you. I heard from another friend in Europe a few minutes ago, someone I called last night to ask about the Holmwoods. After some cajoling, he mentioned a very strange rumor. One or two people have suggested that Arthur and Lucy are killing vampires."

I didn't get it. "Like, in duels? Is that still a thing?"

"No, Scarlett," he said patiently. "I'm saying that Arthur and Lucy Holmwood *are* the skinners you've been seeking."

It took another heartbeat, and then the penny dropped. "Holy fucking shit of shits," I blurted.

"Indeed," Dashiell said dryly.

On the other side of the room, Wyatt had finished his phone call and was pacing back toward me. He gave me a puzzled, slightly alarmed look. I held up a finger, turning away from him.

"I believe they may be hunting their own kind," Dashiell continued. "There's no proof, of course, but if people were starting to talk, that could explain why Arthur and Lucy decided to leave Europe and come to America, after all this time."

For a moment, I was too stunned to speak. All along, I had been making assessments based on my understanding of what vampires do and do not do, and they definitely don't kill each other, except maybe in a serious power struggle. It draws too much attention.

But I had made a mistake. I should never have expected the Holmwoods to think like normal vampires—after all, they'd spent decades proving they were anything but.

"They hate their own kind," I whispered. "They want to wipe out vampires, and they're using Jameson to do it."

What I really wanted in that moment was for Dashiell to laugh at me. I wanted him to come up with an easy explanation for all this that would make me feel like an idiot. I *wanted* him to be snide and condescending. I wanted to feel guilty for ever suspecting Jameson in the first place.

But life doesn't really work like that, not when you want it to. Instead, what Dashiell said was, "I'm sorry, Scarlett, but I think you're correct. It's the only way this whole mess makes sense."

Fuck.

I collapsed onto the couch, unable to speak. I kept the phone pressed to my ear, but I dropped my head into my free hand, squeezing my eyes shut so I didn't have to look at Wyatt, or anything else. Dashiell, to his credit, was silent, giving me the moment I needed.

If I started looking at the situation knowing that the Holmwoods wanted to kill as many vampires as possible, so many things suddenly made sense. In Europe, they had traveled from town to town, killing a few vampires here and there, where they were sure they wouldn't blow their cover. Vampires were notoriously hard to kill, after all, and if the Holmwoods were only in town for a few days, a handful was probably the best they could do.

Eventually, however, that would get frustrating. They would want to go bigger. Like setting up shop in a touristy city and getting the vampires to come to *them*. By putting on a big splashy show, the Holmwoods made sure that vampires from all over North America would make the pilgrimage to Vegas. And if they never came home again, well, who would be the wiser? Any cardinal vampires who noticed would assume that those vampires had just decided to stay in Vegas. This town was, after all, vampire heaven.

It was a great way for the Holmwoods to take out lots of vampires, but one thing could make it even better: having a null to help you do the dirty work. A null could reduce the vampire victims to human again, making them very easy to kill.

Arthur and Lucy must have asked around until they learned of the most disgruntled null on the planet: the one who worked for a controlling, sadistic bully. What had Jameson said to me? *I trust how much they want what they're doing here, and that they need me to do it.* No wonder he was sure that Lucy and Arthur would protect him. He was a big part of their extermination plan.

"It's one big trap," I murmured. "Lure vampires to Vegas, sic Jameson on them, and kill them at your leisure." I should have *seen* it.

"Indeed," Dashiell said gravely. "They've killed relatively few so far, but *Demeter* has only been open for a week, not quite long enough for vampires to make the voyage to Las Vegas. The longer the show goes on, the more vampires will arrive to see it, and the more of them will fall victim."

"But they can't get away with it forever," I protested. "Eventually some cardinal vampire somewhere would notice . . . right?"

"It depends on how much care they took. If you hadn't traveled to Las Vegas and made inquiries, the Holmwoods could likely have spent *years* massacring vampires before anyone noticed."

"And they've got Silvio to hide behind," I realized. Anyone who tried to punish the Holmwoods in the Las Vegas territory would need to go through the cardinal vampire first, and he was a big enough dick to call and warn them.

"I want you to come home," Dashiell declared.

"What?" I forced myself back to the conversation. "Why? What will you do?"

Brief pause. "I'm . . . not sure." That might have been the first time I'd ever heard uncertainty in his voice. "If there was still a vampire council I would go to them, but our highest court was dismantled centuries ago. I will probably have to declare war on the Las Vegas territory, and attack them myself."

"Wait, you mean like, *yourself* yourself? In person?" As powerful as he was, Dashiell rarely left Pasadena, let alone the state. You don't send the president to the front lines; it's just too risky.

"Yes," he said grimly. "I'll have to. The only course I can see would be to defeat Silvio—which shouldn't be terribly hard, if what you're saying is true—take the city, and try Arthur and Lucy for crimes against vampires. At that point I will need to dispatch them."

My head was spinning. I slipped off the edge of the couch, onto the floor, where I could lean my back against something firm. "And Jameson?"

"Him too, I'm afraid," Dashiell said. He had the grace to be somber about it. "If you're right, he has been, at the very least, an accessory to the murder of forty vampires. He needs to die. Or at least be handed over to his old master for punishment."

"You would give him to *Malcolm*?" I echoed. "You can't do that. If Malcolm knows what Jameson has done—"

"Jameson was Malcolm's responsibility," Dashiell said flatly. There was no room in his tone for arguing. "And I suspect that Malcolm already knows. That is why he sent his own team of skinners to kill the null."

Ohhhhh. God, the hits just kept on coming. I'd wondered why the skinners had come after Jameson with the intention of killing him; this explained it. Malcolm wouldn't want Jameson to be able to point a finger of blame at him, or tell anyone Malcolm's secrets in exchange for leniency. Jameson was a liability as long as he was alive. If he were dead, though, Malcolm would bear no responsibility for this mess.

"This isn't Jameson's fault," I whispered. "What Malcolm did to him . . ."

"Jameson is an adult now. He made his choices, Scarlett," Dashiell said, not unkindly. "He has to answer for them."

I sat up. Wyatt had moved around the room into my eyeline and was giving me a desperate *what's going on* look. I shook my head at him, scrubbing at my eyes with the back of my hand. Dashiell was right, of course. Jameson wasn't innocent in this. Jameson had turned vampires human and then murdered them, or stood by while the Holmwoods murdered them. He'd lied to me, and then taken me to bed. I should have been happy to hand him over to Dashiell or Malcolm for punishment . . . but that just wasn't what my heart was telling me. Despite everything, I still wanted to save him.

Jesse's words came back to me. *You are the champion of all the people who fall through those cracks.* I had saved Molly. Why couldn't I save Jameson, too?

Then a terrible new thought struck me. "Dashiell," I said, "if you come to Vegas and attack Silvio first, won't that give the Holmwoods a chance to run?"

Wyatt's jaw clenched with anger. On the phone, there was the briefest pause, and then Dashiell said, "It's likely, yes. But I have no authority to come after the Holmwoods unless they're in my territory. At the very least, this will shut down *Demeter* and stop the immediate killings. If I can get the word out, it may also force the Holmwoods into hiding."

"But then they won't answer for their crimes," I reasoned, thinking of Ellen. Wyatt, who could only hear my side of the conversation, started shaking his head vehemently. He was used to having super hearing, which would make this particularly frustrating. I held up a hand, gesturing again for him to wait.

I felt so conflicted. I didn't want the Holmwoods to get away with murder . . . but at the same time, maybe they would take Jameson with them, and he'd be safe.

As if he could hear me, Dashiell added, "Malcolm won't stop hunting Jameson until he's dead. Even if he escapes with the Holmwoods, Malcolm's skinners will track them down eventually."

"So not only would the Holmwoods have a chance to escape, but you would have to leave LA," I concluded. "The city would be vulnerable. And *you* would be vulnerable, coming here with Jameson running around. No offense, Dashiell, but your plan is crap."

Wyatt's eyes widened—probably he hadn't heard a lot of people talk to a cardinal vampire like that, but I didn't care. We needed Dashiell in

LA. He and I didn't always see eye to eye—okay, we rarely saw eye to eye on anything—but if we lost him, I doubted that Will, Kirsten, and whatever much weaker vampire replaced Dashiell would be able to hold the city for long. And that was assuming the next vampire who stepped up was even willing to work with Will and Kirsten. Not everyone agreed with Dashiell's ideas about sharing power.

For once, he didn't admonish me for my disrespect. He just said, "Arthur and Lucy can't be allowed to continue as they are, Scarlett. I see no other course of action."

I closed my eyes, feeling the tears sliding down my cheeks. "I do," I said into the phone. "And since, as you said, I am here on my own time, in someone else's territory, I am going to hang up before you can forbid it. If I don't come back, please take care of Jack and his family for me."

"*Scarlett*—"

I pushed the button and put the phone down on the coffee table. It began to ring again almost immediately, of course. I looked around for a second, picked up one of my boots that had a small heel, and pounded it on the cell phone until it stopped ringing. Then I kept hitting it for a little while, because it made my hands hurt and I wanted that.

Wyatt watched this whole thing dispassionately. When there were no more pieces on the table big enough to stomp, I dropped the boot and looked at him. "How much of that did you get?" I said in a clear voice. I was weirdly proud of that.

"Most of it, I think."

"Okay. We are going to make a new deal."

Wyatt raised an eyebrow. "Oh?"

I nodded. "Arthur and Lucy Holmwood are responsible for Ellen's death. My friend Jameson, the other null, is probably helping them kill as many vampires as they can. I'll get you the Holmwoods, but in return, I want you to let Jameson slide."

Wyatt immediately began arguing with that, but I stood up and shouted over him until he stopped. "I know! I know Jameson has helped them do terrible things," I said hotly. "Maybe he even pulled the trigger himself. But *you*"—I pointed a finger at him—"do not know what it is to be a null, and neither of us can imagine what Jameson was put through by the cardinal vampire of New York. So you are going to give him a pass, or I will not help you. You can take your money and shove it up your ass."

We stared at each other for a long, tense moment. I didn't say that if he didn't take the deal, I would stop him from leaving the hotel room. I was afraid I would have to back it up . . . actually, I was really scared of the idea that I might back it up. I could throw a knife into this man's neck to save Jameson, and I didn't want to face that about myself.

I just prayed he wouldn't make me.

Nearly a full minute ticked by in agonizing tension before Wyatt's shoulders relaxed. "Fine," he said, looking sullen. I pushed out a breath I hadn't known I'd been holding. "Your boy can walk. But in return, I want your word that if you and I both get through this, you will help me die."

I winced, but how could I say no? Just a second ago, I'd seriously considered killing Wyatt to save Jameson. How was this any different? "Agreed."

To my surprise, Wyatt stepped forward, holding out his hand for me to shake, like we were schoolkids making a bet at recess. He was so deadly serious, though, that there was nothing I could do but stand up and shake hands. His grip was firm.

When I released his hand, I said, "Now we just have to figure out where to find them. The theater is too public, and . . ." I trailed off. Wyatt was smiling under the big handlebar mustache. It was not a happy smile. "What?" I asked.

"I can help with that." He held up his phone. "That call I just got? It was Lucy Holmwood her-goddamned-self. She wanted to invite me to a party tonight."

Chapter 27

"Okay, wait. What *exactly* did she say?" I asked.

"That the Holmwoods are having a VIP party for some of the area vampires at midnight, and they're hoping I'll join them," he reported. "I'm not supposed to tell people about it, but I can invite another vampire to accompany me."

"Do you think they invited you because they know that you hired me?"

"We're not even sure they know you're in town," he pointed out.

"Silvio might have told them." I told him about my little appearance at the cardinal vampire's penthouse. This made Wyatt grin.

"Damn, I would have loved to see that," he said happily. "Anyway, it's possible that Silvio told them about you, but I wouldn't lay any money on it. The whole reason the Holmwoods picked him instead of Minerva is because Silvio is stupid. And arrogant. He won't want the Holmwoods to know that some little girl—pardon me, that's how he would see it—is causing trouble for him. Would your friend Jameson have told the Holmwoods about you?"

"He said he didn't." Of course, he'd said a lot of other things that had turned out to be not true. I knew I couldn't trust Jameson, but . . . dammit, in my gut, I still couldn't believe he'd hurt me. If he wanted me dead, or even out of the way, he could have easily arranged to have me attacked, or done it himself. Instead, he'd twisted himself in knots to get me to leave town voluntarily.

Maybe it was stupid, and maybe I was being naive, but I was going to trust that Jameson didn't want me dead. Therefore, he was probably telling the truth when he said the Holmwoods didn't know I was in town—at least not from him. "But if they *don't* know about me," I said to Wyatt, "why are they inviting you to the party? There are plenty of vampires in Las Vegas."

"Because I've been asking around about the missing vampires," he said sensibly. Right. The list I had asked him to make. "I'm thinking they suspect me of planning something, but they don't know for sure." Wyatt shrugged. "Either way, I'm a loose end. They probably figured I would accompany Ellen to their last killing party, and since I didn't, and I've been poking around, I need to die."

"It's awfully cocky," I said, not liking it. "They think you're onto them, and they invite you to come anyway? That makes no sense."

He suppressed a smile. "That's because you're thinking of me as a vampire, and therefore a threat. Ellen and I, we've always kept to ourselves. We interact"—he caught himself, cleared his throat, and corrected—"*interacted* more with Laurel and her family than with other vampires, which has never gone over real well. No one in the Las Vegas community sees me as anything but a weakling who avoids his own kind."

"Still . . . if they know you've been asking around, they must be expecting you to try something."

He thought about it for a moment. "My guess is, they'll keep your friend Jameson away from everyone at the beginning of the party. That way, if I do storm in there guns blazing, Lucy and Arthur will be able to take me down right quick. Assuming I behave myself, the null shows up and I get killed with everybody else."

He sounded so matter-of-fact about it that it weirded me out a little. But I was convinced. "So where is this shindig, anyway?" I asked.

"They've got it set up at Erson Station." Before I could ask, he added, "It's a historical site, about an hour outside of Vegas, near the Valley of Fire State Park. It's also rented out for events."

"What kind of station?"

California girl that I was, I was thinking fire station or maybe bus station, but Wyatt said, "Back in the 1860s, Samuel Erson's ranch was a regular stop for stagecoaches and the Pony Express line. Sam added on a great big boardinghouse for guests and his own family. The ranch outbuildings are mostly gone now, but the boardinghouse is in good condition. It's sort of a . . . well, not a museum, exactly, but a minor landmark."

"You've been there?"

Wyatt squinted at me. "Miss Scarlett, I helped Sam nail the original shingles on the roof."

Ah yes. Vampires. "Is it a good place to kill a bunch of people?"

He thought about it for a moment, then nodded. "After Sam's death, the property changed hands a few times. Before it became a historical site, the boardinghouse spent a few decades as a gentlemen's shooting club."

"What does *that* mean?"

"Just what it sounds like. There's a lot of land behind the building, so they would bring in pheasants, or sometimes other small game that's not native to the area, and the men would pay to hunt them. The whole back area is a killing ground."

It took me a second, but I finally understood. "It's covered in bullet holes. They're planning to shoot all of you."

"Yes, ma'am. Behind the boardinghouse there's a natural canyon, walls on three sides. It fills with water during the rainy season, but most of the year it's dry enough that they rent it out for weddings. When the property was a shooting club, they would herd animals toward the canyon and trap them there."

"That doesn't sound very sporting," I muttered. "But you're right, it sounds like the perfect place to kill people."

"The Holmwoods could have killing parties every weekend, take out a dozen or more vampires, and no one would be the wiser."

Dashiell had said that the show hadn't been open long enough for many vampires to travel to see it. Once they began arriving, there would be lots more of them to kill. "What about the bodies?"

A shrug. "Like I said, plenty of space on all sides. They can bury them on-site."

"Jesus." Say what you will about LA, but you have to go a long ways out of town before a mass grave would go unnoticed. I got up and paced the room a little, thinking it over. This was usually the moment in any given skirmish when I would step back and let the professional ass-kickers make a plan. I was not the planner. Generally speaking, I would classify myself as "reluctant participant."

"Hold on," I said to Wyatt. I paced a few feet away and called Jesse.

When he answered, I could hear some sort of shouting match going on in the background. "Hey, Scar, it's not really a good time," Jesse yelled.

"What's going on?" I said anxiously. "Is it Shadow?"

"No, Shadow's fine—although she did try to eat a Pomeranian yesterday; Corry stopped her—Hey!" There was a muffled thump, and then Jesse yelled, "Dammit, stay where you are!" To me, he added, "Kirsten caught one of her witches selling 'holistic plastic surgery' to human women in Bel Air."

"You've got to be kidding me."

"Yeah, I wish. Anyway, Kirsten figured it out when one of the 'procedures' went wrong, and now we've got a human with some serious cosmetic issues, and the witch who did it keeps trying to get away before Kirsten can get the spell out of her. Ow!"

"Are you okay?"

"She *bit* me!" he said incredulously. "Scar, I gotta call you back." He hung up the phone.

Well, shit. I felt bad that Jesse was dealing with that situation because of my absence, but there was little I could do to help him.

Meanwhile, I still needed advice from someone accustomed to storming castles. After a moment of hesitation, I placed another call—to Boulder, Colorado. Allison Luther scared me a little, but she also owed me a favor.

It rang twice, and then a brusque voice said, "Scarlett." Lex always answered the phone brusquely. Or maybe that was just when I called. "I heard you met Sashi."

"What—oh, right. Yeah." I had forgotten all about my meeting with the thaumaturge witch. "She's . . . nice."

"I take it that's not what you're calling about," Lex said, her voice guarded. "What's going on?"

"I need advice," I began, hating the way that sounded, like I was a fourteen-year-old with boy problems. "Um . . . tactical advice, I guess? Have you got a minute?"

"Go ahead."

Making an effort to be as concise as possible, I ran her through the situation: *Demeter*, Jameson, the Holmwoods, their intention to kill vampires. I was halfway through the story before I remembered that Lex herself was dating a vampire, last I heard. Boundary witches and vampires were the big exception to that whole "Old World inter-dating" stigma. That might work in my favor: unlike many witches, Lex wouldn't be immediately prejudiced against the undead.

"So you and your client, who wants revenge, are trying to keep them from killing a bunch of vampires," Lex said when I was finished. "But your friend is working for the bad guys."

"Right." Damn. Say what you would about Lex, but the woman could grasp a situation. "The problem is that we have no idea how many people the Holmwoods have working for them, or how many of their employees are actually true believers," I added. "There could be twenty hostile vampires in there, or it might be just the Holmwoods and my friend."

"Who you want to save." Her voice was matter-of-fact, but for some reason I still felt judged.

"Yes. He's like me. And like Charlotte," I said, and immediately regretted it. That had been a little below the belt. Lex was silent for a moment, and I added, "I'm sorry. Just . . . look, Sashi told me that people have tried to kidnap Charlie and brainwash her, or whatever. That could have happened to me, if I hadn't grown up in a small town with no Old World. It *did* happen to Jameson. I want to help him, not kill him. Like you did with Katia."

"Okay." There was a pause, and then she said, "Tell me about the location."

With Wyatt supplying details, I told her as much as I could about Erson Station. She absorbed that without comment, then asked, "What do you have for resources?"

"Resources?"

"People, weapons, vehicles, that kind of thing."

Wyatt was mouthing something at me. "We can get guns, apparently," I relayed to Lex.

"But it's just you and this vampire? Who else do you know in Las Vegas?"

That was a good question. "Well, Sashi, but I got the impression that she's not really a fighter."

"No, she isn't. Anyone else?"

Could I get Cliff back? He was supposedly driving the SUV back to LA, but if they hadn't left yet, maybe Bethany or Tara could drive. But convincing Cliff to help me save a bunch of vampires, without Dashiell's permission, was going to be a hard sell. "I might have one other guy. Human, but a well-trained bodyguard type."

"That's good. And you mentioned a witch?" she asked.

"Yeah, Laurel. But she's pretty weak." I shot an apologetic look at Wyatt, who shrugged in a *you're not wrong* kind of way.

"There may be ways to boost her magic," Lex said immediately. "That's something I've been working on here. Is she a trades witch?"

Most witches did general magic, but a few specialized in something, the way Sashi could do healing magic and Lex worked with death magic. I started to ask Wyatt, then just said, "Hang on, I'm going to put you on speakerphone with Wyatt; he's the family friend."

"Is Laurel a trades witch?" I asked him after I'd hit the speakerphone.

Wyatt hesitated. "Not exactly," he said. "She can do trades magic, but her clan has a sort of talent. I wouldn't call it a specialty so much as a . . . family tradition. It's what brought them to Vegas, actually."

He launched into an explanation, while Lex and I listened silently. I couldn't tell what Lex was thinking, but at the end Wyatt added, "Look, Laurel's already got one kid, and her wife's expecting their second. I don't want to put her in danger, not for me. Not for my revenge."

"That's okay," Lex said. "I think you can use her ability without putting her in harm's way."

"How?" I asked.

"Well, look, you guys are going to have to make your own plan, based on the terrain and the players. But I do have a few . . . suggestions."

Chapter 28

After I hung up with Lex, Wyatt went down to the seating area to call Laurel, while I sat on the bed and called Cliff. When he answered, he was in the Venetian parking lot, driving around to pick up Juliet, Tara, and Bethany to rush them back to Los Angeles. I asked him to pull over for a moment, and explained the situation.

"I don't know, Scarlett," he said, sounding uneasy. "No offense, but I'm not all that invested in saving a bunch of vampires from themselves. And this does not sound like something Dashiell would want you to do."

I heard something in his voice. On a hunch, I said, "Did Hayne already call you?" Dashiell would be pissed that I was going against his wishes, if not his direct orders. And Hayne was Dashiell's human right-hand man.

Heavy silence, and then, "Yeah. I told him you were sending me home, and he said that was a good idea. He didn't say it, but I got the impression that Dashiell is hoping you won't want to go in without backup."

"He's betting on me chickening out?" Well, that just made me more committed.

Stay on task, Scarlett. Chain of command seemed really important to Cliff, so I said, "Look, did Hayne officially order you to go back to LA?"

"Well, no, but—"

I interrupted him. "Then I will give you ten thousand dollars to come along tonight and be my backup. In theory, you won't even be in danger. You'll mostly be protecting Laurel while she does a spell." Without waiting for his response, I outlined the plan that Lex and I had come up with. Well, mostly Lex.

There was a long pause. Then, in a quiet voice, he said, "Ten thousand dollars?"

"Cash. Tonight."

He sighed. "All right, you're on. But if Hayne calls me and gives me a direct order to come back, anytime before we actually leave, I have to do it."

"Deal."

A few minutes later, Wyatt hung up with Laurel. "Cliff is in," I told him. "What did Laurel say?"

"She's in, too," he said, looking grim. I felt a stab of sympathy. Cliff was used to walking into dangerous situations, but Laurel was a relatively weak witch with a relatively normal job. She was only willing to do this for Wyatt. And, to some extent, for Ellen.

Guilt flared in my stomach. If Jesse were here, he'd probably tell me to abort, to go home and let Dashiell come back to Las Vegas with the cavalry. But if I did that, Jameson would almost definitely die. And Dashiell himself would be forced to take a huge risk. I'd like to think I wasn't exactly expendable, but if something happened to me, it wouldn't topple the whole governing system in Los Angeles. In the grand scheme of things, my death would be a brief inconvenience.

"She thinks she knows of a store near the Strip that's open late, so she's going to run and get the items your friend Lex suggested," Wyatt went on. "Meanwhile, you and I need to run an errand."

I raised my eyebrows. "Oh?"

A smile spread across his cowboy face. This particular smile made me nervous. "The guns," I guessed.

A nod. "Can you shoot?"

"I'm better with a blade. I don't like guns much." This was a bit of an understatement—guns freaked me right the shit out.

"That didn't actually answer my question," Wyatt said mildly.

I sighed. Even I couldn't deny that guns were probably necessary here, and I didn't dislike them enough to go to the proverbial gunfight with only some knives. This was exactly why Jesse made me keep practicing with him at the range. "If the situation calls for it, yes. I can shoot."

Wyatt looked at me for a long moment, assessing, then shrugged. "The situation calls for it," he said.

I put on my bulletproof vest and my knife holster, a soft leather belt that looked like a short corset. It sat high on my waist, which let me sit and move around without stabbing myself, and held twelve small throwing knives. I covered this up with a loose long-sleeved shirt. I might get a little hot, but it could have been worse. I added my boots with their knife holsters, too.

Wyatt watched me get ready with an approving—but never lascivious—eye. I was starting to get a serious Old West gunslinger vibe off him, like maybe this wasn't his first time walking into a firefight. When I was ready, the two of us tramped through the noisy casino to the parking garage, where Cliff was waiting at the entrance with a black duffel bag in hand. To my relief, he looked much better than he had that afternoon: more color, less stiffness in his movements. I introduced the two of them, and they shook hands, although Cliff looked a little wary. "He's human in my presence," I reminded him under my breath. Cliff nodded and relaxed slightly.

"How's the injury?" I asked, nodding at his side.

"Pretty good."

"You look like you can handle yourself," Wyatt said, surveying the other man. "You ever been in a firefight?"

"Yeah. You?"

Wyatt nodded, but admitted, "But it's been . . . oh, about a hundred years."

Cliff frowned, and I hurried to change the subject. "So. Where are we going to get a bunch of guns at seven thirty on a Saturday night?" I said to Wyatt.

A wide grin spread over his face. "That, I've got covered."

The three of us had to squeeze into Wyatt's dusty blue pickup truck, which was the kind you see in music videos for country songs. Well, okay, I don't actually watch music videos for country songs, but I'd imagine they're full of small, well-used and well-loved pickup trucks. To my surprise, the interior was perfectly neat, even cleaner than I keep the White Whale. But then, I guess you don't have to worry about fast-food wrappers if you don't eat actual food. I had to sit in the middle because I was the girl. And, in all fairness, the smallest of the three of us.

Traffic on Las Vegas Boulevard was getting hairy, but Wyatt turned us off the main drag, jumping onto a highway for a little bit to form what felt like most of a large circle. At least we got to skip the bumper-to-bumper.

I lost my bearings, but eventually we drove into a part of town that was mostly closed up for the night, unlike the Strip. It was more or less a typical suburban strip mall kind of neighborhood, but Wyatt steered the pickup truck into a dark parking lot, and I squinted to see the building we'd pulled up to. "The Gun Store?" I said aloud. "Seriously?" Cliff didn't say anything.

"Las Vegas's premier indoor shooting range for nearly thirty years," Wyatt said smugly, pulling around to the back lot. "They specialize in guns from throughout history. This is where you go if you want to shoot a tommy gun, or one of James Bond's Walthers."

"That's really cool," Cliff said in an almost reluctant voice, like he hated to admit he was impressed. "But I brought my own weapons."

"Suit yourself." Wyatt put the truck in park and climbed out. "Me, I never did get much of a taste for automatic weapons," he added. "This store stocks the guns I know how to use."

I hurried after him. "Wyatt, a place like this is gonna have state-of-the-art security," I said nervously. "If you break in, the cops will—"

Wyatt held up his key chain, giving it a jingle. Then he inserted a key into the back door and pulled it open. "I'm kind of a silent partner here," he said over his shoulder.

Oh.

Wyatt keyed a password into an alarm keypad. We followed him to a security room, where he did something to the computer, presumably erasing our tracks. Finally he turned to me. "Now," he said, suddenly reminding me of an Old West Willy Wonka. "What do you want to shoot?"

I blinked. "Uh . . . a Glock, if you have it." Jesse owned both a Glock and a Beretta, and made me practice with both. I preferred the grip of the Beretta, which felt more comfortable in my hand, but Jesse always pushed the Glock—a blocky, ugly weapon that would neverthe-less still shoot even if it was underwater or full of dirt.

Wyatt led me to what looked like the main salesroom, flipping on the lights and going behind the counter. Without being asked, Cliff took up a spot near the front door, keeping an eye out for incoming cars. The store had only been closed for a couple of hours, and I could still smell gunfire in the air, that special mix of gunpowder and pro-pellant and ozone. It made me nervous, since I still felt like we were breaking and entering, but then again, Wyatt was a vampire. If the cops showed up, I would suppress my radius and he could press them.

Behind the counter, weapons were hanging on hooks, presumably unloaded. There were little rectangular tubs below them, each one just the right size for a handgun and some ammo. Wyatt grabbed a familiar-looking gun off the wall and dropped it into a tub, then turned to look at me.

"What else?" Wyatt asked.

"Dude. If we're going into a situation where *I* need more than one gun, we're all gonna die."

He wrinkled his nose at me, but shrugged. "You know how to reload, right?"

"*Yes.*" I was mildly insulted. "What about me makes me look like I don't know how to reload a gun?"

He dropped some speed-loaders into the tub along with the Glock and then passed it to me. He pointed to a doorway. "Go in there and get yourself a holster."

The other room had what I guess you'd call shooting accessories. I found an outside-the-waistband holster that looked pretty idiot-proof and carried it back into the other room, still in its package, which I would leave in the truck. Wyatt might not be worried about fingerprints, but I was.

When I got back, Wyatt had removed his duster and was slinging a second rifle across his body on a strap. He had set out boxes of ammunition on the counter. "You know, I saw this scene in *The Matrix*," I remarked. "It didn't end well for Neo."

He grunted. "Better to have them and not need them and all that. You sure you just want the one?"

I looked at the Glock in the holster, hating how crude and violent it looked. "Yeah. I'm sure."

He looked at Cliff. "You good?"

Cliff gave the wall of historical guns a longing glance, but all he said was, "I'm good."

Wyatt shrugged. "Then let's go kill some celebrities."

Chapter 29

We drove to a gas station at the edge of town, where Wyatt did a loop of the parking lot to check for video cameras, and then parked his truck at the very back of the lot, behind the building. The two men got out and leaned against the truck, so I followed suit.

With the sun down, the weather was cooling off quickly, and I probably would have been freezing if I wasn't wearing so many layers. Now I was glad I'd had to pull on a long-sleeved shirt over everything else.

A few minutes later, Laurel pulled up in an actual Range Rover.

Cliff let out a low whistle. "Nice ride," he said.

Laurel climbed out, rolling her eyes a little in embarrassment. She was wearing jeans and a dark green tee shirt, the first time I'd seen her in clothes that I would actually wear. Her chin-length hair was pulled into a short ponytail, and her only jewelry was the same metal wave necklace she'd been wearing all weekend. She looked nervous, and a little excited, like she'd just been called up to the major leagues. Or maybe to the Avengers. "Yeah, well, Wyatt said we'd need to go off-road, so I borrowed this from my father-in-law. It would be best if we didn't get any bullet holes in it. What happened to you?" she asked me, gesturing at my face.

"Oh." I touched my cheekbone, and instantly regretted it. I'd taken four Advil, enough that I didn't have to think about the bruise as long as I didn't move my face around a lot. "You should see the other guy's dead body. Did Juliet and the others get going?"

"Yes." She looked pained. "Juliet is frantic with worry, so Bethany is driving Cliff's vehicle. I take it the car accident was your handiwork?"

"Yes . . . but Jack is completely fine," I promised. "He was just pressed. They're in for a few hours of worry, and some insurance paperwork." I tried to make it sound like no big deal, but the guilt still lanced through me. I had gotten them involved.

Pushing the thought aside, I said to Cliff and Laurel, "Can we get in your fancy car for a minute? Wyatt can show you the map."

Wyatt and I got in the back seats of the Range Rover, and the other two climbed into the front. Wyatt had drawn a little map on Venetian stationery, and after a moment of squinting around he located an overhead light and switched it on.

"This is the boardinghouse, here," he said, tapping at a long rectangle at the bottom of the sheet. "Right behind it and to the left, there's a dirt path that leads to some scrubby forest. If you steer right, however, it leads you into the canyon. If I were planning to kill vampires, I'd tell them there's gonna be an outdoor party back there. Might even set it up with some tables and lights and things. When the shooting starts, there will be nowhere for them to go."

"Okay . . ." Laurel said.

"We want you guys down the other path, near the scrubby forest," I told Cliff. "You're gonna have to come in from the road, work your way around."

Cliff nodded. "I can do that," he said, looking relaxed for maybe the first time since I'd met him. "I've got GPS, and this beast should be able to go just about anywhere." He gave the dashboard a fond pat.

"Where will the two of you be?" Laurel asked.

Wyatt tapped a spot on the map again. "To the right of both paths, there are the remains of an old outbuilding. As far as I remember, there are only three walls still standing, but that should be enough to give us cover until the Holmwoods get close. We wait until they're heading out back, and we ambush them."

Our best chance, Lex had pointed out, would be to go to Erson Station way ahead of the Holmwoods, while they were still busy with the nine thirty *Demeter* show. We would find our hiding place and wait for Arthur and Lucy to appear, and then I would extend my radius so Wyatt could shoot them. We still didn't know how many vampires were working for them, but with the two leaders dead, I didn't think anyone would try to retaliate. They were the engine driving this whole thing.

As for Jameson, his ideology may have been in line with the Holmwoods', but I couldn't see him being devastated by their deaths. And if they were gone, hopefully I could convince him to get out of here, away from Malcolm and the skinners. If he didn't want to come to LA and beg for Dashiell's forgiveness, maybe I could send him to stay with one of the other nulls I knew of, in Europe or Japan.

But that was a problem for Future Scarlett. For now, we would go in, wait for Arthur and Lucy to show up, and kill them immediately.

Which reminded me of something. I gave Wyatt a sidelong glance. "Are you gonna need to do the whole monologue on why they need to die, blah blah vengeance, or can we just shoot them?"

He scoffed. "I just need them dead. I don't need to brag about it beforehand like it's some damn movie."

"How are we going to be able to see them?" Laurel asked, looking at the map. "You said this place is out in the middle of nowhere, right?"

We all looked at Wyatt. "Are there electric lights?" Cliff asked.

"I don't know. But I would assume so, if they've got a null running around."

That made sense. If Jameson was making vampires intermittently human again, they would need to be able to see. "Besides," Wyatt added, "I know the Holmwoods' voices well enough. I'll be able to recognize them. The only thing I'm *not* sure about," he went on, "is the distance between the path and the ruins. We need to keep you far enough away that you won't affect anyone walking by on the path, but stay close enough to see and hear them as they're going by."

Crossing my arms over my chest, I gave him a look and suppressed my radius. Wyatt was about three feet away from me in the big SUV, but I managed to drop it down to about two feet.

As he turned back into a vampire, his eyes widened, and—ironically— a flush of life seemed to overtake him, making him somehow more attractive and dangerous-looking. No, I can't really explain how this works. Maybe it's a pheromone thing, or maybe part of their magic creates some kind of physical illusion, like a filter in Photoshop. The bottom line is that vampires be hot.

"Damn, woman," he marveled, shaking his head. "I've only met you and that Jameson fella, but I didn't know you all could do that. Can you hold it?"

"For a little while, but it makes it hard to concentrate," I told him. "I don't think I could suppress it while I fight, for example, or while holding a really intense conversation. But if we're sitting and waiting, yeah, I can keep it small for maybe a couple of hours. And I can expand it, too."

I needed to conserve energy, so I released my radius, letting it encompass Wyatt again. He stiffened for a second, but his body hadn't had enough time to forget how to breathe, so he adjusted quickly. "All right, that could be useful. How far can you go?"

"Um . . . I'm not sure," I admitted. "Expanding is a hell of a lot easier than suppressing—it's just a matter of willing it bigger, and keeping a little bit of my attention there."

"Could you cover the whole ranch?"

I shrugged. "I really don't know. If I get upset enough, it'll expand on its own. I won't be able to control it. Then it gets really big."

"Huh."

I looked at Laurel. "Did you get what you needed from the crystal store?"

Laurel nodded. "And I followed your friend's instructions for cleansing them; that's why I was late. Are you sure this is going to work?"

"No," I said honestly. "But if Wyatt and I can pull this off, you won't even need to get out of the car. You guys are plan B."

She nodded, slowly pushing out a breath through her mouth in a *whoosh* sound, reminding me of the LA women I know who've done serious Pilates. Then she snapped her fingers. "Oh, before I forget." She reached into a console between the seats and pulled out two small black handsets with belt clips on them. Walkie-talkies. "We use these when we go camping," she explained, handing one to me. It was the size of a fist, but nicely sturdy. I could feel a few tiny nicks and scratches. I hooked it onto the side of my pants. "We've tested the range at like fifteen miles," Laurel added.

"Just make sure you stay outside," Cliff put in. "Or *bring* them outside, if you have to. There's not a lot we can do to help if you're deep in the building and we can't see you."

I nodded and checked my watch. If we were going to get in position before the Holmwoods finished their show, it was time to leave. As the de facto team leader—what a horrible thought—I tried to think of something to say. We were going into this thing to right a wrong, save Jameson, and get Wyatt his revenge. But that didn't make it not scary. Instead, I just glanced at Wyatt, who looked intense and focused despite his overlarge cowboy mustache. "Let's go."

"Good luck, you guys," Laurel said, making eye contact with Wyatt.

"Oh, almost forgot." I reached into my pocket and pulled out a stack of bills wrapped with rubber bands. I handed it to Cliff. "Just in case," I told him.

Laurel's eyes widened, but she didn't say anything. Cliff just nodded and jammed the money into his pants pocket. Wyatt and I had locked the rest of the hundred thousand in the safe back at the Venetian. There was no way I was bringing it along tonight.

"We'll wait to hear from you," Cliff promised me.

I grinned at him. "On my signal, unleash hell."

Chapter 30

Wyatt and I got back into the pickup, and he drove us out of the city. He was quiet, thinking his own thoughts about this mission. As for me, I knew I should be nervous, or at least hyper-focused. Instead, my thoughts kept snapping back to this one memory from New York, like a song stuck in my head.

It had been one of the nights when Jameson and I sat up watching action movies from the nineties, which we both had a serious fondness for. Jameson had just had his third beer, and I was enjoying a full-on buzz. I'd only had a couple of hard ciders, but I wasn't used to being able to drink—in LA I was on call most of the time, and you have to drive everywhere—so my tolerance level was shit. We were watching *Last Action Hero* and giggling like little kids at a slumber party.

"You know Danny went back to school on Monday and *immediately* got a girlfriend," Jameson declared, pointing at the twelve-year-old protagonist.

"What? No way. He's still just a movie nerd. And the real world is harsh, remember."

"Nuh-uh. The kid is confident now. Confidence is half the battle in middle school. No, like, two-thirds of the battle."

"I thought knowing was half the battle."

He sighed, shaking his head. "I'm just not sure you understand fractions, Scarlett."

I tossed a throw pillow at him, which he easily dodged. He finished his beer, set the empty on the coffee table, and gave me a speculative look. "What were you like in middle school, Lady Letts? Did you know what you were by then?"

"No, I didn't find out 'til I was almost nineteen."

"Ah. The age of innocence," he said with a wicked grin. At the time, Jameson was nineteen, and far from innocent. "So who were you back in middle school?"

I tried to make my expression enigmatic, but probably failed. "Guess."

"Hmm." He paused the movie and turned his whole body toward me, making a show of eyeing me up and down. "Well, let's see. I can't picture you as a cheerleader"—I snorted—"and God knows you're too clumsy for sports."

"Hey," I protested. He just looked at me for a second, and I had to duck my head, conceding. "Okay, that's fair."

"You are way too pretty to sit at the losers' table, though, so I'm gonna go with . . . band geek," he decided. "That, or goth chick. I could see you in black lipstick and existential angst."

I laughed. "Nope, neither."

"What, then?"

I shrugged. "I didn't belong to any particular group, I guess. I always had a few friends for sleepovers or going to the mall or whatever, but I didn't have a . . ." I waved my hand, trying to find the right word through my alcohol-induced blanket of fog.

"A tribe?" Jameson offered with a little smile. "That's what white people call it now, right? You never found your tribe?"

"I guess not. I always had people around, but I always felt alone, if that makes any sense. Maybe all nulls are like that, or maybe I was just a freak, I don't know." Suddenly my buzz seemed to be wearing off, and

I was anxious to change the subject. "What about you? Who were you, before you were a null?"

"You gonna guess?"

"Oh, right." I made a point of looking him up and down. Back then he was lean and tall and quick-looking. "Jock," I decided. "I'm gonna say . . . basketball."

"Yeah, because you are racist as shit."

I laughed. "Is that a no?"

His smile faded, and his eyes went distant. "I . . . honestly, I'm not sure I can remember who I was before Malcolm found me. I liked comic books and McDonald's, I remember that much." He leaned back against the couch, and for just a second, his eyes scared me. No one should look that old. Certainly not at nineteen. "That kid seems like a stranger now. More like a dream than an actual person."

The movie was still paused, waiting for us to resume programming, but the atmosphere in the room had shifted. Our eyes met, and for just a second there was an opening, a moment where I could have said . . . something. Maybe I could have made him feel less trapped. Or at least less alone. Jameson never once said a bad word about Malcolm, but I wasn't stupid. I knew that Malcolm was controlling him, that he made his pet null do terrible things. Sometimes Jameson would send me into the city to do touristy stuff, and when I returned to the apartment his knuckles would be skinned and bloody.

"Jameson . . ." I began.

He just looked at me, expectant and maybe even a little hopeful. He *wanted* to talk, I could see that.

But I was still piecing myself back together after learning the truth about Olivia: that she had killed my parents, that she wasn't as out of my life as I had thought. I was sleeping with Eli, and half in love with Jesse, and so emotionally overextended that I didn't have it in me to reach out to the one person I knew was maybe more broken than I was.

I *saw* that Jameson needed help, but I knew damned well that I was in no position to give it. "Uh, I'm getting kind of tired. Bedtime?"

The next day, we both pretended that the previous night's conversation had never happened. I'd told myself that Jameson was a grown-up, that I couldn't save everyone. And I'd gone back to LA to deal with my own shit.

Would things have turned out differently if I had said something else in that moment? Or was that just naive? Dashiell wasn't wrong—Jameson had made his own choices, but it seemed so unfair that he'd had to pick between a shitty choice and a shittier one. It made me realize how lucky I was, despite Olivia, to have found myself in the one city on the continent where everyone in the Old World wanted peace more than they wanted power.

"Miss Scarlett," Wyatt said, breaking the long silence. I jerked upright, turning to look at him. His expression was troubled and serious beneath the cowboy hat. "I need to know that you're going to hold up your end of our bargain."

I blinked. "You're expecting me to have a big ethical panic over killing Arthur and Lucy? Man, you've got the wrong girl." If the only way to save Jameson was to see two murderous vampires dead, I could handle it. Besides, they wouldn't be the first deaths on my hands. I couldn't afford to get sentimental about it.

"That's not what I meant," Wyatt said. "I want to make sure you have your priorities straight, that's all. Killing the Holmwoods needs to come before saving your friend."

"Uh, my hope is that those two things pretty much go hand in hand."

"Yeah, but has it occurred to you that Jameson might *not* choose you over them?" he contended. "He might want to kill as many of us as possible, just like the Holmwoods."

"Then I'll change his mind," I said stubbornly.

"And what if he puts himself between us and the Holmwoods?" Wyatt argued. "What will you do then?"

I hated to admit it, but he had a point there. "It's not going to come to that," I insisted, trying to believe it.

"And if it does?"

"Then I'll try to wound Jameson so you can get to the Holmwoods. Or lure him out of the way. Something. We can make this work."

There was a long moment of silence, and then Wyatt said cautiously, "If you don't mind me asking, why are you so hell-bent on saving him, after . . . what he's done?"

There was a sort of implicit understanding there that I had slept with Jameson, but Wyatt was too much of a gentleman to mention it. Maybe I should have been embarrassed, but I just didn't have it in me.

I thought about not answering the question, but like it or not, Wyatt and I were in this together. We were going into a dangerous situation, and he deserved to know the truth. "Because he's me," I said quietly. "If a few things in my life had gone a little differently . . . he's me."

There wasn't a lot more to say after that.

We were out in the desert, on dirt roads that stretched for miles and miles of uninterrupted nothingness. Finally, Wyatt pulled the truck off the road, seemingly at random. He killed the headlights and pointed forward. "The station is about a half mile up that road," he explained. "We can't park too close without giving ourselves away, and even driving past might look suspicious. We should walk from here."

I tucked the Glock in its holster into my jeans and checked my knife belt, then waited as Wyatt strapped on five different guns: one on his ankle, two in a belt holster, and a shotgun and a rifle on straps that crisscrossed his chest. Then he filled the pockets of his coat with ammunition, and handed me several spare magazines for the Glock, which I managed to tuck into my knife belt. It seemed kind of like overkill to me, but at the same time, it was kind of comforting.

Wyatt led me about fifty yards from the road, and we began to walk parallel to the road, sticking to the desert. He stayed twenty feet ahead of me so he could see better, but the area was surprisingly well-lit, thanks to the three-quarter moon. "What about snakes?" I said to him as we started out. I didn't need to raise my voice; he had enhanced hearing as a vampire. "I'm not a huge fan of death by cottonmouth."

"Cottonmouths live in Florida and Texas," he called over his shoulder. "Around here we have sidewinders and rattlesnakes."

"That wasn't exactly reassuring." I didn't have a particular phobia about snakes, but I am naturally opposed to anything that snaps toward me real fast with fangs. Thank God I was immune to vampires.

He laughed. "I should hear them first, and if one does attack, the venom wouldn't kill me. You just walk where I walk."

After that, I stayed quiet, so I wouldn't distract him, and made an enormous effort to follow his path as closely as possible. A couple of times he paused and suddenly veered to one side, circling an area, and I was careful to do the same. He might have been messing with me, but I'd rather be the butt of a joke than snake food.

After about fifteen minutes of walking, I could make out a brightly lit building just off the road. Wyatt motioned for me to catch up with him. "That's the boardinghouse," he murmured. I didn't know much about architecture, but it actually sort of reminded me of those big plantation buildings you see in the Deep South: white, rectangular, with a big second-story porch held up by Grecian columns. The lights were on inside and out, and as we got closer, I could see a few shadows moving around in front of the windows. It wasn't the Holmwoods, I was certain: it was only nine thirty, and the second *Demeter* show was just starting, an hour away from us. But it would make sense for the Holmwoods to send ahead a couple of guards and maybe a few humans to help with setup and provide snacks. Literally.

At this distance, there was no way to know if I was looking at humans or vampires, but I wondered idly if the Holmwoods were also planning to offer the vampires actual food and drink, which they could consume thanks to Jameson. That would be just the kind of novel gesture that would build trust. Get a bite to eat, then venture back behind the building for a nice moonlit walk and bang! Twice-dead vampires.

We were approaching from the side, but the plan was to avoid the boardinghouse entirely for now, taking up positions in the ruins behind it. I clamped down on my radius and let Wyatt get ahead of me again, so he could use his vampire senses to guide us. He paused, listening hard for a moment, and then eased us around the side of the building, going slow and leaving lots of space between us and the brightly lit windows.

For one surreal moment it felt just like I was a kid playing Ghost in the Graveyard again, only this time the threat wasn't just being caught by one of my brother's friends and having to go wait on the front porch with the other losers. This time we could die. Well, Wyatt could die *again*, I guess.

We crept all the way around behind the boardinghouse, where there was pretty decent lighting coming from a few miniature lampposts. At an angle to the building, I finally spotted the remains of a tiny structure—maybe a smokehouse or outhouse. Something ending in -house. At any rate, Wyatt had been right: there were now three standing walls.

He led the way to the shadows behind the ruins, where we could keep an eye on the building. We were far enough from the light that no humans would be able to see us if we peeked out. Vampires would be a different story, but with all the lights on in the mansion we'd at least see their silhouettes. I hoped.

I could just barely see Wyatt give me a nod and lean back against the ruins, cradling his rifle. I crouched down next to him, getting comfortable, and then slowly released my radius. No one else was back here, and I didn't want to tire out too quickly.

Now all we had to do was wait until Lucy and Arthur showed up. Hopefully they would come out back before the party really got going, but if not, we would wait until we saw a bunch of shadows moving and go peer in the windows until we spotted them. Then I could extend my radius and Wyatt could shoot them through the windows with his little arsenal.

It wasn't the most sophisticated plan, I admit, but one thing I'd learned from my misadventures in LA was that a loose plan was often the best plan.

While we waited, I took occasional quick peeks at the rest of the property. The whole place was a lot bigger than I'd imagined from Wyatt's little sketch. The back of the boardinghouse opened onto a neat gravel patio area that was probably rented out for receptions—I saw stacks of small tables and chairs leaning against the side of the building. At the far edge of the gravel, there were a few feet of green lawn and then the kind of loose wooden fencing used for cattle. I couldn't see the ends of the fence—they just stretched out into the darkness—but in the center was a small metal gate, sized to fit a golf cart or ATV. I could just make out the two paths beyond that. One would go left, meeting up with the dirt road, which was probably how they used to get livestock back there when the place was a hunting club. Hopefully Cliff was working the SUV around to that area right now.

Meanwhile, the path on the right would go to the canyon, forming a kind of kill chute. I wondered where Jameson was positioned. If Wyatt was right about the Holmwoods keeping him away as a precaution, I wasn't sure where they would stash him—maybe he was coming later, after the show, but he could also be back in the canyon right now, getting things ready. I tried to picture him setting out guns and ammunition on a cheap folding table, preparing to execute the vampires as they entered the canyon and became human.

The whole idea made me shudder with disgust. Saying that all vampires were monsters, or even that they should all be put down, was one thing. But going through the actual steps to mass-murder them? It seemed so cold. So . . . well, inhuman, I guess. Could Jameson really do that? This wasn't the first time they were throwing one of these "parties," but I had no idea how involved he was. Did he stay back, extending his radius and letting Lucy and Arthur do the dirty work? Or did he pull the trigger himself?

Stop torturing yourself, Scarlett.

A couple of feet away from me, Wyatt suddenly jerked upright, looking around. He was in my radius at the moment, but he gave me a frantic look that I instantly understood. I pulled in my radius, cinching it as small as I could, and turned so I was facing the inside of the structure. Any threat would likely come from the boardinghouse behind the ruined wall.

I was reaching for the Glock when Wyatt swung his shotgun up at vampire speed. "Scarlett—" he cried, but I never heard what he was going to say. The sound of a gunshot cut him off just as something very fast struck me from behind.

Then everything went dark.

Chapter 31

I didn't want to open my eyes. Judging from the extraordinary frickin' pain radiating from my forehead, any kind of light was going to hurt like hell, and dammit, I had enough pain. In addition to the head thing, and my sore cheekbone from being pistol-whipped, my entire back ached from my shoulder blades to the base of my spine. And I was pretty sure my heels were gonna be cut to hell from being dragged backward like this.

Wait, what?

Reluctantly, I made my eyelids slit open. Someone—a vampire, judging by my radius—had picked me up under my arms and was pulling my body backward. My boots had come off, goddammit, and I could feel little stones cutting and burning my heels where they were dragging on gravel. I could distantly hear arguing voices, but I was still too fuzzy to make out the words. My face was wet, and I could feel a few strands of hair plastered to my cheek. The heavy weight on my hip was gone. They'd taken away the Glock. Or, more likely, I had dropped it when one of the Holmwoods' people had shot me in the back, propelling me into the wall.

At least, that's what I thought must have happened. The wetness on my face was probably blood from where my head had struck the stone, but I didn't think it was bleeding anymore. I wondered about the little walkie-talkie, but instead of moving my hand to check if it was still on my belt, I forced my body to stay limp. I needed a few more minutes to pull my thoughts together before I could fight or even talk.

"Can't just *shoot* someone without checking who it is first," a female voice was complaining. "What if it had just been a lost hiker? I could have pressed her and this would be over in two seconds." The lilting tone was familiar, and after a moment I realized it was Lucy Holmwood. Who was supposed to be at the show. Wait, how long had I been out? And where was Wyatt?

Another, male voice said defensively, "But it *wasn't* just some hiker. And you know she's not dead, right? She has a vest."

"Of course I know," Lucy snapped. "If she were dead, why would I want you to bring her inside? I'm just saying, in the future." Under their bickering, I heard the creak of a door opening, and realized we were on the gravel just behind the boardinghouse.

Oh, shit. They were going to take me into the building. I couldn't let that happen, not if I wanted Cliff and Laurel to be able to bail me out.

From behind me, Lucy's impatient voice said, "Can't you pick her up? She's going to leave a mess all over the carpeting." We paused, and the guy began to adjust his grip, preparing to lift me up. My head still ached, but I wasn't going to get a better chance than this to get away.

While the guy was bending down to scoop up my legs, I planted my feet and launched myself backward and up, slamming the back of my head into his nose. It hurt me a little, but from the sound of it, it hurt him a *lot*. I started to stumble forward, back across the gravel. Then I heard the unfortunately familiar sound of a gun being cocked.

There was a loud pop, and gravel kicked up a foot away from me. "Stop moving," Lucy Holmwood said calmly. I skidded to a halt, the gravel biting into my socks.

"Turn around, please. Hands in the air."

Shit shit *shit*.

Raising my arms, I turned around slowly. Lucy was standing in the doorway of the boardinghouse, silhouetted against the gold-hued glow from the building's exterior lights. I had to squint a little, but even with the backlighting, I couldn't mistake the gun that Lucy was pointing at my head.

"So. You're the null from Los Angeles," she said. "Let's see. Violet? Ruby?"

"Scarlett." How had she known that? I hadn't brought my ID.

"Right. We scouted you, of course. Ultimately we decided you were too comfortable in your position. Too . . . content with the status quo." She wrinkled her nose, like "being content" was the new "doesn't bathe." Then she glanced down at the vampire squatting on the gravel between us, clutching his face. Blood was spurting between his fingers, but Lucy didn't look particularly sympathetic. "Clay? The railing, if you would?"

He lowered his hands, and I realized that Clay had been the fish tank vampire in the show. "Great. Taken down by a backup dancer," I muttered. Clay started to snarl at me, but a sharp look from Lucy warned him off. With my hands up, I glanced at my watch. It was a little after ten. I'd only been out for like ten minutes.

Well, that didn't make sense.

Clay stepped forward and seized my wrist, dragging me into the boardinghouse with more force than was necessary. He might have been stuck as a human, but he was still strong, and I knew I was going to have some serious bruises . . . assuming I survived this.

As my free hand swung down, however, it brushed against the walkie-talkie. A spark of hope hit me, but I would need to look at it to find the right button, and Lucy Holmwood was about two feet away from me. Better to wait until we stopped.

We went through two sort of display rooms, both decorated in what I'd call Early Western Pilgrim, with lots of antiques fronted by little plaques. Finally we reached one that was big, large enough to be rented for private parties. This room had no decorations or furniture, other than curtains on the two side windows, but the far wall was recessed to make a special display spot for a stone bust. There was a bronze rail cordoning off the recessed area, and Clay dragged me straight for it.

Lucy, who had followed along behind us, tossed him something shiny. When he caught it, I saw it was a pair of handcuffs.

Until that moment I'd been able to cling to my natural belligerence, but now I felt an icy stab of fear. A few years earlier, a serial killer had chained me to the floor of his basement, and now I had a thing about handcuffs. I made an effort to keep that off my face.

Clay started to handcuff me to the railing, but Lucy made an impatient noise. "Search her first," she said. She was standing in the doorway, still pointing the gun. Up close, she wasn't terribly intimidating. She was shorter than me, though I was in my stocking feet, and she looked all of twenty years old. She was also even more beautiful than she'd looked onstage, with delicate features that would have been right at home on a porcelain doll. She wore black pants and a black button-down with black heels. Everything looked expensive, even the gun.

"Who are you supposed to be?" I asked. "Ninja Barbie?"

Lucy ignored me. "Get the vest off her," she said to Clay. "No more mistakes."

He had released me to catch the handcuffs, but he immediately took a step toward me. "I'll do it," I said quickly, not anxious to let this guy put his hands on me. He wasn't looking very happy about the blood still trickling from his nose. While Clay watched, and Lucy held the gun, I peeled off my long-sleeved shirt, unbuckled my knife belt, and dropped it to the ancient hardwood floor. I unstrapped the Velcro on the Kevlar vest—a line of blood had snaked down my neck and soaked into the material—and pulled it over my head, dropping it on the floor in front of me. In my tee shirt, jeans, and bloody socks, I held up my hands, turning around in a slow circle.

"Check her," Lucy said. Clay's face nearly split apart with a lewd grin.

My stomach turned over. "Can't I request a female henchman?"

They both ignored me. Still, his pat down was mostly professional. Mostly. If I survived this, I would definitely be taking the Shower of All Showers.

He found the walkie-talkie attached to my jeans, gave it a glance, and tossed it on top of the vest, kicking the pile away with his foot. I felt a little stab of anger. Eli had given me that belt as a gift, dammit.

Finally he stepped back. "No weapons," he reported to Lucy.

"Cuff her." To me, Lucy said, "Put your hands on either side of the rail."

Crap. That was going to seriously restrict my movement, much more than if I had one cuff on me and one on the rail. I considered trying to run again—aside from the door we'd come through, there was one other exit on the long side of the room—but it was pointless as long as Lucy stood in the doorway with the gun. If I'd had my knives, I might have been able to duck and throw and hope for the best, but instead I just put my hands on either side of the railing and allowed Clay to snap on the handcuffs. Then I had to do a sort of awkward half-turn so I could still see the room.

"Go get the other one," Lucy said to Clay. As he went by her, she held out the gun. "I don't think we'll need this."

When he was gone, she stepped over my knife belt, subconsciously wiping her hands on her slacks. "Hate those things," she muttered. Most vampires didn't like guns—scratch that. Most vampires found guns superfluous. Why carry a handgun when you can run over with super speed and break someone's neck? Vampires who hang around with nulls learn to adjust—but that doesn't mean they're comfortable. It was a little funny that she had the same relationship with guns that I did, but I wasn't really in the mood to commiserate.

Lucy disappeared from the room for just a moment, returning with an antique-looking wooden chair. She set it down well away from me, looking me over with a critical eye.

"So . . . why aren't you killing me?" I asked. Okay, I admit, it wasn't the smartest thing to say, but I wanted to take control of the conversation, and it was the first thing that popped into my head.

"Oh, we will eventually," she said in a cheerful voice. "But I figure tonight, at least, we can make use of you. With both you and Jameson here, we'll be able to fit even more people in the killing field."

Glowering at her, I shrank my radius down to two feet around me, just to be contrary. Instead of looking annoyed, Lucy brightened, even more than the average person returning to vampire-hood.

"Ooh, you *are* powerful," she noted. "Maybe we should have tried to recruit you after all."

"I would have turned your ass down."

"Yes, more's the pity," she said with a little sigh. "You can keep your aura sucked in if you'd like, but bear in mind that if you're of no use to me, I have no reason to keep you alive."

I couldn't really argue with that, and I needed to save my strength anyway, so I released my hold on my radius. Lucy took a quick gasping breath as she became human again, then smiled. She'd obviously had a lot of practice being around a null, thanks to Jameson. "Better," she said approvingly.

"Aren't you supposed to be prancing half-naked on a stage right about now?"

Her eyes narrowed for an instant, but then she relaxed. "So you *did* go to the show. I wondered, when I saw you on the lawn. Just think, you could have avoided this whole nightmare by simply coming close to the stage and letting us be killed." She shook her head. "But that's humans for you, I suppose. Always so cautious."

I didn't say anything. When it was clear that I wouldn't be taking the bait, she rolled her eyes. "Come on. Do you really think I'm the only pretty blonde vampire in Las Vegas?" she asked. "I have several . . . oh, I suppose 'understudies' would be the word. On killing nights, they perform for me."

"Thus giving you a rock-solid alibi," I guessed.

She inclined her head in acknowledgment. "We do try to play within human laws as much as possible. It makes everything move more smoothly."

"That's what she said," I muttered.

Clay entered the room, with a completely slack body hefted over his shoulder. The head was facing Clay's back, but I recognized the long coat. Wyatt. Was he dead? No, he couldn't be; he would have decayed down to a skeleton, at the very least. "Where do you want him?" Clay said to Lucy, as though he were moving a sofa.

She gestured to me. "Right next to her."

Clay came closer, hitting my radius and staggering under Wyatt's sudden weight. Carelessly, he dumped Wyatt's body down practically on top of me, so close that I couldn't have kept him out of my radius if I'd tried. When I felt him, though, he seemed *wrong*: even weaker than before, like a tiny ember on its way out. I was about to ask what was wrong with him, but then I realized Wyatt's head was dangling down at an unsettling angle, and I had to swallow my gorge.

They'd broken his neck.

Chapter 32

Clay left the room again, but Lucy was watching my reaction closely. With effort, I didn't allow myself to look away from poor Wyatt and his disturbingly floppy head. I could feel him in my radius, so he was still alive. But if I didn't get him away from me, he wasn't going to be able to heal. How long could a human last with severed vertebrae?

"It's like a science experiment, isn't it?" Lucy said gleefully, as if following my thoughts. "He's alive, but in neurogenic shock. His heartbeat is slowing, and the blood isn't going to his extremities. He's dying, Scarlett." She put her index finger on her chin, looking thoughtful. "How long will it take for him to truly die, beyond the point where vampire magic could still revive him?" She smiled in a sadistic way that creeped me out even more than the broken neck. "I have no idea. Nulls are so interesting. One thing I do know about them, however, is that when their emotions are out of control, their auras expand."

I tried to tamp down on my fear and worry. "Why do I feel an evil plan coming on?"

She sighed, looking disappointed. "Oh, Scarlett. Always hiding behind sarcasm. That was in our reports about you."

I couldn't think of a way to respond to that, but she continued, "At any rate, I do have a plan. We'll wait until the guests arrive, and then if he's still alive, I'll shoot your friend in the head. I do *so* hope that will upset you." She beamed. "We've already invited extra guests, to take full advantage of having a distraught extra null."

She obviously wanted to provoke me, so I met her eyes and didn't look away. Vampires usually need eye contact to press humans, so they aren't used to being looked at directly. It was obvious she didn't like it. "Lucy, go fuck yourself," I said in the most bored voice I could manage.

Ignoring the comment, Lucy checked her watch, crossed her ankles demurely, and continued. "We have a few minutes. Let's chat, shall we? I would just love to know what brought you to my door tonight."

"I get serious lady wood for historical sites," I said in a low voice. "You say 'stagecoach stop,' and I can hardly keep it in my pants."

Lucy let out a dramatic sigh. "Really? Do we really have to go through the whole smacking-around bit? It's so tedious, and honestly, I don't have all night."

"You mean because you have an appointment to kill a whole bunch of your own kind?"

For the first time, Lucy looked genuinely irritated with me. *Finally.* "You ungrateful little bitch," she spat.

"*Ungrateful?* Were you hoping I'd thank you for being a serial killer?"

"We are *trying* to protect your humans," Lucy said severely. "The fewer vampires there are, the safer humanity becomes. Why can't you see that?"

"You forget," I said, "to me, you're all humans."

"Oh, please." She sighed, looking almost . . . disappointed in me? "Don't be such a fang bunny. You, of all people, must know what we are. You've seen what we do. I'm sure you've had to put up with orders and attacks and psychological games—"

I interrupted her. "Sorry, lady, you've got the wrong null. I had a happy childhood. And *my* cardinal vampire is a pretty decent guy, all things considered. Not that that will stop him from completely kicking your ass."

"Hmm. So he *does* know you're here," she said, and I winced internally. Stupid Scarlett. Just keep your mouth shut.

Lucy pulled a phone out of her pocket and started typing out a text, looking mournful. "Have you any idea," she said sadly, without looking up from the screen, "how much time and money we've invested into this little endeavor? The years of planning, recruiting, and research? And then you came along—a stupid, thoughtless child blundering into our business—and ruined years of work." She finished the text and pocketed the phone again. "Now we're going to have to start all *over* again."

"Yeah, obviously *I'm* the bad guy," I replied. I was tired, and frustrated, and worried about Wyatt, and I wanted the walkie-talkie and to get out of the building and for Jesse to be here. I was sick of all of this, and it came through in my voice when I said, "Look, what is the *point* of any of this? If you hate being a vampire so much, just kill yourself and let the rest of us go on with our lives. Hell, I can even make it easy for you. Have your little butt monkey out there shoot you in the head, and I can get home in time for breakfast."

Lucy stood up, her fists clenched. "You think I don't know what you're doing?" she said. "Trying to keep me talking, to tell you all about my feelings? Please. You're just like every vampire sycophant who comes around begging Arthur and me for the real *Dracula* story—"

"Lady, I know the real *Dracula* story," I interrupted, trying to sound bored. "I know all about Claire."

Lucy Holmwood actually flinched. Then she went very still. I'd gotten to her. Interesting. "What did you just say?" she hissed at me.

"I said I know your story, you vapid, parasitic shithead," I said conversationally. "*Dracula* was inspired by a psycho vampire named Claire Clairmont. She cozied up to some idiot personal assistant who fancied himself a writer, and told him all about vampires. He wrote a whole book inspired by Claire, but he changed a good deal of the story to disguise the real players. For starters, he changed his main character's gender." I shrugged. "As for the clichéd creepy castle and three skanky wives, I'm thinking that was just classic Victorian male fears about the horrors of releasing female sexuality, but you'd know more about that than I would."

Lucy's eyes were beginning to bulge in a *very* satisfying manner, so I went on. "That wasn't the only change, though. There's also the small matter of you, Lucy, turning Arthur into a vampire rather than letting him kill you. And, of course, the fact that Claire didn't actually die in London. She died more than three years ago in Pasadena, California." I glared right into Lucy Holmwood's pretty little face. "When *I motherfucking killed her.*"

Lucy fell back in her chair, her hand over her mouth like I'd just slapped it. Okay, technically, *I* hadn't killed Claire/Ariadne (Clariadne?). But I had turned her human again, right before Dashiell killed her.

Lucy held her hand to her mouth for a moment, and then got up and rushed a few steps away, far enough to get out of my radius. "You're lying," she muttered, not looking at me. "You have to be lying."

"When I met her, she had dyed her hair black and wore black clothes. She went by the name Ariadne, and she lived in a great big mansion in Orange County that she let rot all around her like a demented vampire Miss Havisham.

"One thing I never understood, though," I continued, not looking at Lucy, just speaking to the room in general, "when I researched her later, all the sources I found said she died at eighty. But the Claire I saw was *maybe* midtwenties, at the most."

Lucy looked up then, her eyes stricken. "She was twenty-four," she whispered. "After she was turned, she pretended to age for a few years, then she told everyone she'd taken a governess job in Russia. Really, she was looking for a doppelgänger to take her place back in England."

I nodded. It was oddly satisfying to have that piece of the puzzle filled in, like when you find a lost item after you've already replaced it and moved on.

"Did you really kill her?" Lucy said, and her eyes were as intense as any I'd ever seen.

"Yes. She tried to move against the cardinal vampire of Los Angeles, and in the process, hurt a friend of mine," I said. "I turned her human, and then she was killed."

This was a simplification, of course, but not a lie. Lucy would assume I meant that I'd turned Claire into a human temporarily. Instead, I'd somehow taken the vampire magic right out of her, turning her into a human woman again. I hadn't been there when Dashiell killed her, but I was completely certain that he had. Claire had been a thorn in his side for two hundred years, and she'd tried to kill his wife in front of him. Dashiell wouldn't take something like that lightly.

But I didn't understand why Lucy Holmwood was having such a huge reaction to the news about Claire. Had Lucy been in love with her? But why had they parted ways to begin with? I knew Claire had left London after *Dracula* was published, but why hadn't Lucy and Arthur just gone with her?

"Oh shit," I said, understanding. "You weren't *just* trying for some big vampire final solution, were you? All this work, the whole vampire trap . . . you were looking for her." That was why they'd done so much publicity under the *Dracula* names, why they'd made such a big deal of getting vampires from other locations to come to Las Vegas for the show. It wasn't just to exterminate them. They wanted to lure Claire to Vegas.

"You were hoping to kill her, too."

Chapter 33

Lucy's pretty rosebud mouth opened, but for once she said nothing. Then she closed her eyes, and actual tears slipped down her face.

Staggering, she came back and sat down in the chair, looking like she couldn't bear to stand up anymore. "I promised him," she whispered. She bent her head over her knees, clutching handfuls of her hair.

"Arthur?" I guessed. "What did you promise?"

She had no reason to answer me, not really. At that moment, though, I didn't think she was really aware of who she was talking to, and the words came tumbling out in a broken whisper. "If he let me live, if he joined me, we would fight against she who cursed me with this plague. She who tried to come between us. We would find her, together. We would punish her, and then we would die." Lucy winced. She didn't want to die, at least not anymore.

"*That's* what all this was about?" I said, flabbergasted. "You hated Claire for turning you into a vampire?"

A momentary panic hit me—did the Holmwoods know that Dashiell was the one who'd turned Claire into a vampire to begin with? But no, I didn't think so—they had never made any effort to draw him into this plan, so either they didn't know or they didn't hold him responsible for Claire's actions. But I wasn't about to bring it up now, in case Lucy decided that put Dashiell on her personal hit list.

"Do you think I wanted this?" Lucy demanded. She gestured down at herself. "Do you think I chose this existence over the life I had planned? I was going to marry Arthur, and we were going to have children and a beautiful estate, everything I'd wanted my whole silly, simple life. And she took all that away from me just for . . . for a *demonstration*."

She'd lost me. "What? What demonstration?"

Lucy sat back, waving a hand. "Claire had some ridiculous notion that telling the world about vampires would force vampire societies to get along. She wanted to expose us, so she needed to show that hack writer what it was to feed, to turn someone." Her face twisted sourly. "She picked *me*. Because I was naive, and because I was there." Her lower lip trembled again. "I was going to have *children*."

"Why wait so long?" I blurted. "Why not go after Claire back then? There were two of you."

Lucy glowered at me. "Claire went into hiding," she snapped. "It wasn't exactly difficult, in those days, but she cut all her old ties with other vampires. Why do you think we spent so long traveling? It's a big world. It took decades just to narrow it down to the United States." Her glare deepened. "And then you took my revenge away from me." She couldn't keep up the anger, though. After a moment, she crumpled, her head falling into her hands.

Then I had an idea. It was not a *great* idea, and it would generally suck, but it was all I had.

I made myself scoff loudly. "What kind of *moron* goes to this much trouble just to find someone?" Lucy's head shot up, her eyes burning. "Honestly, Luce," I went on, "you've got to be pretty pathetic to chase some chick around the world for a century because of some imagined slight."

"*Imagined slight?*" She reached down to my discarded belt and snatched a knife, then stalked over to me, grabbing my hair and yanking my head sideways to expose my throat. "I could kill you," she hissed, holding the blade close. "Or so much worse. Don't you see that? Have you no respect for—"

I spat in her face.

"Ugh!" She jerked back, disgusted. But I'd already hooked one socked foot behind her ankles, so she tipped backward, her arms flailing, and landed hard on her back. I wanted to kick her face, but without my boots I might break a toe, so instead I lifted my leg and stomped my heel down on her chest, forcing the air out of her lungs. A classic Marko move.

The knife fell out of her hands with a little clatter. Her face went pale and shocked, like she couldn't believe someone had dared turn the tables on *her*, the famous Lucy Holmwood.

Even vampires who spend time around nulls aren't used to having the wind knocked out of them. Hell, it throws most humans. God knew it threw *me* every time I took a bad fall during my training with Marko. While Lucy lay there trying to suck in air, I worked my handcuffs around the railing to get closer to her. If she got enough breath to scream, I was fucked.

I turned as far as I could in the handcuffs, straining my shoulders, but I was able to pull the knife out of her reach with my heel. I hooked my foot around her neck and slid her just a little closer. I managed to position my body over her, and I placed my foot over her neck, pressing down just a tiny bit. "If I step down hard, I'll crush your larynx and you'll die," I told her. Okay, I didn't actually know if this was true, but the odds were good that a vampire would know even less about the physiological need to breathe than I did. "So just shake your head yes or no. Do you have the handcuff keys?"

She shook her head no. Her delicate face looked terrified as she struggled to regulate her restored breathing. "Does Clay have them?"

She nodded.

Shit. "Call him," I told her. "Just his name."

I eased up the pressure of my foot, and she yelled, "Clay!"

The big vampire poked his head in the room, then immediately reached for the holster on his belt. "Stop!" I hollered. "Or I'll stomp on her throat and she'll die. Toss the handcuff keys to Lucy's left hand. Slowly." God, I felt like I was writing my own bad movie dialogue.

Clay looked at Lucy. I was pushing my foot down on her throat again, but she had rolled her eyes sideways so she could see him. She nodded her head, almost imperceptibly.

Digging into his pocket, Clay pulled out a tiny set of silver keys and carefully tossed them to Lucy. They hit the old floorboards, slid, and came to a stop near her left hand, just within reach.

"Pick them up and put them in my hand," I told her.

Her brow furrowed into a horrible glare, but she did as she was told, raising her arm and leaning upward a little to reach my hand. I lifted my foot along with her body, ready to stomp it back down if she screwed me over. But Lucy pushed the keys into my palm. Her fingers were damp. I'd made Lucy Holmwood nervous. Yay me.

I kept my foot on her neck, hoping my feet were smelly. The fear and adrenaline pumping through my body were urging me to *hurry hurry hurry*, but I forced myself to move slowly as I unlocked one of the handcuffs, and then the other. When I finally had my hands free, I dropped down and snatched up the knife Lucy had dropped. With my left hand, I held it to Lucy's throat as I pulled back my leg, which had begun to ache with tension. I was still practically on top of her, and I had the bizarre thought that it probably looked like we were playing Twister. Hopefully I was winning.

"Clay, I'm gonna need that knife belt now," I said, sparing a quick glance at him. "Kick it over." Grimacing, he kicked the belt, which slid over and came to rest against Lucy's leg. Keeping the blade near her neck with one hand, I reached for the belt with the other, fumbling the buckle closed. Then I looped it over my right shoulder, removing one more knife.

"Stand up very slowly," I told Lucy. "I'll take a step back to give you room, but you should know that I can throw these things as well as I can hold them."

I backed up a tiny step, but I wasn't even watching Lucy: I was watching Clay. Sure enough, when he thought I was distracted with Lucy's movement, his hand shot toward his holster.

I extended my radius and threw the first knife, hitting him high in the shoulder. He groaned but kept moving, so I switched the other knife into my right hand and *chunked* it into his throat.

In action movies, you always see someone throwing a knife into the bad guy's heart, and when it comes to vampires, everyone automatically thinks of the heart as the best place to hurt them. But it's *really* difficult to get enough power behind a throwing knife to push all the way through the breastbone, even of an ordinary human, and I wasn't sure I had the upper-body strength. The throat, however, was right there in the open, and it was vulnerable as shit.

The blade buried itself in Clay's trachea. He dropped the gun, his hands shooting up to clutch at the knife. He made a couple of strangled, unbearable attempts to breathe, and then collapsed, his eyes going dull. Lucy, who was facing him, gave a little gasp of surprise, but she didn't seem all that broken up. She'd probably seen a lot of vampires-turned-human die in a null's radius lately.

Speaking of which, I could still feel Wyatt's vampire magic, but it seemed to be dimming. I forced Lucy to move across the large room toward the door we'd come through, mostly so I could get Wyatt out of my radius without shrinking it. I picked up Clay's gun where it had fallen, and glanced at it just long enough to make sure I could figure it out. Thank God, it was a Beretta. It was a little different from Jesse's, but close enough for me to use. I tucked the knives back into my belt and pointed the gun at Lucy, who instinctively raised her hands.

Then I paused. I wasn't actually sure what to do now. I couldn't leave Wyatt with these people, and I couldn't carry him out of here, especially not if I was keeping a gun on someone. I was stuck.

Think, Scarlett.

Lucy must have seen the uncertainty on my face, because she sneered. "You're out of time, little null. Arthur and the boys will be here any minute, and they've got a lot more firepower than you can handle with one gun and a couple of pig stickers. If you run right now, you might get away before they kill you."

I glanced over my shoulder at Wyatt. He hadn't moved.

"Where is Jameson?" I asked Lucy.

Confusion flickered over her face, followed by comprehension. "*That's* why you're here? He's your little friend, is he?" She looked at me with pity. "Oh, you poor dear. Do you think you can *save* him?"

I gritted my teeth. "I can try."

"But he doesn't want to be saved," she reasoned, as if she were explaining something very obvious to someone very stupid. Which, okay, maybe I was. "He hates vampires more than we do. My goodness, he's just *loved* killing my kind. I've barely needed to lift a finger; he's been so happy to—"

"*Where is he?*" I repeated loudly. The gun was getting heavy.

"I'm right here, Letts," came a tired, familiar voice from the side doorway.

I was unwilling to look fully away from Lucy Holmwood, so I turned my head to the left and peeked out of the corner of my eye. Jameson was standing just inside the room, his hands and his eyebrows raised. "And I think maybe we need to talk."

Lucy sighed with relief. "It took you long enough," she snapped, tossing her pretty blonde hair. She paid no attention to the gun I was still holding.

"Sorry," Jameson said, stepping slowly into the room, his hands still up. He glanced curiously at first Wyatt and then Clay, but all he said was, "The first two gas stations I tried were out."

"Out of what?" I asked. My hands seemed to want to move the gun toward Jameson, the moving threat, but I forced myself to keep it pointed at Lucy.

Jameson's lips quirked up in a wry smile. "Ice, believe it or not. I was making a run for ice before our guests arrive."

A snort burst through my lips. It was so ridiculous it had to be true. "Please move away from him," I said to Jameson, who had sidled closer to Wyatt. "I want him to heal."

"Oh." Jameson looked down at Wyatt for a moment, then shrugged and moved closer to Lucy and me. It was a huge room; there was still plenty of space.

Jameson looked between us. "So I see you two have met," he said cautiously.

"Yes, and I'm ready for you to kill her now," Lucy said imperiously. "At first I thought she might be of use to us, but she's more trouble than she's worth."

I glared at her. "Um, hello? I have the gun."

She scoffed. Now that her guy was here to back her up, her confidence had returned. "Please. I doubt you even know how to use it."

I raised the Beretta, flicked off the safety, and sent one bullet straight into the forehead of the poor stone bust behind the bronze railing.

Both Jameson and Lucy jumped at the sound, and I made a mental note to thank Jesse for forcing me to the stupid range all those times. It might have been my imagination, but in my peripheral vision I thought I saw Wyatt stir. Maybe it was just wishful thinking.

"Scarlett, what the hell?" Jameson burst out. "What are you doing?"

"What am *I* doing?" I said incredulously. "You're killing people! You literally came here tonight to *kill people!*" He tried to answer, but I wasn't finished. "You've been lying to me this whole time, and for *what?*"

I gestured to Lucy. "For them? For their fucked up genocide plan? You and me, we could have—" My voice broke then, and I stopped talking before I started crying in earnest. Lucy was smirking at me, but she knew better than to say anything at that moment, while I had the gun.

There was no chance for Jameson and me, not anymore. I knew that, but it still pissed me off that he'd thrown us away. Now the best-case scenario was me getting him out of the country alive, and that would require a hell of a lot of luck.

"To kill *vampires*," Jameson corrected, his eyes hard.

"What?"

"I did all this to kill *vampires*. Not people."

"That might be how she sees it," I said, gesturing to Lucy. The gun was getting sooo heavy. "That's how she thinks. But you and me . . . God, Jameson, when we get close to them they're humans again. You of all people know that beneath the magic, they're just like anyone else."

His face went to stone. It had been the wrong thing to say. "Malcolm is *not* like anyone else," he hissed. "And neither is Claire, or even your precious Dashiell. They think they get to decide, Scarlett. The think they control us. At best, we're chess pieces to them, and at worst, we're goddamn Happy Meals. A snack and a toy, all in one package."

"Good analogy," I muttered.

"It's wrong," he said, his voice starting to shake. "What they do is *wrong*."

"What about my Ellen?" said a gravelly voice from the floor. Wyatt's eyes were open, and his neck was no longer at that disturbing angle. He still lay on the floor on his stomach, but his head was turned sideways so he could see and speak to us. "She never hurt no one. Hell, most of our blood comes from a family of willing volunteers. Witches, who have called her Auntie Ellen for five generations now. Why did my Ellen deserve to die?"

"I . . ." Jameson looked like he'd been slapped. He glanced from Wyatt to me, as if to ask *is this guy with you?*

I nodded. "It has to stop, Jameson," I said quietly. My hand holding the gun was officially shaking, but I managed to keep it pointed at Lucy Holmwood. "Listen to me. If you want to go to New York and kill the shit out of Malcolm, I'll come along and back you up, every step. But Old World or not, you can't exterminate a massive group of people just because some of them mistreated you." I took a breath. "I won't let you."

Jameson's eyes welled up. He opened his mouth to speak, but before he could, I felt a quick flash of *new vampire in my radius*, and then Arthur Holmwood appeared in the doorway and shot me.

Chapter 34

At the range, Jesse was always telling me to *wait* before I pulled the trigger, that if I rushed to take the first shot I could, I was going to miss my target. Apparently no one had given Arthur Holmwood this advice, because he'd fired the gun before he had a good angle. The bullet hit me from the side, going into my upper right arm, coming through, and digging a furrow of skin out of my shoulder. It wasn't fatal, but it hurt like hell, and fresh blood immediately soaked the side of my tee shirt. I dropped the knife belt *and* the gun, instinctively clutching at the wound with my left hand, trying to staunch the bleeding and duck away from the doorway at the same time.

But Arthur simply walked through it, stepping forward as he took aim again.

"No, wait," Jameson cried, stepping between me and Arthur. He held up his hands. "You don't have to do that."

"Oh for *heaven's* sake," Lucy sputtered. "Just kill her and be done with it. The guests will start to arrive soon."

"You don't have to kill her," Jameson pleaded, looking at Arthur, who was glancing at his wife for his cue. "There are handcuffs right here. We can—"

"Oh, this bitch *has* to die," Lucy said, glaring at me. "Even if she weren't irksome and unpredictable, I simply see no reason to keep her alive."

"You say the sweetest things," I muttered.

"How about because I asked?" Jameson said to Lucy, a little heat in his voice now. "I've come along with you on this twisted little kamikaze mission, and I haven't asked for a single thing. But I'm asking now."

The three of them began to argue, but I stopped listening. I was getting light-headed. I'd donated blood to Cliff—oh, God, had that been just this morning?—and now I was on my second wound of the night, after the gash in my forehead. Not to mention all the bruising from my cheekbone and my back, where my vest had stopped a bullet. The pain seemed to suddenly crystalize, and I could feel myself starting to sway.

But my eyes caught motion: Wyatt was beginning to move his arm. Right toward the bulletproof vest. I didn't understand why he was bothering—until I realized the walkie-talkie was still resting on top of it.

Wyatt's hand crawled over to it, and he fumbled at the emergency button. Which was nice and all, but I wasn't sure how much good it was going to do when we were stuck *inside* the house.

Still, I didn't want Jameson or the Holmwoods to see what he was doing. "I could cure you," I blurted.

All three of them turned to stare at me. I looked at Lucy. "I can turn you into a human again. Isn't that what you want? To undo what Claire did to you?"

She hesitated, her eyes jumping around the room. "That's impossible," she said uncertainly.

"I can do it. I have before." I tried to concentrate on the outline of my radius so I could start the process, but I had nowhere near enough focus. I was in too much pain. "Well, not right now, but, you know, later. I can."

Arthur looked at Jameson. "Is this true?" he asked hopefully. "Can you really cure us of this filthy curse?"

Jameson looked at me, his eyes weighing me. "I've never heard of a null being able to do that," he said at last. "*I* couldn't."

Lucy snorted. "You see? She's just a lying piece of trash."

I almost laughed at the irony. I was the only one who could give Lucy Holmwood the one thing she wanted . . . except she was going to kill me before I could.

She looked at Jameson. "She dies."

"Fine," he snapped. "At least give me a minute to say goodbye to her. You owe me that much."

Looking victorious, Lucy held out her hands in a *be my guest* gesture. "I need to go get cleaned up, anyway," she said imperiously, glancing down at her dusty outfit. She seemed more offended that I'd made her lie on the floor than by the actual assault. "Arthur, you'll see to this?" she asked her husband. She was intentionally not looking at me now, wanting me to know that I wasn't even worth her sticking around to watch me die.

"Of course, my love." He actually blew a kiss at her back as she walked out. What a douche.

Jameson stepped toward me, crowding me into the corner, his back to Arthur. With some effort, I focused on his face. "Scarlett," he said softly. "I begged you to go home."

I raised my chin to meet his eyes. I might be going out, but I wasn't going quietly. "And I begged *you* to come with me," I replied in as strong a voice as I could manage.

"You were free. You could have just gone home and tattled on us to your boss," Jameson said, almost accusingly. "Why did you come back here?"

"You know why." I felt my lower lip tremble, but I didn't look away from him. "It's Vegas, right?" I said, trying for a lighter tone. "I thought I'd bet everything that you didn't want me to die."

For a moment I thought Jameson might cry, but then he pulled his face together with a huff. "I'm not sorry," he snapped. "I don't take it back. If I had to do it all again, I'd still kill them."

"Yeah, I'm getting that." My good hand was sticky with blood, but I wiped it on my jeans, reached up, and rested my palm on his cheek.

He closed his eyes for a moment, leaning into it, and I felt a tear slide between my fingers, and then another. His anger had drained out of him, and he just looked . . . tired.

A throat cleared behind him. "Jameson, my good man," came Arthur Holmwood's voice. "I'm afraid we need to wrap this up. Our guests will be arriving."

I leaned sideways so I could see Arthur's face. He looked politely regretful, like he'd just told a bunch of nice kids their slumber party had to end.

If I had to die, at least I could get in one last dig. "By the way, Arthur," I said conversationally, "I killed Claire, *years* ago. She's been dead for *all* of your little revenge tour."

His mouth dropped open. "No, she isn't."

"She is." I gestured around. "You know, Lucy said you guys were going to kill yourselves after Claire was dead. So why not let me go?" I shrugged. "Yeah, I'm going to send my boss to stop you guys, but isn't that what you *want*?"

It was stupid, but for a second I actually thought I had him. Then Arthur's gaze hardened. "My wife was right. You *are* a lying piece of trash." He raised the gun again. "Say goodbye, Jameson."

That's when I knew it was over. I was out of ideas, and I was going to die. You'd think that would scare me, but everything hurt so much, and my mind was numb. I was just hoping that I'd bought Wyatt enough time to recover so he could get out of here, or at least kill the Holmwoods like he wanted. Thoughts of Jack and Jesse and Molly jumped into my brain, but I pushed them away, because I would *not* cry.

"Dammit, Letts," Jameson sighed. Slowly, he leaned forward and kissed my forehead. Then he pulled his gun out of its holster, turned quickly, and shot Arthur in the head.

Chapter 35

Now it was my turn to be stunned. Jameson turned back to me. "I was planning to work on him," he complained, re-holstering the gun. "Arthur's more pliable than Lucy. Maybe I could have talked him out of . . ." He shook his head. "Never mind now. Come on."

He picked up my knife belt, looped it over my head, and took my left hand, pulling me toward the door he'd come through. I stumbled after him for a moment, then dug my heels in. "Wait! Wyatt—"

"I'm okay, Miss Scarlett," came a wry voice from the floor. Wyatt was struggling to his hands and knees. "Go. The sooner you two get away, the faster I'll heal. I'll find another way out." He glanced at the window behind him, then turned to eye Arthur's prone form. The other vampire *looked* dead, but I could still feel a faint buzz in my radius. As soon as we were gone, he would start to heal. "After I finish what I came for."

"Good luck," I said, and then I let Jameson pull me out of the room and down an unfamiliar hallway.

"You have a car nearby?" he whispered over his shoulder, hurrying me along.

Swallowing hard, I nodded. "If we can get away from the board-inghouse and the lights, I can get us out of here."

"I'm not going with you."

I stopped dead in the hallway. Jameson turned back to me, looking jumpy. A couple of vampire lackeys were crossing the hallway up ahead; they looked at us and whispered to each other, then scurried away. We were running out of time here. "What?" I blurted. "Why not? We can get away—"

He shook his head. "Assuming your friend finished off Arthur, Lucy's going to punch my ticket. If she doesn't, it'll be Malcolm's people. He's not going to stop until I'm dead, Letts, not ever. And I won't let you or your boss get caught in the crossfire."

"But—"

He stepped close. "This was always a one-way trip for me, Scarlett," he said hoarsely. "I knew that coming in. I just never expected . . . well, you." He smoothed hair away from my face, reminding me of that kiss on the gondola at the Venetian.

"Jameson—" I was absolutely going to keep arguing with him, but from behind us we heard a gunshot, then the crash of breaking glass, followed by a terrible, bloodcurdling shriek. There were two more gunshots, and then the sound of running.

"Come *on*." Jameson yanked at my arm, and I was too weak and off-balance from blood loss to do anything but follow. He was pulling me toward what looked like a foyer, complete with a grandiose front door. *Yes*. Outside. For the first time since Arthur had shot me, actual hope bloomed in my chest.

But the big door was opening, and I could hear chattering voices and two hits in my radius: vampires about to walk in. Quickly, Jameson dodged to the right, pulling me into a darkened side room. We froze. The voices on the other side were talking with renewed excitement, about the gunshots. There were four vampires altogether, and they'd never been near a null before. They thought it was fascinating. Hopefully that meant they wouldn't realize how close we were right now.

Jameson leaned down to put his mouth near my ear. "Watch your step in here."

Keeping my feet where they were, I carefully turned my body to look at the room behind me. We hadn't turned on the lights—they would have given us away—but there was a little light coming in from the curtainless floor-to-ceiling windows on the opposite wall. It was just enough for me to see outlines of sheet-covered furniture pushed against the walls, as well as some of the rotting or missing floorboards Jameson had been warning me about. Great. If I put my weight on any one of those, I'd go straight through. And could there be snakes under there?

Shit. I really wished I hadn't had that thought.

I held still and tried to breathe as quietly as possible, my thoughts flying to the sounds we'd heard. I was hoping the crash had been Wyatt escaping through the window. The scream had definitely been Lucy's, but I could only hope that Wyatt had gotten out before she found Arthur. Or, preferably, Arthur's dead body.

Still chatting, the four vampires *finally* moved away from the foyer and headed deeper into the building. I counted to ten, and then Jameson opened the door a crack to peer out. The stripe of light revealed a telltale red smear on the floor just outside. Blood. My blood. Leading right into this room. Any vampire could follow that.

"Jameson—" I whispered, but I was too late.

The door exploded inward, or at least that was what it felt like. Someone had fired a shotgun right through the door, hitting Jameson in the chest and knocking us both backward.

I fell hard on my butt, bruising my tailbone, with Jameson tangled in my legs. His breathing immediately went shallow. Struggling to sit up, I felt his chest. He'd been wearing his vest, thank God, but some of the shot must have gotten through or around it, because my hand still came away bloody.

Then the room flooded with light, and I saw Lucy Holmwood standing beside the old-fashioned light switch, breathing hard as she clutched Wyatt's shotgun. Her hair was wild, her eyes practically feral.

"You killed him!" she screamed at us. "My love!" She raised the shotgun to her shoulder again. "You have destroyed everything I care about. I hope you rot in hell."

"Actually, I don't think anyone *rots* in hell," I said brightly. "I mean, your body rots in its grave, but my understanding is that hell is more of a burning, fire-type situation."

Lucy froze, her brow furrowing. *This* was what I was wasting my last words on? "Also, you might want to look down at your chest," I added.

Her chin dropped, and she saw what I'd already seen: a small red dot, hovering on her breastbone. She screamed with rage. She didn't look quite so pretty and delicate anymore. "You think I care?" she cried. "If you both die, I can heal from any gunshot." She sighted down the shotgun.

"That's probably true," I admitted. In my lap, Jameson was getting pale. I needed to take him to a hospital, *now*. "But hopefully it'll be hard to move fast enough once the other thing happens."

"What other thing?" Lucy demanded.

For once, my timing was pretty excellent. At that exact moment, the floor began to shake. No, not the floor, the ground below it. There was a bit of cracking and crashing as some of the rotting floorboards fell in. "What's—" Lucy began, but at that moment a torrent of water exploded through the floor between us like a geyser from hell.

Chapter 36

I'd known for a while that different witch clans used magic in different ways, even the ones without a particular specialty. But most of the magic I'd encountered was some form of sympathetic magic—a small thing standing in for a big thing, like when you torture a voodoo doll and the magic actually injures your ex-husband.

As Wyatt had explained earlier that evening, however, Laurel and her clan were experts in elemental magic, specifically the manipulation of water. A hundred years earlier they had been employed as dowsers, finding small veins of water in the desert, then merging and cultivating them to create springs. Their witchblood had diluted as more and more of them married non-witches, until the current generation, which was pretty weak on Scarlett's Internal Magical Power Scale.

Laurel had spent years designing fountains on the Strip, using water magic in many tiny ways, but so much manipulation of water had started burning her out—hence the career change.

When I first heard about Laurel's talent I thought it was interesting, but I couldn't really see how it could be useful in our situation. How would nudging an underground stream to move over a few inches— which was about the most Laurel or anyone in her clan could manage anymore—help us stop the Holmwoods?

Then Lex told us about enhancing witch power with crystals, and I realized Laurel's value as a diversion. The original idea had been to either draw the Holmwoods to one specific spot so we—or Cliff, with his rifle—could take them out, *or* to create a distraction somewhere away from Wyatt and me, so we could escape, depending on what the situation required.

But we were still in the desert. I'd expected Laurel to produce a garden hose–sized spray of water, you know, *outdoors*. I hadn't banked on an actual geyser that caused the windows to explode outward. Cliff could have shot Lucy, but if he hadn't been expecting the geyser either, I wasn't sure he'd recover quickly enough to take her out.

As the column of water continued to surge upward through the floor, Jameson and I were immediately drenched, although the water was raining down on us after it hit the ceiling, so it had lost most of its force. I wondered how long the wood ceiling could take that kind of abuse before the second story came crashing down. I couldn't even see Lucy Holmwood anymore. Had Cliff managed to shoot her after all? I felt around, but there were no vampires in our immediate vicinity, and I couldn't afford to concentrate on expanding it at the moment. Shit. Was she dead, or had she escaped back through the door?

Or was she working her way around the geyser to us?

The sound of water roared in my ears, and I shouted down to Jameson, "We gotta get out of here! How bad are you?"

He shook his head a little, grimacing. "I'm fine. Vest caught most of it," he yelled. "Broke some ribs."

"Come on." As the cold water continued to pour down on us, I picked up my knife belt again and struggled to stand, feeling every bit of the pain in my body, including my heels in my drenched, shredded socks. Then I had to reach down and help Jameson up, and everything hurt even worse. With his arm draped over my shoulders, I stepped toward the doorway—but I could feel vampires in my radius, obviously moving closer, so I turned around again and we made our way to the big windows, picking our way around the rotten floor. I didn't think we would ever make it there, and I was braced for another shot in my back or for the ceiling to drop on me.

But that didn't happen. We finally reached the blown-out windows, where I helped Jameson step through, onto the ground. He reached up to help me, groaning with pain.

And suddenly Cliff was there, an assault rifle slung across his back with a leather strap. He reached up to my waist, helping me down to the ground. "Where's Laurel?" I yelled over the noise of the water.

Cliff was careful to put me a little ways away from the glass—he'd seen my socks, which were now smeared with dirt and watery blood. I could barely feel my feet. That water was *cold*. "Twenty yards away, protected in a circle," he shouted. They'd stayed back a little, so us nulls wouldn't undo her magic. Smart.

"Help me get this thing on," I said, holding up my knife belt.

Cliff helped me unbuckle it, looping it around my waist and refastening it. I was swaying again, so he ducked under my arm, choosing the side without the wound. With me still half holding up Jameson, we probably looked like a demented kick line, but we managed to inch away from the house. As my eyes adjusted to the dim light, I saw the Range Rover parked haphazardly a little ways away. With everyone focused on the gunshots and the arriving vampires, he'd been able to pull up practically onto the lawn.

"That is a lot bigger than I pictured," I said, jerking my head toward the geyser.

"Yeah, she tapped into the house's water main," Cliff replied. "She said the crystal Lex recommended is spectacular."

We stopped just in front of the car, where I had to squint against the headlights. "Jameson, get in," I said to the other null. He looked bad, and was now shivering from the cold water, on top of it. "I've got to go back for Wyatt."

"Lucy must have killed him," Jameson pointed out. His color was terrible. "We heard those shots."

"He might have gone through the window. I have to be sure," I said firmly. Even if Wyatt *had* wanted to be put out of his misery, I wasn't leaving him behind. If Lucy Holmwood was still alive, she would use him to vent her frustrations.

I didn't say it to Jameson, but in that moment I decided that I also wouldn't leave until I knew for sure that Lucy Holmwood was dead. She couldn't be allowed to run away and start this whole thing again somewhere else, or provoke a war with Los Angeles. I had started this hero bullshit, and I was going to finish it.

I looked at Cliff. "Do you have a gun I can borrow?"

Cliff reached into a back holster and pulled out a Glock. It was *my* Glock. Well, the one I'd had earlier. I looked at him with surprise, and he smiled at me. "I've been scouting the property for half an hour. I've got your boots in the car, too, if you want to grab them."

"Can you? I don't want to get too close to Laurel while—"

Beside us, with no warning, Jameson fell to his knees.

I yelped and dropped down beside him, setting the gun on the dirt. "Jameson!" I looked for a wound, but he'd fallen away from the head-lights, and between the low lighting and his black clothes, it was like trying to find a shadow inside another shadow. Cliff, who had squatted next to us, pulled a flashlight out of one of his coat pockets and flicked it on, shining the beam on Jameson's shirt. "Here," he said, pointing to holes above and below the Kevlar. "Looks like they were using buck-shot. Nasty." He palpated one of the upper wounds for a moment, and Jameson screamed with pain. "Broken collarbone," Cliff announced. "And he's losing blood too fast. We gotta get him to a hospital."

"You stupid lying *liar!*" I screamed at Jameson. "You are *not* fine!"

"I didn't want to slow you down, Letts." He gave me a weak grin that tore into my heart. I groaned and fought the urge to tear at my hair. "Argh!" Why did this have to be so *hard?!*

As I looked down at Jameson's ashen face, fear and despair started to overtake me, and I felt my radius practically explode outward, farther than it had ever gone before. But I didn't care. I wasn't paying any attention to what was happening back at the boardinghouse. I only had eyes for the null in front of me.

Because he was dying.

Don't cry, I told myself, though my eyes were burning. *Don't cry.* Somewhere in the distance, I vaguely heard more gunfire, but it barely even registered in my thoughts. Jameson was dying. Wyatt was still out there. I needed to focus. With effort, I forced myself to look at Cliff. "Take Laurel, get him to the closest ER. Right now."

He shook his head. "Look at you, you're barely upright. *You* go to the hospital; I'll find Wyatt."

"That would be awesome," I said tiredly, "except without a null, these guys are . . . you know. Vampires."

"Oh," he said in a small voice. "Okay. I'll go get Laurel." He turned and disappeared into the darkness behind the SUV.

I looked down at Jameson, who was blinking really hard, like he was trying to keep himself awake. I bent and kissed him on the lips. They were cold, but then, so were mine. "Don't die," I told him, brushing wet hair off my face. "I'll be really pissed if you die."

"Scarlett . . ." His fingers fluttered where they lay on his stomach, trying to find my hand. I grabbed them. "Come with me. Wyatt will be okay. He's a vampire." He didn't say it, but his tone suggested that because Wyatt was a vampire, it didn't really matter if he was okay.

"I'm not like you," I whispered. His face shifted, becoming infinitely sad. "But I don't hold it against you," I added.

Cliff ran back toward us, with Laurel a few feet behind him. "Let's get you up," he said to Jameson, but before he could a loud crackle erupted from the direction of his belt. I jumped, then remembered the other walkie-talkie. We'd left it in that big room with the bust, along with my bulletproof vest.

Cliff and I had just enough time to exchange a look before the walkie-talkie crackled again. "Attention, useless bitch," came Lucy Holmwood's seething voice. "I have your little pet here, with a stake positioned right over his heart. If you want him, come fetch him. I fucking dare you."

Cliff and Jameson both started to shake their heads, but I was already picking up the Glock and struggling to my feet. I leaned toward Cliff and pulled the handset off his belt. "Get them out of here," I said quietly, and without listening to his response, I turned and began trudging back toward the boardinghouse, shivering with cold.

I forgot to get my damned boots.

Chapter 37

As I returned to the boardinghouse, I saw that I'd been right: the closest corner of the big white building had actually collapsed, right where Laurel had created the geyser. I could still see a bit of water spurting out, but it was dying down now, and with Laurel leaving it wouldn't last much longer.

I held the walkie-talkie to my mouth. "Where are you?"

Lucy's voice cackled at me. "Just behind the building. Come and get me, bitch."

Name-calling? Really? But I clipped the handset to my belt loop and walked, trying to focus on my still-expanded radius. Behind me, I could feel a witch moving away. Laurel. Okay. I tuned out her signal and searched forward.

In the past, they'd killed four or five at each of these parties, but Lucy had said she'd invited more vampires to take advantage of having two nulls. The last time I'd paid attention like this, there were maybe a dozen vampires moving inside the boardinghouse and on the grounds around it. Now, though, I only felt two, one much weaker than the other. Lucy and Wyatt. But where were the others? Had they run away? Did Lucy persuade them to go back into the kill chute?

Cautiously, I kept walking around the side of the building, trying to slow my breathing. I might need to suppress my radius again, and that couldn't happen until I calmed the fuck down. At the corner, I paused and peeked around the side of the building. There were some shrubs in my way, so I eased my body around them, trying to peek through to see the back gravel area I'd become all too familiar with earlier.

Then I saw them.

The gravel and the area immediately surrounding it were strewn with bodies. Dead bodies. No buzz of life at all.

There were maybe fifteen of them, all between the ages of twenty and forty, and where I could see their faces, they were all good-looking. So your typical vampire sample group. Some of them had tried to run, judging by the way they were positioned, and others had even crawled a few feet away before being cut down. Jesus. I'd heard shots earlier, but I'd been too distracted to count them.

This was my doing. I'd been upset, and I'd completely lost track of my radius and how it was expanding. Lucy had used my carelessness against these poor people.

In the center of all this carnage, Wyatt lay flat on his back, with Lucy Holmwood sitting on his chest. Her skinny legs were splayed out to either side of him, and there were discarded guns around her—probably Wyatt's own weapons. Lucy had both hands wrapped around a large wooden stake, which had already pierced Wyatt's chest. He was breathing shallowly, and I wondered if she'd punctured a lung.

I must have made some kind of noise, because her head suddenly shot up, her eyes finding me in the shadows. "Come out, come out, wherever you are," she sang, her now-human eyes scanning the bushes.

I pushed out a deep breath and stepped around the shrub, into the light. "Hello, Lucy. Did you run out of bullets?"

She beamed, and I saw the wildness in her eyes, something I'd only seen before on a werewolf about to lose control entirely. Uh-oh. I didn't know if it was my actions, Jameson shooting Arthur, or the news about Claire, but we'd definitely broken Lucy Holmwood's brain. "Yes, more's the pity. This *creature*"—she wiggled the stake a little bit, and a guttural moan escaped Wyatt—"has extra bullets, but I don't know how to put them in." She shrugged. "Ah, well. I never did mind getting my hands dirty." She smirked at me. "I couldn't have done it without your help, though."

Guilt lanced through me, but no, I wasn't taking responsibility for this massacre. This was all Lucy. "And what exactly is your goal here?" I asked, walking closer. I had the Glock tucked in the back of my jeans, right below the knife belt, but my hands and arms were shaky from cold and blood loss, and I didn't trust my aim, especially with my injured right arm. If I missed, she would kill Wyatt, so I would need to be nearly within arm's reach before I drew the gun, or even a throwing knife. "You could have run away just now, with or without killing Wyatt there. Why are you still here?"

Her eyes burned. "Because none of it *matters*," she spat. "You killed Arthur. You killed Claire. You killed the show. I have nothing left, and it's all because of *you*, you *beastly* little tart."

Victorian insult words really don't have much sting these days, I've noticed. "You want to fight, is that it?" I asked. "I'm right here." I doubted I could even pull together a basic aikido throw, but if I could get her to step away from Wyatt, I could shrink my radius and he could heal and—

But Lucy shook her head. "First I'm going to make you watch me kill this little worm," she said through gritted teeth, looking back at Wyatt. "This *traitor* who came here to—"

Enough. Wyatt was out of time, and I wasn't going to get another chance. I didn't want to risk the gun, in case I missed and hit Wyatt, so I whipped a knife out of my belt and threw it at her.

I was aiming for the neck again, but the blade flashed in the air and buried itself in Lucy's right shoulder. She screamed, and her human instincts told her to retreat, so she scrambled off Wyatt and scooted away from me, moving toward the building door and escape.

The second knife hit her in the belly. I tried to focus, to get my hands to stop shaking, but the third knife glanced off her cheek, leaving a long gash of gore. I stumbled forward to stop her, to get closer, to protect Wyatt, but she managed to grab the doorknob with bloody fingers, yank it open, and stumble inside. She was still in my expanded radius, still human, but getting away fast.

Fuck her. I went to Wyatt and dropped down onto my knees beside him. He was still human, too, but he was alive, though his breath came in short gasps.

Then I felt a third vampire suddenly pop into my radius, but before I could react Lucy Holmwood came backing through the doorway again, her hands raised. I was confused until I saw the gun come through the doorway, followed by the man holding it. My jaw dropped open.

"*Dashiell?*"

Chapter 38

He was dressed like an FBI agent in a movie: a black bulletproof vest over nice slacks and a white shirt that he'd unbuttoned at the collar. His face was grim but controlled. Lucy, who hadn't removed the knives from her shoulder or stomach yet, was glaring at him with feral rage.

"How the hell did you get here so fast?" I blurted.

Dashiell shot me an amused look. "I have a plane, remember?"

"Ohhhhh." I'd forgotten, actually. Dashiell didn't advertise his wealth, and since I'd first met him I'd only heard of him using his private aircraft a handful of times, usually when Beatrice wanted to visit friends. I'd never even seen it.

Without moving the gun away from the enraged-looking Lucy, Dashiell gave the gravel area a quick look. "I see you've been busy," he remarked, the way you comment on the traffic report.

"Uh, this was mostly her," I said. Then a thought struck me, and I added in a weak voice, "Please don't kill her."

"What?" Now Dashiell did look at me, incredulous. "Surely you're not going to suggest we take her to her sycophantic cardinal vampire for judgment?"

"Ohhhhh no. No. But I promised this dude *he* could kill her." I gestured at Wyatt, who was conscious but breathing shallowly. "We made a deal."

Dashiell just raised his eyebrows, looking a little doubtful. Wyatt seemed to be barely hanging on. Then, to my immense surprise, the vampire actually clapped one hand over the stake wound in his chest and climbed to his feet, with only a little help from me.

"Do you mind, sir?" he said to Dashiell.

My cardinal vampire looked at me. I nodded, letting my trust for Wyatt show on my face. Dashiell shrugged and handed the gun over. The cowboy kept one hand over his injury, and raised the weapon with the other.

"You fuckers, you have no idea what's coming to you," Lucy snarled. Her hands were clutched into fists, but she stood her ground. "You think we were the only skinners in town? The only ones looking for revenge? I've made calls. You have no idea what will happen to Las Vegas without us here keeping the balance—"

"Ms. Holmwood," Dashiell said formally, "you are, in some ways, my responsibility. I turned Claire Clairmont, who turned you. I apologize for the pain and suffering my actions have apparently caused in this chain of events. But for the crime of murdering your fellow vampires, I sentence you to death."

Lucy's eyes widened. Dashiell nodded at Wyatt, who gritted his teeth and pulled the trigger.

I looked away. It felt a little cowardly, but my nightmares were crowded enough. When Lucy's body hit the dirt, Wyatt stepped forward and put two more shots in her heart. I felt her presence blink out of my radius. She was just another corpse now.

It was over.

Wyatt turned to look at me, swaying on his feet. "Miss Scarlett?" he said faintly. "I'd be much obliged."

"What? Oh." I suppressed my radius, pulling it in tight around me. Wyatt became a vampire again, and his chest wound instantly started healing.

He smiled with tired relief. "Thank you." He turned to Dashiell, holding out the gun, handle first. "And thank *you*, sir."

Dashiell took it, watching Wyatt with those cautious eyes. "You are quite welcome. Scarlett has informed me that you've been of great service."

Had I said that? I must have. Or Cliff had overheard me talking about it. It didn't really matter now. I was kind of dizzy. "She also said you'd like her to help you move on," he added carefully.

"Yes, sir," Wyatt replied, guarded. "We made a bargain."

Dashiell's face grew stern. "Scarlett is my employee, and should not have agreed to kill another vampire without checking with me."

"Hey—" I began, but Dashiell spoke over me.

"Moreover, I'm inclined to believe that enough vampires have died here tonight." He gestured to the carnage around us. "I would therefore consider it a great favor if you would come back to Los Angeles with us and work in my service. For . . . let's say a year. At that point, if you still want to die, I'm happy to get out of your way, and Scarlett will not be in trouble."

Oh. I got it then. I wasn't actually in trouble—Dashiell didn't actually have much say in what I did on someone else's territory, unless I threw his name around while I did it. But he was either trying to spare me or save Wyatt—maybe both—so I kept my mouth shut.

Wyatt eyed him for a long moment, considering the offer. "Please, Wyatt," I put in. "Please don't make me kill anyone else tonight."

He turned and met my eyes. He looked so sad, and alone, and just . . . *done.* For a moment I almost considered opening my mouth and recanting, but I held my ground.

Finally, Wyatt said, "You didn't have to come back to save me, Miss Scarlett, but you did." To Dashiell, he added, "All right, Mr. Dashiell. I accept your proposal of a year of service. For her."

I felt my shoulders sag with relief. I wouldn't lose any sleep over the Holmwoods, but playing a role in Wyatt's death would have haunted me. Now I had at least a year to not worry about it.

"Excellent. Now." Dashiell glanced at me with aristocratic curiosity. "You are all wet. And you are not wearing shoes."

I looked down at my clothes. My tee shirt, leather knife belt, and jeans were soaked through, as were my now-dirt-colored socks. "It's a long story."

Dashiell hesitated, and I was so sure he was going to ask me about Jameson, I could practically see it. Then he looked around and said, "I suppose the next item on our agenda is cleaning up this mess."

I relaxed infinitesimally. Dashiell would have to ask eventually, of course—Jameson *had* helped the Holmwoods—but he was giving him a head start. The cardinal vampire sighed, considering the bodies all around us. "We're going to need help to get this done by sunrise. I can make some calls."

Make some calls. It was only in that moment that my brain began to process Lucy's final words. "Oh my God."

Both men turned to stare at me. "Dashiell, I need a car," I said desperately. "Right now."

Dashiell gave me the cell phone he was carrying—mine was still in a zillion pieces back at the hotel room—and the keys to a late-model Jeep. I had the feeling it wasn't a rental, but I didn't care. Heat blasting, I followed the Internet's directions to the closest ER, which was in Boulder City. It was a manic, reckless drive, fueled by adrenaline and fear, and if the Jeep hadn't been a four-wheel-drive vehicle, I would have flipped it at least twice.

Finally, I saw the signs for the hospital. I dumped the Jeep in the short-term ER parking and rushed inside, my head swiveling around. The waiting room wasn't large. There was a cluster of worried-looking people sitting around, waiting for loved ones, but none of them seemed particularly agitated. It was the normal, barely tamed frenzy of any other night at the emergency room.

I spotted Cliff in a cluster of those fake wood and fake leather chairs, underneath an equally cheap TV. He was slumped down, his head propped on one palm. Blood streaked down the front of his shirt, but it didn't look like it was his.

I rushed toward him as fast as my injuries would allow, my wet socks slipping on the linoleum. Cliff looked up, and I saw his face go flat, like he was trying to keep feelings off it for my sake.

He stood up as I arrived, automatically holding out his arms to steady me. "He's in surgery," Cliff reported. "The doctors aren't optimistic, but . . . he has a chance. I sent Laurel home to be with her family. She was exhausted."

I processed all that quickly, and said breathlessly, "We need to get in there. I think Lucy may have told the skinners where to find Jameson."

"How?" he demanded. "When would she have had time?"

"After Jameson shot Arthur," I explained. "If she called Malcolm and told him about Jameson betraying her, and if he googled the closest ER . . ."

"Shit." Cliff scrubbed his hands through his hair and started toward the big airlock door that led into the patient area. "Come on. We'll see if we can talk our way—"

The sound of gunshots burst into the relative calm of the waiting room, and the intake nurses looked up in alarm. I started toward the door leading into the hospital, but just then lights on the wall began to flash, and a siren wailed. Someone had pulled the fire alarm.

The waiting room occupants began to rush toward the exit. Then the airlock door I'd been about to enter slammed open, and a flood of people rushed through it, nearly trampling each other.

"We gotta get in there," I yelled to Cliff over my shoulder.

He caught my upper arm, the one still oozing blood. I cried out, and he let go instantly. "Sorry! But look, you're never gonna be able to get back there—"

"Are you coming with me or not?" I demanded. I was already beginning to push against the wave of people.

Cliff clenched his teeth, but he nodded. I wormed my way through the doorway, snarling at everyone who tried to shove me. It probably helped that I looked like I'd just run through a blood sprinkler. I wove my way through the panicking stampede, following the signs to the surgical suites.

This hallway was already deserted. Cliff and I exchanged a look, and he drew a handgun from the small of his back. I followed suit with the Glock. We crept forward, stopping at each doorway, where I would hang back and Cliff would do a quick sweep of the room. We checked three doors on the left and two on the right. They were all empty, although two of them had lots of instruments and discarded gowns. Probably the surgeons had wheeled patients out of there when the fire alarm sounded.

Then we found a surgical suite that wasn't empty.

"Oh my God," I breathed. Cliff, who had swung the door open, motioned for me to stay back, but I ignored him and forced myself to step inside. My legs felt like lead posts in damp jeans.

There were three bodies in surgical scrubs on the floor, all dead of obvious gunshot wounds. A fourth body leaned against the wall in the far corner. If there had been anyone else in here when the shooting started, they had fled.

I stepped over them and approached the table. Jameson's large body was stretched across it, partially covered by a gown. His chest and upper legs were exposed and bloody where the surgeons had started to extract the buckshot. His eyes were closed, and his face looked peaceful.

He didn't seem at all troubled by the three new gunshot wounds in his chest.

I knew what I'd find, but I had to check anyway. I stepped up and put trembling fingers on his wrist to feel his pulse. I waited. Waited.

Nothing. I began to sob.

A gentle hand was placed on my arm. "He didn't feel anything," Cliff said quietly. "He just went to sleep."

I shook my head, the tears pouring down my cheeks. I was so *tired*. And dizzy. Was this even real? Hadn't I just been checking the ground for cottonmouths, and now I was in the middle of a hospital massacre? This *couldn't* be right.

In the distance, we could hear the wail of sirens. The fire engines. "We need to go, Scarlett," Cliff added in the same careful tone. "He's gone."

I reached up and touched Jameson's cheek, below the black eye. He was still warm. He felt like he might wake up at any moment, but I knew better. I went on tiptoes and leaned forward to brush a kiss on his forehead. "I'm sorry," I whispered, though I didn't even know what I was sorry for. For sending him to the hospital without me? For the shitty hand he'd been dealt as a null? Or was I sorry that we hadn't gotten a chance to see what this was? We could have loved each other. It felt like we had been on our way there.

I turned to Cliff, but just then the dizziness rose up to take me. I let it.

Chapter 39

"*Scarlett. Wake up, babe,*" came the familiar, teasing voice.

I bolted upright, but of course Jameson wasn't really there. Instead, Cliff and I were in Dashiell's Jeep, where I'd passed out with my head leaning against the glass. Some of my hair was still stuck there with tacky blood.

"Yes, sir." Cliff was talking on the cell phone, but he glanced over at me with concern on his face. I shook my head. "We'll be there in about fifteen minutes."

I let my eyes drift closed again, and didn't open them until Cliff pulled open the door and held out a hand to help me climb down. "Where are we?" I croaked.

"Regional airport just outside Vegas," Cliff reported. We had driven right onto the tarmac. He pointed. "That's Dashiell's plane."

I didn't bother to nod, just rested my head against the glass and stared out. From the outside, it looked like a mini version of any other aircraft, but when we climbed the steps and crossed the threshold, I saw that the inside was configured as a nice lounge area for humans and awake vampires. Instead of rows of seats, there were groups of four soft leather armchairs that could be swiveled around to form conversation clusters. There was a separate room at the far end, and I knew without checking that it would be full of airtight sleeping pods—Dashiell didn't like the word "coffins"—for vampires. I stumbled to the closest chair and collapsed.

Cliff had climbed up behind me and was standing in the doorway, shifting his weight from one foot to another. "Dashiell and Wyatt are smoothing things over at Erson Station," he said, using the slow, cautious tone that one reserves for the mentally ill. His shirt was damp where he'd carried me out of the hospital. "Apparently the Holmwoods had already dug a big pit out back for bodies. Dashiell and Wyatt will bury everyone and make it look like an exploding water pipe caused all the damage."

I think I nodded.

"I know you're in shock," he continued. "But I need to check on your injuries. Um, your physical injuries."

He stepped toward me, but I shrank back, shaking my head.

"I'm fine," I said. "Leave me alone."

"You might have a concussion," he insisted. "And the bullet wound on your arm is still bleeding."

When he tried to come close, I cringed away from him, hearing a voice say, "No, no, no, no." Oh. It was my voice. Cliff said something else, but I'd stopped listening. Eventually he put a blanket over me and went to sit somewhere else.

I just sat there for the longest time in my bloodstained clothes, staring at nothing. After a while, the plane's inside door opened again, and I heard footsteps on the ladder. Without really thinking about it, I instinctively felt for two vampires in my radius, but I sensed only witch magic. Powerful witch magic.

I blinked, looking up. Sashi Brighton was in the doorway, looking down at me. "Hi," she said, her voice cracking a little. She was wheeling the little first-aid suitcase I'd seen in her house. "What happened to your shoes?"

I looked around, without really seeing anything. "They're . . . somewhere."

"Cliff says you won't let him check on your injuries." I just looked at her. "I can't use magic on you, obviously, but I'm still a proper physician's assistant." Sashi glanced at Cliff.

On cue, he stood up. "I'm just going to take a look around outside." He squeezed past Sashi and climbed down the exterior stairs.

Sashi looked around for a moment before swiveling one of the large chairs so she could sit right across from me. I sat passively while she took my blood pressure and shone a light in my eyes.

"Do you feel light-headed?" she asked, pulling on sterile gloves. "Headaches?"

I nodded.

She examined the bump on my forehead. It wasn't bleeding anymore, but it hurt when she touched it. She asked me some more questions about my head injury, and then some stupid stuff about the president and the date. Then she sighed. "Well, you're in shock, and you've got a pretty severe concussion. Your blood pressure is dangerously low. You should be in the hospital."

It wasn't a direct question, so I didn't bother to answer. After a while she took a few materials out of her kit and put butterfly tape over the cut on my forehead. She told me it would probably leave a scar, as if that was something I would care about. Then she cut away the sleeve of my ruined tee shirt so she could examine where Arthur Holmwood's bullet had gone through my arm. "This needs stitches. God, your skin is so cold. All right, that's it," she announced. "We're taking it all off. I have a hospital gown in here somewhere."

She unbuckled my knife belt and helped me get my arms into the gown. After she tied the back, I had to stand up long enough for her to pull down my jeans. She peeled them off matter-of-factly, taking what was left of my socks too. "Ouch," she said when she saw my feet.

"Just scrapes."

"Still." She put some disinfectant on gauze and used it to clean the scrapes on my feet, which hurt. She rolled some bandages around each foot before covering my feet and legs with an airplane blanket. "Better," she said, and took some more supplies out of her case. She pulled down the shoulder of my gown and began applying iodine to the bullet wound. I winced at the sting.

"Cliff said that you lost someone tonight," Sashi said gently, probably trying to distract me. When I didn't respond, she asked, "Was he human?"

It seemed like a strange question for a second, and then I realized she was probably wondering if she could have done something to save him. "No. A null, like me."

"I'm so sorry, Scarlett. Were you close?"

I had no idea how to answer that. After a moment I settled on, "He saved my life tonight."

"So he was a good man."

"I think . . . he was trying to be." My voice wobbled. "He was complicated."

After another moment, Sashi said, "There," and put down her instruments. I hadn't even noticed her doing the stitches. She pulled off her surgical gloves with a snap, looking at me directly until I finally met her eyes.

"This world . . . the one in the shadows. It isolates us into these little bubbles," she said, covering my cold hand with her warmer one. "As a result, we have so little say in who we get to be with."

"That's why you don't want to be with Will?"

She sighed. "I've been thinking about that. Say I took your cure, and say Will would even have me. I could move to LA and take a human job at a hospital. But Will's whole life is in the Old World, and I would no longer have a place in it. How many hours a week do you think he spends dealing with pack business?"

"No idea. A lot."

"As he should. But me being there would be a constant pull away from what he needs to do. Away from being alpha. It would divide him, force him to choose. Every hour of every day, he would have to pick between me and the pack." She shook her head. "Even setting aside the good I can do as a witch . . . I think we would eventually tear apart. Or he would ask you to cure him, too, and that would tear *him* apart." She reached over and pushed a lock of my hair behind my ear. It was a maternal gesture.

Very, very gently, she said, "Scarlett . . . sometimes it's not supposed to work out."

I cried then, for a long time. Sashi held me, smoothing back my hair and just generally making a fuss over me. When I was done, she helped recline the leather chair and then covered my lap and chest with more airplane blankets, which smelled like plastic wrap. The last thing I heard her say was, "I'm going to start some IV fluids, all right?"

I just nodded, already half-asleep. I felt her moving aside the sleeve of my gown to tie the tourniquet, and then I was out.

The next thing I was aware of was the sunshine. Someone had opened the window shades on the plane, and a beam of sunlight was warming the right side of my face. Just as it got uncomfortable, someone crossed in front of the window, cutting off the heat. I opened my eyes . . . and saw a familiar figure in a tee shirt and hoodie.

"Jesse?"

He looked down at me with that thousand-watt grin. "Hey, lazy. Geez, I thought this was a work trip. I wish I got paid to sleep all weekend."

I burst out laughing, but it quickly turned into more of a sob. "You know me. Shows, spas, and shopping. It's what I live for."

"Yeah, that sounds about right." There was a whine from next to Jesse, and I looked down—sort of—to see Shadow. She was sitting politely, but when I sat up and really looked I could see her tail wagging frantically. "Hey, Shadow."

The bargest took that as permission to put her front paws on my lap and take one long swipe of my face with her tongue. "Ack! All right, fine. I missed you, too."

Point made, the huge bargest dropped back down to all fours, her nose snuffling over my blankets and the hospital gown. I looked around. The plane was empty except for some of Hayne's men, in their signature black polo shirts. They were carrying a couple of the airtight sleeping pods out of the plane. "Where are we?"

"Burbank airport. Dashiell called a few hours ago, said you were flying back and you had some minor injuries." He gave me a skeptical look, but was smart enough not to point out that my injuries didn't look so minor. "Corry's waiting in the car."

People. I was back home, where I had my people. My eyes pricked with tears again. Stupid fucking Las Vegas. "I'm never, *ever* going back there," I said to Jesse. "Where's Cliff?"

"He already left. Said to tell you he'd talk to you later."

"Okay." I hit the button to make the seat un-recline. My skin was still stained red, and more red had rubbed off onto the leather seats from when I'd been sitting there in my blood-soaked clothes. Dashiell was going to kill me when he saw it. Actually, scratch that. He'd probably make me come back later and clean it up.

Jesse was watching me again. "Hey, are you aware that you're covered in a great deal of blood?"

"Yeah, but most of it's mine. Speaking of which . . ." I peeled off the clear tape holding the needle in place and pulled out the IV.

"Hey!" Jesse protested, but I was already pressing my fingers down on the small spurt of blood. "Seriously, Scar. What the hell happened this weekend?"

"It's a long story." I pushed the remaining blankets down, aching in so many places that there was no point in taking inventory. I saw that someone had left my boots set out neatly near the door, which cheered me up a little.

I shivered from the plane's air conditioning. "Here." Jesse shrugged out of the hoodie and helped me get it on. I zipped it up gratefully, breathing in his comforting scent of oranges and cologne. The warmth felt amazing. "Is it still Sunday?" I asked.

He gave the bump on my head a very concerned look. "Yes."

"Take me home?"

"You bet."

I started to stand up, and felt something tucked between my hip and the armchair. I reached down and pulled out a small paper bag, rolled up. When I held it up, the bottom of the bag began to tear, and tightly bound chunks of money spilled out onto my lap.

Jesse's eyes got huge. "Whoa. That's gotta be like . . ."

"Ninety thousand dollars," I said in a hollow voice. Wyatt had seen me lock the hotel safe. I hadn't killed him like I'd promised, but maybe he was counting on me doing it when his service to Dashiell was up.

If they'd stopped back at the hotel, my suitcase might be around here somewhere, too, but I'd get it later. Or never. Who fucking cared.

I looked at the money for a long moment. I could feel Jesse practically vibrating with questions, but I just shook my head. "Let's go."

Chapter 40

Jesse let me borrow his phone so I could call Abby as we walked out to the parking lot where he'd left the White Whale. She crabbed at me for making her work on Sunday, but she promised to messenger over a new phone. In the meantime, she checked on my old phone and managed to retrieve a voice mail that had come in just before sunrise. She sent it right to Jesse's phone with her technical wizardry, and I plugged one ear so I could listen.

The message was from Silvio, the head vampire in Las Vegas. Apparently, the Venetian wasn't Dashiell and Wyatt's only stop after they were finished at the boardinghouse. They had also made a quick visit to the penthouse suite at the Mandarin Oriental.

I didn't know what Dashiell had said or done to Las Vegas's leading vampire, but in the voice mail Silvio promised that by the time we landed in LA all footage from the hospital shooting would have gone missing, including everything from the waiting room. He ended by apologizing for any trouble I might have found in Las Vegas, and assured me that I was welcome back anytime. He sounded nervous as hell, which made me smile. Scary encounter with Dashiell aside, Silvio's backers were dead, and now he was going to have to try to hold Las

Vegas all by himself. I gave it maybe three months before some enterprising newcomer showed up to take him out. Served him right.

I couldn't reach my injury very well, so after we got home Corry helped me Saran Wrap and tape my stitches, then stood next to the shower to help me wash off the blood. To her credit, she didn't say anything about all the bruises that decorated my body—several of which I didn't even remember getting. Behind her, Shadow kept ducking in and out of the bathroom to check on us.

"You're a lifesaver," I told Corry.

She smiled. "Which is a nice change of pace. Usually you're the one saving me."

With her help, I got dressed in some loose-fitting sweatpants and a soft bra that was designed for yoga, but which I saved for when I was lying around the house and couldn't be bothered with underwire. I put a plain tee shirt on over that and Corry helped me into my favorite jacket, the one Jesse had bought me a few months earlier. He was waiting for us out front, swinging his keys around his finger. "Are you sure this is a good idea?" he said, looking me over. "You still look like shit, no offense, and that bruise on your cheek makes you look like you were pistol-whipped."

"That is only because I was, in fact, pistol-whipped." I had told Jesse most of the story, leaving out my feelings for Jameson. Jesse and I weren't romantic or anything; I just wasn't ready to talk about that yet. Then again, Jesse used to be a detective with the LAPD. He probably figured it out by himself.

"Do you even have a story prepared?" Jesse asked.

"Nope." I started shuffling out to the car with Shadow right beside me. "Are you coming or not? Because I could *totally* drive myself. Concussion be damned, you know?"

Jesse sighed and followed me to the van.

It had only been—what, a week?—since I'd been to Jack and Juliet's place, but it felt like years. Or like a dream. Or maybe I was still kind of in shock. At any rate, when Jesse knocked on the door of their condo, I felt like a total stranger.

The door popped open. "Scarlett!" Juliet rushed forward to hug me, moving fast enough to make Shadow twitch a little. I squeaked with pain. She pulled back, taking in my bruised face and the butterfly bandages on my forehead. "Oh my *God*! What happened?"

"You really shouldn't drive when you're upset," Jesse said with a smile, holding out his hand. "Hi, I'm Jesse Cruz."

Juliet automatically took his hand, blinking as she looked up at him. "Oh, okay. Wow. Um, hi, I'm Scarlett's sister-in-law, Juliet." She stepped to the side. "Come in, come in. Jack's on the couch. Jack, honey," she called. "Your sister's here, and she looks like she has a better story than you."

I shuffled inside, with Jesse's hand subtly resting on my back for support. Jack was sitting on one half of their L-shaped couch, holding an icepack to his head. A football game was playing on the flatscreen. When he turned his head to look I saw a bruised lump on his forehead that matched mine pretty well. We should take our Christmas card photos early.

Jack sat up as he saw us walk in, picking up a remote to flick off the television. "Holy shhhh-crap," he blurted, and I heard Jesse snicker. I glared at him.

"Sorry, you sound just like your sister. Hi, I'm Scarlett's friend Jesse," he said again, stepping forward to shake Jack's hand, too.

"I've mentioned him before," I put in.

"Yeah, but you didn't say he looked like *that*," Juliet said under her breath, so only I could hear her. "The kids are in their rooms," she added. "I can get them, but . . . um . . ." She looked from Jack to me, totally uncertain. Would I want the kids to see me in this condition? We were a little bit beyond normal social protocol here.

"Why don't we sit down?" Jesse suggested. He led me toward the open half of the couch, while Juliet sank into the corresponding armchair.

Jack watched as I lowered myself gingerly to the cushions. I'd taken a bunch of ibuprofen, but the bruised tailbone still hurt like a bitch. "Scarbo? What happened?"

"I rented a car to come back this morning," I said, using the story that Jesse had come up with on the way. He was really coming along nicely in the "make up lies" department. "I was worried about you, and excited, and I guess I drove too fast. I got into an accident getting off the freeway. Hit the steering wheel, and I fell on my tailbone climbing out of the car."

I had told Jesse that using a car accident story twice in two days was ridiculous, but he'd argued that that was exactly why it would work. It was too lame to be a lie.

And he was right. Jack and Juliet made the appropriate exclamations of sympathy, and I assured them that I'd be fine.

"You know, in like, a month, we're going to be laughing about this," my brother said, shaking his head ruefully. "I can't believe we both had a crash in the same weekend!"

"Yeah. It's weird. How are you?" I asked, looking him over. My stomach twisted with guilt. I'd wanted him to walk away without a scratch, but Molly had insisted we needed a bump on the head to sell it. The bump seemed huge, but he didn't look like he was in terrible pain . . . right?

He gestured toward his forehead. "It's nothing, honestly. Barely more than a fender bender. And insurance will take care of everything." He glanced at his wife. "I'm just sorry there was a mix-up at the nurse's station and they made my situation sound way worse than it was."

Juliet was wringing her hands in her lap. "And then I made it sound terrible to *you*, and look what happened." She shook her head. "I should never have left you there to drive yourself back, knowing how upset you were. I just didn't think—"

"It's not your fault, Jules," I said, carefully leaning over to pat her hand. See, I could do casual touching if I had to. "Besides, I wasn't just worried about Jack. I was excited. I've got some other news."

Jack instantly looked between me and Jesse, so I rushed to add, "I, um, won some money at the roulette table. And I want you to use it for Logan's bills."

They started to protest, so I picked up the purse and upended it on the coffee table. The money from Wyatt fell out.

As Jesse had pointed out in the car, stacks of falling cash was a pretty attention-grabbing visual aid. Both Jack and Juliet went totally silent.

"It's about a hundred grand," I added. "I won ninety, after taxes, and there's a check on the bottom with what I've been saving up from freelance jobs for the last couple of months. I want you to have it for Logan," I said again, because they both looked so stunned, I wasn't sure how much was getting through to them. "Are, um, you guys okay?"

Jesse, for his part, was grinning.

There were tears, and denials, but eventually I convinced them to keep the damned money. I didn't say it out loud, but if they'd refused it I would have made Jesse drive me to the nearest homeless shelter and pushed it through the mail slot. I didn't want to have anything to do with that money, not after losing Jameson. His death hurt, and it was going to hurt for a long time, especially because I couldn't help but agonize over whether I'd been responsible. Would he still have died if I hadn't investigated the vampire disappearances? If I hadn't pushed him so hard? Why hadn't I understood Lucy's warning just a little faster? Or driven faster, or tried to find a phone number for Cliff to warn him while I was driving . . . the list of my own bad choices went on and on. At any rate, I couldn't look at that money without seeing the gaping holes in Jameson's chest. It was hard enough trying to deal with the sight of Jack's giant head bump.

When we finally left the condo, I had to lean on Jesse a little for support. Shadow kept pace with me, but she was constantly glancing up at me with worry. I couldn't really blame her.

In the elevator, Jesse eyed me and said, "I know what you're thinking, you know."

"Oh, really?"

"You think you fucked up, both by going along with the bachelorette party cover story in the first place and by using Jack to end it. You're blaming yourself for his injury, for Juliet being worried, all that. But they're *fine*, Scarlett. Hell, they're elated. You've taken a tremendous weight off their shoulders."

I didn't answer. He was right, of course. But . . . "It could have been so much worse," I whispered. "If anyone else found out we were connected, Juliet and her friends could have been killed." Bethany sucked, but Tara was a genuinely nice person. And neither of them deserved to die. "Jameson *was* killed. I feel like . . ." I shook my head.

The elevator dinged. We got out, but Jesse stopped in the lobby, turning to face me. "Like what?"

"Poison."

Not so long ago, *Jesse* had accused me of something similar. I'd pushed that idea away, and our friendship had gotten past it, but . . . "Maybe you were right about me," I whispered.

Jesse sighed and wrapped his arms around me. "You're not poison," he said into my hair. "You just have a complicated life."

I accepted the hug, but inside, I was thinking that I needed to stay away from Jack and Juliet for a while. Maybe forever. They didn't deserve the risks that I carried.

It was ironic, of course: not so long ago, I'd missed my brother terribly, and resented him for pushing me away while he was grieving for our parents. Now he was doing everything he could to make room for me in his life, and I was going to put distance between us again. And Juliet, and Riley and Logan, too. At the end of the day, they were too nice, too normal, to be a part of my life.

How sick was that?

Chapter 41

When we returned to the cottage house Jesse decided to stick around, watching a movie with Corry while he set up my new phone for me. I told him I could have done it myself, but he rolled his eyes and shooed me off to my room to sleep.

By the time I woke up, stiff and hurting, Jesse was gone and night had fallen. Shadow was lying on the bed next to me, and started thumping her tail when she saw that I was awake. I took four Advil from a bottle on my nightstand and lay back down, staring at the ceiling for a long time. Then the doorbell rang.

Shadow jumped up and sort of pointed at the door, but I ignored it. Molly would be awake by now, if Corry hadn't woken her early to hang out. My null apprentice wasn't returning to college until tomorrow. "They probably ordered pizza or something," I told Shadow. The bargest gave me a hopeful look. "We'll get you some later, okay?"

Someone knocked on my door. I pretended not to hear it. "Uh, Scarlett?" came Corry's voice. "You should probably get out here."

She sounded afraid. I sat up, nearly crying out at the pain in my tailbone, and started moving toward the door. "What's wrong?" I said as I jerked it open.

She was wearing flannel pajama pants and a Berkeley tee shirt. Her eyes were wide. In a low voice, she said, "Um . . . Dashiell is here."

I stared at her dumbly. "Dashiell is *here*? Like, at the house?"

The cardinal vampire did leave his mansion to handle his business affairs, but in all the years that I had known him, he'd *never* come to me. I always went to him. Corry nodded. "What do I do?" she whispered.

"I don't know," I said, which was honest. I led her back down the hall to the front door. Dashiell was standing just inside the house, talking to Molly in low tones. My roommate had her head bent down, looking submissive and meek. I hated that.

I would have to take charge, goddammit. I decided to treat Dashiell like any other guest. "Hi, guys," I said to them, but I looked at my roommate. "Molls, would you and Corry take Shadow outside for a bit?" I asked.

Molly scrutinized my expression for a moment and then nodded. Shadow gave me a look that said, *I know what you're doing, and I don't like it.* "It's fine," I told the bargest. She didn't look like she believed me, but when Molly and Corry stepped into flip-flops and went out into the yard, Shadow reluctantly followed.

Dashiell was looking around the cottage, with its funky paint colors and pieces of Hollywood memorabilia that Molly had hung on the walls. He was wearing a gray suit with a narrow black tie, and he looked about as out of place as a time traveler from the future. "Would you like something to drink?" I asked him.

He shook his head, stifling his amusement. "Thank you, but no. I simply wanted to check on you. Cliff reported that you were injured. We should sit."

For once, I didn't have a snarky comment. I just ushered him into the living room, lowering myself carefully onto the couch. Dashiell perched on the edge of the armchair, his eyes searching me like he was doing inventory. "Are you all right?" he said quietly, his eyes lingering on the bruises on my face and wrist.

I thought about it for a moment, and decided to be honest. "Not really." Then I told him everything that had happened after I'd hung up on him, leaving out only the parts about Jameson and me, as I had with Jesse. Dashiell listened quietly until I got to my conversation with Lucy Holmwood, and then he wanted every detail. When I was finished, he leaned back in the chair, looking pensive. "I hadn't realized just how much damage she did," he said.

"Claire or Lucy?"

Rueful smile. "Well, both, but I was talking about Claire."

It was a good opening for the question that had been nagging at me. "Did her plan work?" I asked him. "Did Claire really unite the vampires with *Dracula*?"

He sighed. "It was a complicated time. The vampire council had fallen a century earlier, and many of us were getting reckless." He shook his head. "I know you've seen jostling for power, but this was on a different level. Vampires stopped caring how many human bystanders were killed in their machinations. In a way, yes, the book did force us to put aside our differences and create the loose feudal system we have now. But it caused as many problems as it solved, because for the first time, humans organized themselves to hunt us." He chuckled. "Claire did at least manage to build a few fail-safes into Stoker's narrative—the garlic, the holy objects, walking around in daylight—but still. There were many vampires who called for her head on a pike, and that's not a metaphor."

I studied him. "You helped her get away, didn't you?"

His gaze slashed over at me, and I immediately regretted my words. "I withdraw the question," I said quickly, but I'd seen in his face that I was right: Dashiell had helped Claire escape from the mess she'd made in Europe.

I had to wonder if *that* was the real reason he'd sent me to Las Vegas to look into the Holmwoods' actions. If he'd suspected that the Holmwoods were after Claire, he might have felt responsible, since he'd prevented Lucy and Arthur from getting the revenge they needed. It might have stopped all of this. And that was on top of him killing the last cardinal vampire, and him turning Claire into a vampire to begin with.

"We live long lives. We cannot know how a single choice we make might ripple out," Dashiell said quietly. "But, for what it's worth, Scarlett, I am sorry if any of my actions contributed to Jameson's death."

I stared at him, surprised. I didn't think Dashiell had ever apologized to me before, unless it was in a *sorry for your loss* kind of way. He looked away from me, which was another first. "I had a weakness for Claire once," he went on, his eyes wandering around Molly's artistic contributions to the living room. "I felt sorry for her because of her circumstances, and I thought I had the power to reshape her life as I saw fit."

His meaning wasn't lost on me. "Jameson wasn't Claire," I said, angry.

"No, he wasn't. But my point, Scarlett, is that, like it or not, some people are beyond saving."

Fuck you was what I really wanted to say. I needed him to get out of there before I actually did. "Was there anything else?" I said sharply.

He shook his head and stood up. "We'll have a meeting with Kirsten and Will tomorrow night, to discuss the Las Vegas situation. For now, I can see that you need rest. I'll see myself out."

He took a few steps toward the door, paused, and turned back. "I am glad you're back," he said simply. And then he was gone.

Epilogue

Life is funny. Wait, scratch that. People say that all the time, but what they really mean is that life is cruel, tragic, and unfair—but not without a sense of humor about it.

On Monday night, I made the drive up to Pasadena for the follow-up "state of the union" meeting with all three Old World leaders. I did not say anything to Will about seeing Sashi. Part of me longed to, but who was I to interfere in someone else's personal relationships? Mine were a mess. I hoped that Sashi would find a way to tell Will about his daughter, but it wasn't my decision. If I didn't hear anything about it, I promised myself I'd try calling her in a month or two, just to check in.

Meanwhile, Dashiell had a few updates from Las Vegas. All upcoming productions of *Demeter* had been canceled. There was a rumor floating around that the Holmwoods had left town with the show's profits, though the Bellagio declined to press charges. A new Cirque du Soleil show was announced for the Bellagio theater a few days later, and after a couple of weeks of speculative newspaper articles, everyone moved on.

The hospital shooting in Boulder City was blamed on one of the orderlies, who had, the story went, killed a bunch of his colleagues before turning the gun on himself. I felt a little bad about that, but ultimately I had too many other things to feel guilty about.

I spent a couple of days resting and healing, and then my life got more or less back to normal, at least on the outside. I cleaned up supernatural messes, worked on Dashiell's security with Hayne and his team, trained with Marko, and watched TV with Molly. I went through all the motions, but I couldn't help but *feel* different. Older, mostly.

The one bright spot that came out of the whole mess was Wyatt's surprisingly smooth transition into life in LA. Dashiell had offered him a job on a security team at one of his companies, but Wyatt turned him down and got his own part-time gig, as a bartender at a gay cowboy bar in West Hollywood. The job kept him busy and distracted, and gave him somewhere to go every night. And after decades in Las Vegas, there was nothing the homosexual cowpokes of Los Angeles could do that would so much as raise an eyebrow on the old vampire. When he wasn't working, Wyatt stuck close to the mansion, running nighttime errands for Dashiell or working on Beatrice's garden under floodlights. I saw him fairly often, and every time Laurel called me to check on him, I could truthfully say he seemed at peace with his new life.

At least for the next year or so.

As for me, grief seemed to have taken root in my chest again. I'd lost people before, God knows, but Jameson's death hit me harder than I would have expected. Maybe it was because he was a null too, or because I had seen a romantic future for us, but I began having nightmares about him that rattled me. In the dreams I saw him dead, or bleeding out, or—worst of all—perfectly fine and laughing, in bed with me. There were nightmares about Malcolm, too. In those dreams, it was me he found, me he shaped into what he wanted. There were many nights when Molly shook me awake, her eyes wide with alarm, because I'd extended my radius in my sleep.

After a couple of weeks of this, I started researching what it would take to go to New York and assassinate Malcolm. He may not have pulled the trigger himself, but in so many ways, he had orchestrated Jameson's death. I wanted him to pay for that.

Dashiell somehow figured out what I was doing, though, and warned me off. Actually, he *didn't* warn me off, which was sort of refreshing. He just told me I needed to work on my timing. "You're not ready," he said sternly. "And he'll be expecting it now. Better to wait a bit, and let him think he's won."

So I put the idea on hold, but the nightmares persisted. Eventually I wondered if my subconscious might be tormenting me because we'd never held a funeral. Jameson's body was buried in a mass grave in the Nevada desert, but it wasn't like the lack of a body made it impossible to pay my respects. When my friend Caroline had died, we'd at least had a memorial service. I guess I just hadn't realized how important it was to say a real goodbye until the opportunity was taken from me. Which was another terrible irony, because getting rid of dead bodies was part of what I did for a living. For years, I had refused to think about what destroying bodies did to the victims' loved ones. Now it was me.

I could have asked Beatrice to put together a memorial service, of course, or maybe even done it myself . . . but who would I invite? Who was left to remember Jameson besides me and the horrible Malcolm, who was responsible for his death? That was the worst tragedy of all. Jameson had lived a short life filled with pain and bitterness, and now he was gone, with almost no evidence that he'd ever lived.

Well. That was what I thought, anyway.

It was Shadow who clued me in. She went from her normal level of "attached and protective" to suddenly giving me the full Secret Service treatment. She stuck to my side even in our own yard, where she'd always enjoyed roaming around, and even came into the bathroom when I showered, standing guard just outside the tub. Sometimes she would paw and whine at me for no apparent reason, getting frustrated, like she was trying to tell me something that I was just too oblivious to understand.

Until, with a growing sense of terror, I did.

"Scaaaaaaaaaaarlett," Molly yelled. It was a Thursday night, three weeks into April, and we were all set up for house movie night. It was Molly's turn to pick what we watched, but she had surprised me by eschewing the usual romantic comedies in favor of an Ingrid Bergman mini-marathon. Jesse had promised to come by for the second feature, *Notorious*, after he finished family dinner at his parents' house.

"Are you coming or what?" Molly called. "I know humans spend a lot of time in the bathroom, but this is getting ridiculous!"

Dazed, I swung the bathroom door open and shuffled into the living room like the living dead. Shadow, who had managed to wedge herself into the small bathroom with me by standing in the dry tub, followed at my heels, keeping to my slow pace like she was spotting me for a fall. Which maybe she was.

"Scarlett?" Molly asked, her eyes filling with concern. "Have you been crying?" When I didn't answer, she rushed to add, "Uh, I didn't mean to hassle you about the bathroom; you can stay in there as long as you want."

I just shook my head. "I don't know how to . . . this is so . . . so . . ." I didn't have the words.

Looking panicked, Molly vaulted off the couch and rushed over to me, grasping my arms. "What happened?" she asked, searching my face. "Did someone hurt you?"

In answer, I held up my fist, clenched so tightly that my knuckles ached, so Molly could see the test.

"I'm pregnant."

Acknowledgments

Being exposed to the work of Joss Whedon at a formative age taught me maybe my hardest lesson about writing: no matter how much you like your guy, you gotta keep knocking them down. Your hero can win the biggest of battles, but having a series means you will have to knock them back down again. It's not always fun, or easy, but it's also the only way readers can watch your hero learn to pick herself back up.

Over the course of five novels I have had a great time watching Scarlett pick herself back up again, each time a little stronger and smarter than before. If I'm being totally honest, somewhere along the way I began to enjoy devising ways to knock her down, too. For me, that was the final hurdle to becoming a writer: when I finally got past the urge to only be *nice* to my darling protagonists. Life isn't nice, and there's no reason why life in a world full of magic should be any nicer. The key thing for me, and the reason I love being a writer, is that Scarlett always gets up, and she's always a little better for having fallen.

In many ways *Blood Gamble* is the culmination of both Scarlett's journey and my own. It's a fish-out-of-water story about someone who *just* learned to swim in their own pond, and it ends with a game-changer (sorry, that was a lot of metaphors just there). Believe it or not, the twist at the end of *Blood Gamble* has been part of my plan since *Dead Spots*, and I'm so excited and grateful to have *finally* reached this plotline, possibly the most epic of all my knockdowns.

I do understand—I've understood all along—that this ending will worry or aggravate some longtime readers. I have agonized over the upcoming response to this book, but ultimately I decided I needed to stick to my plan for Scarlett and the series. If this alienates you to the point of needing to quit reading my books, I thank you for taking the journey with me thus far. But to those of you on the fence, or worried about the novels "jumping the shark" (oh, how I loathe that expression), I say: Wait. Watch. There is a plan.

Meanwhile, as usual, there are many people I need to thank for helping me make *Blood Gamble* a book I can be proud of. My enormous gratitude to Tara Erson (pronounced TAR-uh, like the sticky stuff), a great friend who welcomed me into her home in Las Vegas and took time out of a crazy schedule to show me around the city—despite suffering from an excruciating toothache pretty much the whole time. Like Scarlett, I'm not particularly fond of the Strip, but visiting Tara always helps me understand the fascinating, vibrant, and always-evolving city beyond the casinos, where real people live completely sequin-free lives. A disclaimer: this book mentions a number of real-life locations, and a couple that I made up so I could trash them. Because this is fiction, I have taken many liberties with layout, security, hours, etc. in order to tell a better story. All resulting inaccuracies are mine alone.

My thanks also goes out to Alex Bledsoe, a great writer and friend, who was gracious enough to do a signing with me at Barnes & Noble in Madison when I was promoting my novella *Nightshades*. The topic was vampires, and the discussion inevitably turned to *Dracula*. Because the Transylvanian count has appeared so many times, in so many formats, someone asked us if we would ever write Dracula in our own books. Alex said no, because *Dracula* is sacrosanct, and because putting him into a book would result in comparisons to the original, which is a fight you can't win.

I said, "Hold my beer."

Kidding. I don't drink beer. But the conversation did get me thinking that while I wouldn't necessarily write Count Dracula, it could be fun to dip a toe into the lore. And that became the seed of the Holmwoods' story you see here.

Thank you to the team at 47North: my acquisitions editor, Adrienne Procaccini, my amazing developmental editor, Angela Polidoro, and the other behind-the-scenes people who are instrumental to putting out the finished product you now hold. I also want to thank my husband, Tyler, who gave me an idea that became the engine for much of the plot, and my wonderful extended family, who read my books and act as my champions in so many ways. Thank you to my parents, not because they particularly helped with *this* book (although Dad did have a few nice Vegas tips), but because they raised me and are therefore kind of responsible for everything I do. Actually, if you have issues with the book, maybe take it up with them? Just a thought. (See how I just complimented them and threw them under the bus in the same paragraph? My dad taught me that.)

Scarlett Bernard will return in *Shadow Hunt*.

Melissa Olson

March 10, 2017

About the Author

Photo © 2013 Elizabeth Kraft

Melissa F. Olson was raised in Chippewa Falls, Wisconsin, and studied film and literature at the University of Southern California in Los Angeles. Melissa is the author of eight Old World novels for 47North as well as the Tor. com novella *Nightshades* and its two sequels. She now lives in Madison, Wisconsin, with her husband, two kids, three dogs, and two jittery chinchillas. Read more about her work and strange life at www.MelissaFOlson.com.